CUT THE DECK

B BASKERVILLE

-CHAPTER 1-

UNTIL LAST YEAR, RACHEL Pearson had never considered her own mortality. Now she thought about it twice a week, every week. The fifteen-year-old attended yoga classes to rebuild her strength after an accident left her with fractures to her C4 and C5 vertebrae. She'd been bed-bound for four months; the physiotherapy to get her walking again had been brutal.

Yoga class always ended in *shavasana*, or corpse pose. Twice a week, Rachel would lie on the yoga mat, exhausted, sweaty and frustrated. The old Rachel would find yoga tediously easy. The new Rachel struggled to stand on one leg.

"Empty your mind," said the instructor in a voice that was supposed to be soothing but made Rachel feel like she was back in primary school.

She could never empty her mind in *shavasana*; instead, she thought of the day she'd fallen and couldn't get back up. It was the day Great Britain's

1

hot prospect for the next Olympics spectacularly dropped out of contention. Literally.

Rachel rolled up her mat, gathered her things and braced herself for the climb down the stairs.

"Take care, Rach. I'll see you next session."

Rachel tucked waist-length plaits down the back of her sweatshirt and waved over her shoulder. She rarely said a word to anyone at yoga. After all, what did she have in common with these women in their forties and fifties with cardio butts and incessant talk of daytime soaps and PTA meetings?

It was a bitterly cold night at Prior's Haven. The little beach on the North Sea coast was home to Tynemouth's rowing and sailing clubs. Yoga class was held above the sailing club, and it had the most beautiful views of the mouth of the Tyne. The frosty ground cracked beneath Rachel's feet as she made her way up the slope towards the main road. The first snowfall of the year had begun, and snowflakes clung to the fur trim of her coat.

If Rachel Pearson had known tonight would be her last, she would have stopped to appreciate the beauty of a thousand stars twinkling above the North Sea. She would've called her parents and told them that she loved them. She would've called her boyfriend and forgiven him for the horrible things he'd said.

She would have stuck to the main road instead of taking a shortcut.

Rachel pushed headphones into her ears and selected a Christmas playlist. It was still November, but as far as Rachel was concerned, once Guy Fawkes night was out of the way, Christmas tunes were fair game. She loved anything festive, and she was currently halfway through hand-making Christmas cards for her friends and family. Standing at the crossroads between the steep bank up to Tynemouth village and a deserted, unlit car park, Rachel weighed up her options. It would take twenty minutes to walk home through the village but eight minutes tops if she took the shortcut. She had promised her dad that she wouldn't, but the sooner she got home, the sooner she could shower, get into her pyjamas and finish her stupid biology assignment before calling Will to see if he was ready to apologise.

The shortcut won.

Rachel activated the torch on her phone and scanned it back and forth over the frosty ground as she carefully made her way across the car park. Despite the joyful music that made her bob her head and tap her candy-pink nails against the inside of her pocket, prickles ran down the back of Rachel's neck. This route home always gave her the heebie-jeebies. Perhaps it was the pitch-black or the chilling sea breeze, or maybe it was the unshakable suspicion that she was being followed.

A well-worn path connected the back of the car park to a large field dominated by the Collingwood Monument, a tribute to local-born Lord Collingwood, Nelson's partner in the Napoleonic wars.

Rachel was careful of her footing where the ground changed from asphalt to mud. She dug her toes into the frozen earth and pushed herself through the narrow gap between the bushes.

She couldn't wait to get home and back into the warmth.

Baby, It's Cold Outside began to play. She loved this number as a little girl, but the older she got, the creepier it sounded. Rachel skipped the song. The lull in the music happened just in time to hear the crack of a twig behind her. It was not in time to stop the plastic bag from being pulled over her head.

-CHAPTER 2-

TERRY PARKE SHOOK HIS head at his wife.

"You're stark raving mad. It's brass monkeys today, or haven't you noticed?"

Gwen smiled at him as she removed her coat and jumper. He was right about the weather, and though she'd never admit it, he was probably right about her; she was an absolute lunatic for wanting to go for a swim in the North Sea on a day like this. To be fair, she'd thought the same thing when she first saw Doris strip off and run straight into the sea wearing nothing but a polka dot bikini.

The Ageing Disgracefully Club liked to meet every Wednesday morning come rain or shine to have a quick energising dip, boost their endorphins and get the blood flowing. There were eight of them in total, all women, all in their sixties and seventies, and all of whom had husbands who thought they were completely bonkers.

TERRY THREW A TENNIS ball for his daft-as-a-brush Patterdale terrier and watched him shoot off across the beach, his tail wagging with every step. It was three below zero and even the sand was frosted over. Terry blew into his hands, desperately trying to warm them before shoving them deep into his pockets and walking in pursuit of the dog. The little dafty was more than happy to chase the ball but would never bring the damn thing back.

"Should've got a retriever," mumbled Terry.

Behind him, Gwen was running gleefully towards the water's edge, knees high, arms flailing, and all Terry's favourite bits wobbling. Doris and the others weren't far behind. He could hear their excited squeals as their feet touched the bracing North Sea for the first time that week. Only toddlers and women over forty could reach that pitch. Terry was surprised the terrier's floppy ears hadn't pricked up.

"Come on, Jasper. Get over here. Good boy. How's about when your mother's finished playing silly buggers we pop to the café in the village and get ourselves a nice cup of tea and a bacon butty? Sound good, lad?"

The terrier sat and wagged his tail. Terry was convinced the dog knew exactly what he was saying. He puffed out his breath and watched it condense in the icy air.

"Then it's a deal. Bacon butties it is. Now FETCH!"

The dog hightailed it across Prior's Haven, kicking up plumes of sand in his wake. Tennis ball in mouth, he turned and considered a return to his master only to become distracted by something in one of the sailing boats. Terry tutted, the boats should've been moved to storage for the winter, and in fairness, most of them had been. Some people, however, had more money than sense and had left the laser dinghies to face a north-eastern winter unprotected from the elements.

"Leave it, Jasper."

The dog scurried up to the edge of the laser, his nose peering into the boat, his tail rigid.

"Jasper, whatever it is, leave it alone, ya daft mutt. Get your ball. Come on, for once in ya life, fetch the damn ball."

Wendy, the eldest member of the group, was out of the water now; the quick splash had been more than enough for her. She wrapped herself in a thick white towel and giggled as she watched her friends bounce in the gentle waves.

"Jasper, leave it! Honestly, I've never known a more disobedient dog."

Terry huffed under his breath. He needed to get Gwen's towel ready and pour her some coffee from his flask. Jasper had better not be nose deep in a dead seagull like he had been the last time. Disgusting flying rats. The mangy thing had been full of maggots.

Oh dear God.

Terry fell over backwards and cursed as his behind hit the cold, hard sand. *Dear God.* He tried to yell, but no sound escaped his lips. The girl was young, a teenager most likely, and thin, painfully thin. Her long spindly legs were pale and folded into the boat at such an angle she appeared knock-kneed. She wore shiny black stilettos but no trousers or skirt. Above the waist she was dressed in a white, bloodstained shirt and a black blazer. Bizarrely, a top hat was perched jauntily atop her head, and a magic wand stuck out of her blazer pocket. Long, dark plaits that reached her waist were crossed over her chest. It took a while for Terry to notice that a white rabbit, its pink eyes foggy from death, had been tucked into the crook of her arm.

"Oh sweet Jesus," he stammered, trying to push himself back to his feet. The scream finally came and he bellowed, "POLICE. We n-need to c-call the POLICE."

Terry grabbed Jasper's collar and pulled him into his chest.

"Terrence? Is everything all right?" called Doris. She shuffled out of the water, a goosebump-covered woman with rapidly reddening legs.

Gwen frowned and followed her friend. "What's going on, Terry?"

Terry turned as eight shivering ladies in their swimwear plodded up the beach to see what all the fuss was about.

"Police, you say?" asked Susan, who was rapidly approaching seventy. "What's the fettle?"

Terry's protective instincts kicked in. He had been raised in an age of chivalry, a time when it was good manners - not offensive - to offer your seat on the bus to a pregnant lady. But times were changing, and only last week he'd been called a sexist for telling a young lad off for swearing when there were ladies present. Sexist or not, Terry didn't want his wife or her friends to see what he'd just seen. He was old-fashioned and proudly so.

"No. NO!" He ran towards them. "Don't look. Please, Gwen." His arms were extended as he tried in vain to shepherd the women away from the scene. "You don't need to see that. You don't need—"

"Holy Mary, mother of God."

Gwen collapsed to her knees; sand clung to her damp, pink skin.

"Poor child. Poor, poor child."

"Please, Gwen," begged Terry. "Please get dry. Get dressed. There's nothing we can do. The poor bairn—"

"CPR. Start CPR." Susan's voice was shrill - as high-pitched as it had been only minutes earlier when she'd raced into the sea - only now it was with horror, not joy.

"She's gone," said Terry. He felt helpless, a feeling he was experiencing more and more since shifting to the wrong side of sixty-five. "Please darling, we can't do anything... Oh Gwen, you're turning blue. Please, you'll catch your death."

-CHAPTER 3-

"But Mum."

"But nothing, Tina. I said no, and I mean no."

Tina sighed. Her eyes were locked on her mother's. She didn't want to give an inch, didn't want to back down.

"I'll be in the spare room. Josh's parents will be there."

"It's still a no, Tina."

"You can call them; they're called Reg and Lucy. They said it's fine."

"And I said it's not. There's no way on Earth I am letting my fourteen-year-old *crash* at her boyfriend's house. Spare room or not. Ask again in two years."

Tina's face crumpled. "Honestly, you are such a BITCH." She stormed upstairs, slamming her bedroom door behind her.

DCI Erica Cooper closed her eyes. This was all she needed. In other homes, one parent would turn to the other for backup, but this was a single-parent household. Tina's father had been nothing more than a monthly child support payment for twelve years. Two years ago, he'd flounced back onto Tyneside after eight years in the south and four years in Qatar and had expected to instantly bond with his estranged daughter. Both Cooper and Tina had understandably been less than impressed at the idea, but lately, Tina had agreed to weekly visits.

Cooper heard Tina's bedroom door creak on its hinges.

"It's 'cause I'm an aspie, isn't it? If I was normal you'd let me."

Cooper propped her elbows on the kitchen table and lowered her head into her hands. As much as she wanted to tell herself that Tina's ASD had nothing to do with this, it probably did. Her daughter wasn't slow; in fact, the opposite was true. Academically, she was gifted. The term *prodigy* had been bandied about by more than one of Tina's teachers. But Tina struggled to make friends, and her longing for acceptance meant she was easily led. She'd do anything to fit in. Anything to be liked.

"Mum!"

"I heard you," shouted Cooper. She hated talking through walls. "And one, no, it has nothing to do with that. Two, there's no such thing as normal. And three, I'm not going to keep repeating myself. Come down and finish your breakfast."

"I'm going to ask Dad."

The door slammed shut again. Cooper took a deep breath and counted to ten. "Yeah, good luck with that," she muttered through clenched teeth.

Tina had timed this tantrum to perfection, thought Cooper as she looked at her reflection in a stainless steel kettle. The wig wasn't convincing. It was made from real hair, and the light brown colour matched her own. Still, the cut wasn't quite right, nor was the texture. Cooper's hair had a natural kink to it and it fell in gentle waves to her collarbones, or at least it had done until chemo caused it to fall out. Then there was the fringe. Cooper tilted her head back and forth and tried to convince herself that she quite suited a fringe and poker-straight locks, but it was no use, she didn't look like her old self, and she hadn't for many months. A tailored suit that had previously hugged her thirty-something curves was now baggy and hung off the edges of her shoulders like an adult-sized shirt on a child-sized hanger. Cooper's belt was fastened two notches tighter, and her energy levels had dropped from bordering on hyperactive to being in desperate need of recharging. Had she been naive in thinking her first day back at CID after four months of sick leave was going to go smoothly?

Cooper checked her watch. Perhaps she could salvage the day once Tina had been packed off to school by treating herself to a Starbucks and a pastry en route to HQ.

Her phone rang.

"Have you lost your mind?" It was Kenny, the monthly child support payment. "Telling our daughter she can have a sleepover at that cretin's house? No daughter of mine is going to become another teenage pregnancy statistic."

"Like I was, you mean? I seem to remember you playing a minor role in that debacle."

There was a snort at the other end of the phone.

"Besides," Cooper continued, "I never told Tina she could stay at Josh's. In fact, I told her the opposite. Let me guess, she said that *I'd say yes if you said yes*, and she buttered you up by saying she'd spend the whole weekend with you so you two could have some quality daddy-daughter time?"

"How'd you know that?" he asked, a bark still in his voice.

"Because I've lived with her for fourteen years, Kenneth." Cooper's voice was harsh, she hadn't intended to snap at Kenny, but he made it so bloody easy. She ran a hand over her forehead and played with her new fringe. "Sorry. Look, our daughter is a sneaky little genius. Now don't blame me. She gets it from you. I have to go, Kenny. I'm back at work today; I need to get off."

"That's today?"

Cooper could hear the guilt in his voice.

"Right, well, best of luck. Not that you need it. Sorry about going off on you. Should have known."

Cooper ended the call and took a long gulp of coffee. It was cold and bitter but she needed the caffeine.

"Tina, time for school," she called up the stairs.

The door creaked. "I'm not going." Then it slammed again.

It was a bluff - Tina was a stickler for routine - but it was a bluff Cooper could do without. She was about to march up the stairs when her phone rang again.

"Cooper. You live in Tynemouth. How quickly can you be at the Priory?"

Detective Chief Superintendent Howard Nixon was a gruffly spoken man with little time for *hi, how are yous*. The Priory, Cooper knew, was the ruined remains of Tynemouth Castle and a Benedictine monastery where the old kings of Northumberland were buried. It sat atop Ben Pal Crag, sporting views of King Edward's Bay to the north and the river Tyne to the south.

Cooper pinched the bridge of her nose. "I can be there in under ten, sir. What do I need to know?"

"Body of a young woman found in one of the boats at the sailing club. She's in fancy dress and cuddling a dead rabbit."

Cooper's brows knitted together. "Sir?"

"Aye. Might be some student initiation gone wrong. Got drunk, got separated, fell asleep in the cold. But the gent who called it in reported the woman had no trousers or skirt on, and there's blood on her shirt. You still got a field kit, Cooper?"

"Yes, sir. I'm looking at it right now."

Cooper got to her feet; she tucked her phone between her ear and shoulder and pulled on a thick woollen coat.

"Good. Uniforms are securing the scene. Forensics are on the way."

"Who's the SOCO, sir?"

"Atkinson," replied Nixon.

Cooper nodded. She had a good relationship with Justin Atkinson. He was the first scene of crime officer she'd dealt with upon joining the force. He was there when she saw her first dead body, and he was the only one not to take the piss because she'd thrown up all over her own shoes at the sight of it.

"I'm putting Daniel on this. He'll meet you there."

Cooper was about to respond when Nixon hung up.

"*How are you feeling, Cooper?*" the detective drawled in a facsimile of Nixon's voice while she cleared her breakfast items into the dishwasher. "*Good to have you back, Cooper... Let us know how we can ease you back into the swing of things, Cooper.*"

"Tina!" she called, more loudly this time. She picked up her field kit and pulled sheep-skin gloves over her hands. "Got to go. You'll have to walk to school."

A grunt of annoyance echoed down the hallway, but if Tina had anything else to say to her mother, it would have to wait until dinner.

-CHAPTER 4-

Cooper parked her beat-up old Mazda in a short-stay car park near the sailing club. She pulled up the collar of her coat to protect her neck from the icy wind and stepped out into the crisp morning air.

"So much for a Starbucks and a pastry," she grumbled to herself.

She wrapped her arms around her torso and shuffled down the bank towards Prior's Haven.

Police tape cordoned off access to the beach. As Cooper approached, she flashed her warrant card at two uniforms who stood aside and held up the tape for her to manoeuvre herself under. Steep cliffs overlooked both sides of Prior's Haven. Numerous nosy parkers had already gathered on the Spanish Battery to the south. They were angling morbidly to catch a glimpse of the victim. They'd be disappointed; a sizable forensic tent protected the young woman's dignity.

"Morning, Tennessee," greeted Cooper to Detective Sergeant Jack Daniel.

Tennessee was a statuesque young man with an angelic face that would be better suited to modelling Armani than to patrolling the streets of North Tyneside. He had unruly blond curls and the sort of healthy complexion Cooper would've killed for, even before her illness.

"Ma'am! It's good to have you back." He clasped her gloved hands in his and beamed at her. He looked like he wanted to hug her. Cooper instinctively took a step backwards. Hugging officers at a possible murder scene would not go down well with the crowd of onlookers.

"Ma'am?" asked Cooper with raised eyebrows. "Surely I'm not old enough to warrant the ma'am treatment? You know it's Cooper. Any more ma'am nonsense and I'll have you transferred to Sunderland."

Tennessee nodded formally. "Yes, ma'am. I mean Cooper. Ah, please don't transfer me to Sunderland. My dad will never let me hear the end of it, ma'am. I mean Cooper. Ah, shit."

Cooper held in her giggle and remained poker-faced.

"Bring me up to speed, Tennessee."

"The vic looks to be in her mid to late teens. She's dressed in some sort of magician's outfit with a top hat and magic wand. Uniforms are taking statements from local residents, but most of them have already left for work. Atkinson's in the tent, and his assistant's scouring the beach for evidence. We've been trying to get hold of someone from the sailing and rowing clubs. Both buildings have CCTV on the entranceways. There's no street lighting down here, but the clubs have movement-activated lighting on the doors. I'll let you know when we've tracked down the committee members who have access to the cameras."

Cooper nodded and looked around. She knew this area well. When Tina was an infant, Cooper would bring her to the secluded beach for picnics. They'd amble hand-in-hand along the kilometre-long pier keeping their eyes peeled for dolphins.

Tennessee's phone buzzed and he retrieved it from his pocket.

"DS Daniel," he said. He paused for a second while the person on the other end of the call spoke. "Cooper," he covered the microphone on his mobile. "It's one of the geezers from the sailing club." He put the phone back to his ear and strode towards the water's edge. "Yes, we'd appreciate your help on this matter... As soon as possible, sir."

Cooper readied herself as she pulled on a bunny suit and gloves. She still hadn't grown used to the sight or smell of death, and part of her hoped she never would. She didn't want to become one of those jaded old coppers who could look at a corpse and make an inappropriate joke. Nixon came to mind.

Taking a deep breath of sea air, Cooper bowed her head and entered the forensics tent. Justin Atkinson was crouched next to the body of what had once been a beautiful young lady. She had stalk-thin legs and her brown hair was styled in two long braids that reached her waist. From where Cooper stood, she could see a patch of blood on her white shirt and bruising around the girl's neck. She watched as Atkinson worked, taking samples from behind the girl's fingernails, bagging and labelling as he went. To the left of the boat, a collapsible table was set up. Atkinson's equipment and storage boxes were laid out in perfect right angles, and five pens lay precisely parallel to each other.

Only when Cooper spotted the dead rabbit, bagged and sealed, did she let out a gasp. "Bloody hell."

Atkinson looked up. "Well, if it isn't Erica Cooper."

"Good to see you, Justin." And it was. "I just wish it were under better circumstances."

"Yes. Same here." Justin Atkinson's frameless glasses perched on the tip of his nose, and his pronounced Adam's apple bounced as he talked. He straightened up to his full height of six-foot-four and looked down at Cooper with sadness in his eyes. "I try to stay professional, you know that, but it's hard when they're so young. So much wasted potential."

"How old was she?"

"I'd guess fourteen to seventeen. The pathologist will be able to narrow it down if she's not identified."

Cooper bit her lip and looked at the bruising. "Strangled?"

"Looks that way. Again, Margot will tell us more."

"Margot Swanson? They're taking her to the Freeman?" she asked, referring to a hospital in

B BASKERVILLE

Heaton where Cooper had undergone most of her cancer treatment.

"Yeah," answered Atkinson. He deposited a swab into a little transparent tube, tightened the lid and removed his gloves. "She's on her way. The Royal Victoria's overrun at the moment. Big multi-vehicle in the West End last night. Anything new's being directed to the Freeman until we're told otherwise."

Cooper swallowed and stuck her head back outside the tent under the guise of needing some fresh air. Rumour had it Margot Swanson was romantically involved with Detective Neil Fuller. Fuller had been Cooper's on again off again lover for over a year; he'd become permanently off again two days after Cooper found the lump in her right breast.

Dealing with Margot Swanson was the last thing Cooper wanted to do. She ran the back of her hands over her mouth and stared out to sea. In the distance, a score of seagulls chased a fishing trawler that was returning to port and headed for the Fish Quay.

"Okay," she said with artificial pep. "What do you have so far?"

Atkinson rubbed the grey stubble on his chin. "Bruising to the neck, probable strangulation. Additional dark powder residue on the neck and ankles. Charcoal perhaps. Samples are off to the lab this afternoon. I was hoping to lift prints from the ankles, but the marks are heavily smudged; I can't get a thing."

Atkinson used tongs to lift the girl's shirt back and revealed a cut to her chest. "She's been sliced open and stitched back up. I shudder to think. I've taken hair samples from the jacket and examined her nails."

Cooper's eyes darted to the victim's nails. They were painted Barbie pink, and all but one were talon-long.

"There's no blood under the nails from what I can tell," continued Atkinson, "but there's plenty of mud, a few blades of grass too."

"Mud?" Cooper met Atkinson's eyes.

"Indeed. Mud, not sand."

"Suggesting she was killed elsewhere and then dumped in the boat?"

"I wouldn't say she was dumped," said Atkinson. "I think *displayed* would be a better term."

"You're right," sighed Cooper, wondering what sort of depraved individual she was dealing with. "The outfit? The rabbit? Whoever did this wanted her to be found; otherwise, he could have pushed her off North Pier, and she'd never have been seen again."

"Or he could've rolled her off the clifftop and made it look like an accident."

"Any prints on the boat? Her clothes?"

"The boat's riddled with prints. Every sailor in the club will have helped haul it up the beach. Then you've got all the kids and dog walkers who come down here. As for the clothes, there are partial prints on the shoes. They're a few sizes too big for her. Look." He pointed to where the shiny leather gaped behind the girl's heels. "And there are numerous mismatched fibres and hairs on the jacket. Hong has started checking the field directly behind us, but he hasn't found signs of a struggle there. There are tyre marks where cars have clipped the edge of the field. We'll take impressions, of course. Just in case."

"Right," said Cooper. The beach may have been tiny, but it had a high volume of traffic between the two clubs and the dog walkers. There was likely to be over a hundred different cars using this stretch of road on any given week.

The sub-zero temperature was beginning to affect Cooper's body. She started to shiver; under the wig, her scalp was itchy.

"Good start, Justin. Keep me in the loop."

Atkinson bobbed his head, then he pushed one of the pens on the table a millimetre to the left.

Cooper stepped out of the tent and found Tennessee talking to Hong, Atkinson's assistant. He held a condom with a pair of tweezers and dropped it into an evidence bag.

"Detective," she called, grabbing Tennessee's attention. "We need more manpower. Request a team down here to scour the area. Have the uniforms extend the perimeter to cover the fields on the Spanish Battery and around the Collingwood monument. We're looking for the victim's clothing. Those clothes aren't her own. For one thing, the shoes don't fit. And look for any signs of a struggle, including evidence of nails being dragged through mud or grassland. She's missing a nail. Pink varnish."

Tennessee closed his notepad and tucked it into his inside pocket. "I'll get on it right away." The young man's eyes darted over Cooper's face. "You doing okay? I am allowed to ask that, right? It's just, you look a little pale."

Cooper felt chilled to her bones. "Just hitting the ground running, Tennessee." She reached out and patted the man on his arm. "And yes, you're allowed to ask."

- CHAPTER 5 -

THE HEADQUARTERS FOR NORTHUMBRIA Police were housed in Wallsend. An area three miles east of Newcastle upon Tyne and so named for being the end of Hadrian's Wall, the seventy-mile fortification that marked the northern boundary of the Roman Empire.

Cooper paced back and forth along a magnolia corridor. She clutched a file to her chest and wished she'd worn her navy suit; navy commanded more respect. Beyond the double doors at the end of the hall, her team were waiting to be briefed. She hadn't seen some of the people in the room for months. Would they treat her differently? Cooper didn't know how to play it. Cool and calm? She could go in with all guns blazing, but that would be obvious over-compensation. She thought honesty was the best policy, but Cooper couldn't bring herself to tell the team she wanted to go home and get into bed. She could barely admit it to herself.

Cooper tapped her feet and looked at the strip lighting on the ceiling for inspiration. When none came, she pulled her shoulders back and strode into CID.

"Right, take your seats. Phones down, eyes up."

The room fell silent. Cooper quickly scanned the place; it looked just as dreary it always had. She hadn't expected banners and balloons, but some cake would have been nice.

"The body of a teenage girl was discovered at Prior's Haven this morning by a...." She checked her notes and took a breath to steady her voice. "Terry Parke. She was dressed up to look like a magician, complete with, I'm sure you've heard, a dead rabbit."

Cooper paused to make eye contact with some of the group.

"Initial impressions indicate strangulation. The SOCOs have an overabundance of prints and DNA from the boat, as well as the clothes she was dressed in. It's going to take Atkinson a while to sift through his findings, so in the meantime, we need to need to get down to business. Who is she?"

Cooper stuck a photo of the girl's face to a whiteboard and turned to face the other detectives.

A man with a middle-aged hairline and a middle-aged spread coughed and got to his feet.

"I might be able to answer that."

"Go ahead, Sutherland."

Sam Sutherland opened his notepad and spoke with a heavy northern accent. "Fifteen-year-old

Rachel Pearson of Oxford Street, Tynemouth was reported missing at nine-thirty last night. Parents reported it after she didn't come home from yoga. Guess where her yoga classes were held?"

"The sailing club?"

"Bingo. Physical description matches the victim. Long dark hair, slim build, five-foot-three. When she left home at ten past six, she was wearing cloud-print leggings, a blue Adidas sweatshirt and a black, knee-length winter coat with a fur trim hood."

Tennessee raised his pen in the air. "I have a girl in a fur trim coat and blue and white leggings on CCTV leaving the sailing club shortly after seven-thirty."

"That's our girl," said Sutherland. He walked around his desk, opened a file and flicked through some papers for a moment. "Yes. When she didn't come home, the parents called her friends and her boyfriend, but no one knew where she was."

Cooper perched herself on the edge of a desk and crossed her legs. "Do we have more from the scene? Keaton?"

DS Paula Keaton was round-faced with an upturned nose. At five-ten and a former rugby player, Keaton was built - as Superintendent Nixon would describe - like a brick shithouse.

"We have, boss. A pink yoga mat was found in the bushes at the back of Haven car park."

Cooper looked to Sutherland.

"Aye," he answered. "The girl's mother said she'd be carrying a pink mat."

"Any sign of the clothing?"

26

"Not that I've heard, boss. But Atkinson's just been on the phone. The uniforms have possible clawing marks in the ground at the back of the car park. Photos should be in your inbox within the hour, and they're taking casts."

Cooper unlocked her phone and opened Google Maps. "Oxford Street?" The map showed a corner of green where the river met the sea. The southern end of Oxford Street connected to a pathway that, if followed west, would reach the Fish Quay, and if followed east, would reach the Spanish Battery. "She might have been taking a shortcut home. There looks to be worn trails crisscrossing the fields between the coast and her street."

Keaton shuffled and began clicking the top of her pen. "The lighting down there's atrocious. Gives me the creeps at night time. Be a miracle if anyone saw anything."

Cooper couldn't help but agree. "What's the media situation?"

"The switchboard's been inundated," said Tennessee. "We've asked the press to keep a lid on things until we inform the family."

"The mainstream press might hold the story," started Sutherland, "But social media's already swamped with photos of the forensics tent down at the Haven."

"Right," said Cooper with a sigh. "Well, we'd better get a wiggle on, hadn't we? Sutherland and Keaton, head back to Prior's Haven and check in with the guys doing door-to-doors. Get hold of the yoga instructor. We need a list of everyone at the class last night. Track them down, find out who saw what."

Sutherland was already pulling his coat on.

"Tennessee, you're with me. Get an FLO ready," she added, referring to family liaison officers. "We need to tell the Pearsons."

Tennessee's shoulders slumped; his eyes lowered. It was part of the job every officer dreaded. Keaton patted the younger man on his back as she passed. When she reached the doorway - which she filled - Keaton turned to Cooper.

"Welcome back, boss."

"HOW'S HAYLEY?" ASKED COOPER.

"Eight months gone now. Turn left here." He pointed right.

Cooper had learned long ago that Tennessee's verbal directions were never to be trusted. Left meant right, north meant south, and *it's a seventy* almost always meant *it's a fifty and there's a speed camera up ahead.*

"Hard to believe I'm going to be a dad in a few weeks."

"Tell me about it," answered Cooper. "You look barely old enough to drink. Do you know if you're having a girl or a boy?"

"A boy. Left again. Hayley wants to name the little guy Alfred after her pa, but I think it's too old-fashioned."

"And let me guess. You want to name him after United's starting eleven?"

Cooper parked the Mazda in front of a semi-detached new-build in a small cul-de-sac and killed the engine. Immediately the temperature inside the car began to drop.

"I was thinking Bobby."

Cooper chuckled. Bobby Robson had been a local hero, a great manager and an upstanding gentleman. There were worse people to name your kid after.

Tennessee doubled over, and Cooper swore she saw his eyes darken a shade. "I can't stand this bit."

"None of us can, Jack. But it's nothing compared to how Mr and Mrs Pearson are about to feel." Cooper exhaled and watched her breath fog in front of her face. "Is the FLO on the way?"

Tennessee's knees bounced up and down. "ETA's ten minutes."

Cooper exited the vehicle and walked up to the house. Tennessee lagged behind by two steps. The Pearson's front door was dusty and covered in cobwebs, the paintwork around the window frames flaked, and a large crack ran through the doorstep. Cooper gave her DS a supportive look as she rang the doorbell. The young man had a great future ahead of him in CID, and Cooper recognised her responsibility in helping to shape his career. She had to lead by example.

There was a rush of footsteps before the door swung open. An exhausted-looking woman with frantic eyes and smoker's lips looked expectantly up and down the street.

"Rachel? Is she with you? Did you find her?"

"Mrs Pearson? I'm DCI Erica Cooper," she held up her warrant card. "This is DS Daniel. May we come in?"

Mrs Pearson must have read something in the expressions on the detectives' faces because she crumbled, folding herself in two, arms cradling her stomach.

"No, no," she began to wail. "It's her, isn't it? I saw on Facebook. The body? Please say it's not her."

The slim woman began to hyperventilate.

"Sally?" A heavy-set man emerged in the Pearson's hallway. He pushed his phone into the back pocket of his jeans and rushed to his wife. "What's happened?" he asked Cooper. "Haven't you found her yet? Where's Rachel?"

"Mr Pearson." Tennessee's voice had a stillness to it. "We really need to come inside."

The man pulled his wife to her feet. "Right," he said. "This way."

The Pearsons led Cooper and Tennessee to their living room, and Cooper motioned for them to take a seat. Their sofa was covered in protective plastic sheeting; it emitted a squeaking noise as Mr Pearson sat and adjusted his weight. He squeezed his wife's hand and looked up at Cooper with bloodshot eyes.

Cooper knew there was no sense in delaying the inevitable or trying to soften the blow. "I'm afraid the body of a young woman matching Rachel's description was found at Prior's Haven early this morning—"

"It's not her," snapped Rachel's father. "She's at a friend's."

Sally Pearson's eyes were red with tears. "She's not at a friend's, Lou. We tried all her friends. We called them all. We Facebooked everyone."

"It's not her," he repeated.

"We can't know that for certain, Mr Pearson, but given the location and the discovery of a pink yoga mat nearby...." Cooper's voice trailed away for a moment. "We're going to need you to attend the Freeman Hospital to make an identification." She checked her watch; the FLO should be there soon. Sally and Lou Pearson would need all the help they could provide. "If you don't feel you can perform the identification, please let us know, and we can arrange for someone else who was close to Rachel to attend. An aunt or uncle, perhaps."

Sally Pearson clutched a cushion with both hands. "No. It should be us. I need to see."

Lou Pearson wrapped an arm around his wife. "It won't be her," he said. "You'll see. It'll be some other poor lass. It won't be her."

Cooper's stomach was turning over. The denial mixed with grief and dread was hard to watch.

"I'm very sorry," said Tennessee. He straightened his posture and removed a notepad from his coat pocket. "But we need to ask you some questions. I know you went over a lot of this when you reported your daughter missing, but it would really help us if we could go over a few things again."

Lou Pearson's brows lowered half an inch, and he removed his arm from his wife's shoulders so he could fold his arms across his chest. "Hold on a minute. Are you saying we're suspects? You have a nerve, lad."

Tennessee hadn't said that. Not even close. But Cooper noted how quickly Lou Pearson jumped to that conclusion.

"No, Mr Pearson. But I do need to get a gauge of Rachel's movements."

Sally Pearson placed a calming hand on her husband's knee. When he swiped it away, she got to her feet and began pacing the room, wringing her hands. "I need a smoke," she declared before heading to the back door of the home.

"Mr Pearson," said Tennessee. "Can you go over the events of last night for me?"

The man's eyes returned from following his wife. He clenched his hands into fists and hid his face behind them for a moment. "Rachel goes to yoga every Tuesday and Thursday," he started. "It's part of her rehab. She fell down the stairs, you see. Last year. She couldn't walk for a long time, needed surgery and physio, the works. She can walk again now, but with a bit of a limp, and she still struggles on uneven ground. She won't accept lifts. Very independent girl. Always has been."

His eyes flicked to the front window as he saw Pru Wilson, the family liaison officer approach.

"I'll get it," said Tennessee.

Lou Pearson's tone began to relax. "She was wearing leggings with clouds on them and a blue sweatshirt. Adidas, I think. Her coat is black with a furry hood. It's one of those padded ones, like a quilt."

Cooper nodded. "This is good, Mr Pearson. You're doing really well. Can you tell us the timings? When she left, what time she'd usually be back?"

"The class is six-thirty to seven-thirty," he looked up and watched Tennessee guide the FLO towards the back of the house to introduce her to Sally Pearson. "She usually sets off from here at ten past six, a little earlier if she wants a spot at the front of the class. Most of the time, she's back home by eight, but sometimes she'll pop by Will's, so we didn't worry at first."

"And Will is?"

"Will Harper. Rachel's boyfriend." His voice was tinged with objection. "We called her at half eight, but it went straight through to her answerphone. I called Will shortly after. I was in two minds 'cause Rachel doesn't like being checked up on. Typical teen, right?"

"Very typical," said Cooper. She could relate.

"But her dinner was getting cold, so I called. Will said he hadn't seen or heard from her since school."

"Which school does Rachel attend?"

"Tynemouth Academy."

Cooper's back tensed. "How was Rachel's demeanour yesterday?"

"She was quiet. She can be tetchy. Never used to be, mind you. The accident changed her. She gets frustrated easily, very sarcastic, can fly off the handle."

"It must have been difficult. Learning to walk again."

Lou Pearson's hands formed back into fists. "Gymnastics was her life. She wanted to go to the Olympics. I know lots of kids say that, but Rachel was actually on track for it." He motioned to the mantlepiece where rosettes and trophies surrounded framed photos of Rachel in her leotard. "She was on the under sixteen's England team. Got a silver medal at the junior Europeans."

The Rachel in the photographs was lean and muscular. Her thighs were thick, a stark contrast to the stalk thin ones Cooper had seen that morning. The atrophy after her accident must have been immense.

Cooper's eyes flicked to the coal fire underneath the mantlepiece. It was beginning to die down. The sound of the back door clicking back into place preceded Tennessee, Sally Pearson and Pru Wilson's return to the living room. Sally Pearson was a broken woman. Her body shook as she walked, and she supported herself on the furniture as she passed. She looked as if she might collapse at any moment.

Cooper acknowledged the newcomer with a nod. "Mr Pearson, this is Pru Wilson. She's a family liaison officer with Northumbria Police. Her role is to support you and Mrs Pearson, act as a point of contact and keep you updated with the case."

Pru was young and blonde, with a spread of freckles across her cheeks.

"I'm going to make us all a cup of tea," said Pru. "Then it would be a great help to us if you could make a list of all of Rachel's friends, including the ones you contacted yesterday evening."

Lou Pearson nodded.

Cooper followed Pru to the kitchen and had a quick chat with her to make sure she was up to date with everything that had occurred. Then Cooper and Tennessee let themselves out, catching a glimpse of Lou Pearson adding a few lumps of coal to the fire.

The winter air hit Cooper's chest, knocking the wind out of her. "Did you get anything from the mother?" she asked, her voice wheezy.

Tennessee jumped into the car and buckled up. "Not a lot. She was hysterical. Understandably. I've got an address for the boyfriend, a William Harper. Apparently, the father didn't approve."

"They never do."

"I asked if she knew of anyone who would want to harm Rachel, but the mother says she was a popular girl. Had loads of friends. Always invited to birthday parties, shopping, the usual. The mother didn't know of any fallings out and is adamant her daughter never touched drugs.

Cooper's phone buzzed. She selected speakerphone before answering.

"Cooper here."

"Erica, it's Margot Swanson from the Freeman," her voice had a sing-song Highlands lilt to it.

Cooper's teeth ground as she started the engine and put the car into reverse. "You received the body?"

"Yes." There was a pause. "Erica, erm... You might want to see this."

-CHAPTER 6-

THE THIN HAIRS ON Cooper's arms stood on end. The cooling system in the morgue was somewhat excessive on a winter's day such as this. Keeping her coat and gloves on, she held the door for Tennessee and followed the route to the post-mortem room where she'd been told Margot Swanson would be waiting in room B.

Rows of stainless steel drawers reminded Cooper of filing cabinets, only these housed the recently deceased rather than folders of accounts and reports. The morgue had a stench made up of death, bleach and anti-bacterial gel. Every time Cooper encountered it, her mind conjured up an image of vomit-splattered Kurt Geiger shoes.

"Erica." A side door leading off from the morgue opened, and Margot poked her head out. "This way, please. Jack, good to see you. Is it still snowing out there?"

"Just a dusting," answered Tennessee. "More forecast for later."

Margot shuddered dramatically. "Only one cure for this weather. A roaring fire, a bottle of port and an epic cheeseboard. Am I right?"

Cooper didn't answer, but Tennessee's eyes drifted to the right. Presumably, he was picturing the curvaceous pathologist lazing by an open fire. Margot Swanson was Scottish, fifty-something, voluptuous and a known flirt. She had double D's, full lips and a penchant for younger men. Cooper believed the technical term was: *Cougar.*

"Shall we get this over with? What couldn't I be told over the phone?"

Margot bristled and ran her hands down the sides of her lab coat. How she made it look like a designer dress, Cooper would never know. She pulled the sheets back from Rachel's face and waited a moment for Cooper and Tennessee to gather themselves.

"Well, I'm not nearly done, and we're going to be waiting a few days for toxicology - they're backed up - but I'll run through what I have so far. We have ligature marks on the neck," she pointed to red and purple marks that looped around Rachel's neck like a macabre necklace. "Justin found some shredded plastic under the victim's nails in his initial assessment and I've found more of the same in her throat."

Tennessee swallowed. "She was suffocated with a plastic bag?"

"That would be my assumption," started Margot. "However, we also have finger and thumb-sized bruises to the neck. I would suggest there was an attempt at suffocation. When she clawed through the bag, our lad or lassie changed their MO to strangulation."

Cooper was sceptical at Margot's use of the word *lassie*. Females rarely conducted this sort of crime. It wasn't sexism; it was statistics. "You think a woman could have done this?"

"The size of the bruising would suggest male, but a larger female would be a possibility." Margot pointed to the girl's neck. "It's also worth noting that her larynx is fractured. Whoever did this didn't just stop her from breathing; they completely throttled her."

Tennessee turned away from the stainless steel examination table and wrinkled up his eyes.

"But moving on," continued Margot. "Taking account of the temperature last night, which would have delayed rigor and algor mortis somewhat, I'd put an estimated time of death at eight p.m. last night."

"That fits with our timeline," confirmed Tennessee, his back still to the table.

Cooper ran her gloved hand over the back of her neck. "Any evidence of sexual assault?"

Margot steepled her fingers. "Well, as I said earlier, we're not done yet." She moved to her left and rested her hands on the edge of the table. "But I can say at this time it looks unlikely. There is no sign of trauma to her pelvis, and we haven't found any semen on the victim." Her eyes moved to Tennessee. "Are you doing all right, sweetheart? Need some fresh air?"

"He's fine," said Cooper, cutting in. "Keep going."

"It's just... it's not going to get any easier."

"Whatever you need to show us, just show us." Cooper was losing patience. She didn't want to be in this refrigeration unit any longer than necessary, and frankly, everything Margot had told them could've been handled over the phone.

Margot's lip twitched. "Okay," she said, pulling the sheets that covered Rachel further down to reveal her shoulders and upper chest.

"Bloody hell," said Tennessee, his voice weaker than Cooper was used to hearing.

"As you can see, she's been cut open and stitched back together. From what I can tell, the tool used to do this was a flat, very sharp blade. Something akin to a Stanley knife or even a scalpel. The accuracy would indicate that this was conducted by someone with a steady hand."

"What was she stitched back together with?" asked Cooper, leaning in for a closer look at the wound.

"We can run some tests," answered Margot, "but to be honest, it looks like standard sewing thread, the sort you could buy anywhere."

Cooper's hand moved to her chest without thinking. A subconscious show of empathy to Rachel. It was a disturbing truth that some killers got a thrill out of taking a memento from their victims. Usually, they took photographs to preserve the memory forever; sometimes, they'd take an item of jewellery or clothing. Now and again, a special breed of psychopath would take something from the victim's body. Last year Cooper saw a murder victim with all of her fingers and toes removed. And Yorkshire Police dealt with a killer who took teeth from his victims: *The Dentist*, they'd called him.

"And why?" she asked Margot, her hand still on her chest. "Tell me this sicko didn't cut out her heart."

"Actually," said Margot, pausing to pick up an evidence bag from a shelf behind her. "They put something in."

Cooper took the bag and turned it over in her hands. She could sense Tennessee join her, his shadow falling over her shoulder.

"What the actual—?"

Cooper stared down at a small laminated business card. Cream-coloured and texturised, it was plain apart from two words printed in black ink: *The Priestess*.

-CHAPTER 7-

THE PRIESTESS? NOT PRIEST. Priestess. That's why Margot said, *lad or lassie*. That's why she said a larger female could have been responsible.

Cooper opened the front door to her Georgian terrace and was relieved to feel that the heating had come on automatically. Tina's shoes and backpack were in the porch area and sounds from the living room suggested Tina was watching television.

The calling card wouldn't leave Cooper's mind. She pulled her wig from her head and ran her nails over the fine hair on her scalp. *Heaven.* She'd dealt with all kinds of offenders since joining Northumbria CID. Still, she'd never come across a killer who'd left an actual calling card. This was a first. Who the bloody hell was The Priestess?

"Is it true?" Tina was stood in the doorway to the living room. Still dressed in her school uniform, she looked dishevelled.

41

"Have you brushed your hair today?" asked Cooper with narrowed eyes.

"Of course," lied Tina, hastily pulling her locks back into a ponytail and securing it with a bobble from her wrist. "So... Is it true? Is Rachel Pearson dead?"

Bad news obviously travelled fast through Tynemouth Academy.

Cooper exhaled and filled the kettle. "Who told you that?"

"No one. But there's obviously something big going down at Prior's Haven; the pictures of the tent are all over Twitter. Then Rachel didn't show up to school this morning, and Chloe said Rachel's mum called her last night because she hadn't come home." Tina motioned for her mother to sit down while she took over tea-making duties. "Then Will Harper was called out of art class this morning," she said, wagging a teaspoon about, "and he never came back. Not to mention Linda's been running about like a headless chicken all day and looks like she's about to start tearing her hair out. No offence."

"None taken."

Tina might well have a future in CID.

"Thank you," said Cooper when Tina handed her the warm mug. "Sit, and please don't call her Linda. It's Ms Webb."

"When she's at Dad's, I have to call her Linda."

"We're not at Dad's."

Tina sipped her tea but kept her eyes lowered to the table. Cooper reached out and placed a hand over hers.

"Look, Tina, this morning, someone found a body on the beach. Rachel's parents visited the morgue this afternoon and confirmed it was Rachel."

"Fuck."

"Tina!"

"Sorry, Mum, but I can't think of a better word right now."

Cooper's mouth curled at the corner. She had a point. "No, I'm sorry. Were you and Rachel close? We'll need to speak to her friends over the next few days."

Tina huffed and got back to her feet. "As if someone like Rachel would be friends with someone like me."

Tina began to rummage through the kitchen cupboards.

"What do you mean?"

Tina's eyes scanned over a cupboard that was bare apart from a tin of chopped tomatoes and half a pack of spaghetti.

"Tina."

"Can we have fish and chips?"

Cooper had to hold her tongue when it came to Tina's lack of focus. "Yes, if that's what you'd like. Now, what did you mean by *someone like Rachel?*"

Tina closed the cupboard door and rested her back against the worktop. "She's beautiful and popular, and I'm a grade-A weirdo. We don't exactly move in the same circles."

"You're not a weirdo. Don't talk about yourself like that." Cooper's heart broke a little each time she heard her daughter self-deprecate. "Did you have classes with Rachel?"

"Just music, art and PE. We're in different sets for science and English and stuff." Tina opened Cooper's purse and removed a tenner. "This'll be enough, right?"

Cooper nodded. "You and Rachel never chatted during the classes you shared?"

Tina made a noise that resembled *pfft* and started to lace up her shoes. "I mainly keep out of her way. She's the kind of girl who can turn the whole school against you if she wants. Or she was. Anyway, back in ten. Curry sauce?"

Cooper shook her head.

WITH A BELLY FULL of complex carbs, and Tina settled for the night, Cooper poured herself a glass of pinot noir. She wasn't one for midweek drinking, but today had been no ordinary day. She lay down on the sofa and propped her feet up over the armrest. She opened her laptop, rested it on her bloated stomach and began searching Rachel Pearson's social media profiles.

Sally Pearson said her daughter was popular. Cooper thought back to her own teenage years and distinctly remembered that there were two types of popular: the type where everyone loves you, and the type where everyone secretly hates you. From speaking to Tina, it was possible that Rachel fell into the latter category.

Rachel's Twitter feed was an endless commentary of how annoying her teachers were and how the wrong person had been voted off *Strictly*. There were occasional messages to celebrities, with Ariana Grande being a clear frontrunner for Rachel's approval. She was, by all accounts, the *GOAT*. Cooper had to google that one; it was an acronym for the *greatest of all time*.

Rachel's Instagram was set to private, as was Rachel's Facebook profile. However, a few photos had been uploaded to the public. Cooper scanned these photos but didn't see any connection to a church. Rachel was never pictured wearing a crucifix or a cross. Under her *About* section, she described her religion as *fundamentalist atheist*. Cooper clicked on a photo of Rachel surrounded by school friends. They were all doing what Cooper believed were *trout pouts*. Could one of the posing girls be The Priestess? Some of the taller ones certainly looked strong enough to throttle the stick-thin, five-foot-three Rachel. The following picture showed Rachel with two friends. They'd used a filter to give themselves bunny ears and whiskers. The girls looked like Disney cartoons. She clicked right, and a photo of Rachel in her gymnastics leotard appeared. She had a medal hanging around her neck, and she was being carried on the shoulders of two muscular young men. There was a string of comments attached to the photograph, mainly congratulations messages for her medal-winning performance. Will Harper's comment caught Cooper's eye. He'd posted a red, angry-faced emoji. It would appear Will Harper was the jealous type.

-CHAPTER 8-

TENNESSEE WAS HALFWAY THROUGH a Gregg's steak bake when Cooper picked him up en route to the Pearson's house on Oxford Street.

"Want a bite?" he asked with his mouth full.

Cooper ignored the flakes of pastry that fluttered into the car's footwell. When she'd first bought the car, she'd vowed to keep it clean and take it for weekly valets. Her vow had lasted less than a month, and these days it wasn't unusual for the dashboard of Cooper's car to be under a thick layer of dust.

"Please," she answered. "I'm famished."

Without thinking, Cooper finished the steak bake and looked apologetically at Tennessee. "Oh."

"Eyes on the road," he replied, "and it's fine. We'll grab some real grub when we're finished at the Pearsons."

"Good shout," she said, crumpling up the paper bag packaging and shoving it into a cupholder. "So, were you all right last night? Manage to switch off when you got home?" Cooper was thinking back to the morgue and remembering Tennessee's face when Margot revealed the card that had been stuck inside Rachel's chest.

"Truth be told, I didn't have a moment to think about it. Had to finish painting the baby's room. Hayley's picked out this hideous shade of purple."

"I thought you said you were having a boy."

"We are," grunted Tennessee, folding his arms over his chest. "She started banging on about not conforming to gender stereotypes. Anyway, when I was done with the painting, I had to put the crib together. Guess what colour that is."

Cooper parked the car and put it in neutral. "Not pink?"

"It might as well be, ma'am, sorry Coop. The damn thing's covered in purple and yellow butter-flies."

Cooper chuckled. "Well, if I know you, and I think I do, you'll repaint it in black and white stripes the first chance you get." Black and white being the home colours of Newcastle United FC.

"You read my mind," answered Tennessee as he stepped out of the car.

When Cooper and Tennessee knocked on the Pearson's door, it was answered by Pru Wilson, the FLO.

"How're things, Pru?" asked Cooper.

"As you would expect," answered the petite blonde in a hushed voice. "Come on through."

Pru led the pair of them to the living room, where Sally Pearson was sat on the sofa with her legs pulled up to her chest. She was smoking as she stared out the window. An ashtray balanced on the armrest overflowed with cigarette butts. Since her daughter's death, Sally Pearson's smoking had moved from the back step to the sofa.

"Good morning," said Cooper. Of course, there was nothing good about it.

Lou Pearson stomped through from the kitchen with an armful of freshly laundered clothes. He dumped them on an armchair and began furiously folding.

"I can take care of that," said Pru, taking a step towards him.

"I can manage the bloody laundry. Please stop your infernal fussing," he snapped.

Cooper's eyes caught a large bouquet of lilies on the dining table. They were still wrapped in cellophane, yet to be put in a vase. She opened the card and read; *To Sally and Lou, I'm not sure what to write. I'm so sorry for your loss. Our loss. I loved Rachel. I'm lost without her. If you need anything, please call. Will.*

"He dropped them off this morning," said Rachel's father. "He didn't look well, truth be told. Doubt he got any sleep, not that we did either." Lou's jaw clenched. "Said he's not going to school today. His mum's taking him to the GP." He turned back to his pile of laundry and started pairing socks.

Pru laid a blanket over Sally Pearson's shoulders and nodded to Cooper and Tennessee to follow her to the kitchen.

The three of them huddled close to the back door while Pru began to make some toast.

"She won't eat," started Pru, "but I'll keep trying. It was brutal at the morgue. It was a positive ID."

"Nixon told me," said Cooper. "Do you know about the card?"

Pru nodded. "That's some fucked up shit," she hissed. "Leaving a calling card inside the victim? Never in all my days... Margot didn't show it to the parents."

"Good," said Cooper. "We're keeping that under wraps for now. What did she tell them?"

"She kept it brief. Once they ID'd her, they asked how. They always ask how." The toast popped, and Pru fetched a plate from the cupboard and some spread from the fridge. "Margot explained that it was strangulation and that there was no evidence of sexual assault."

Cooper's stomach rumbled. "Okay," she said.

"It was dreadful, as you can imagine. Sally had a panic attack. She was shaking uncontrollably, started talking about running into the road, poor woman. She had to be given a sedative; I've made an appointment for her with Talking Therapies at eleven."

Pru picked up the toast and took it through to the living room. "Here you go, Sally."

Sally Pearson didn't look up.

"I'll just leave it here on the windowsill, tuck in when you're ready."

"Mr Pearson," said Cooper. "I know this is terribly difficult, but I need to ask you some more questions. Perhaps we should move to the dining room?"

Lou Pearson looked at his wife with concern, then he nodded. "Yes, yes, we'll go through to the other room."

He sat down and rummaged through a pile of papers on the dining table. "Here," he said, handing a piece of paper to Tennessee. "You asked for a list of Rachel's friends."

"Thank you," said Tennessee. "This will be very helpful."

Cooper glanced at the paper. It was a long list. Every girl in the year must be named. All but Tina, she noted.

"Mr Pearson, can you tell me where you were on Tuesday evening?"

His face reddened. "Are you having a—"

"It's routine," said Cooper in a quiet, calm manner. "I'm not implying anything."

"I was here. At home. All night. Worried sick." He spoke in quick bursts like a dog barking at a postman. "And so was Sally. Rach went off to yoga then we had our dinner. Spaghetti bolognese. Rachel's was kept in the pan, ready to have once she got home and showered. We watched television, and when she wasn't back by half eight, we started making phone calls."

"Thank you," said Cooper, keeping her voice neutral. "Apart from yourself and your wife, who else knew Rachel's routine?"

Lou Pearson sat back in his chair and slowly exhaled. His eyes darted back and forth across the table as he thought. "Well, Will, obviously. I was never too keen on that lad, but the kid's in pieces. We all are. I don't know how many other friends she told about yoga; you'd have to ask them. The yoga teacher, I guess. She had Rachel's details from her sign-up form. Have you spoken to the other women in the class? Someone must have seen or heard something?"

Cooper leant forward and interlaced her fingers. "We have a list of everyone who attended the class. Our colleagues are taking statements from all of them."

Her answer seemed to satisfy him as his shoulders lowered and the colour started to fade from his cheeks.

"This might seem like an odd question, but did Rachel own a pair of black stilettos?"

His eyes flicked to Cooper's. "She always wore flats. Walking was hard enough for her as it was. She had one pair of heels, not big ones though, just little ones. What are they called?"

Cooper shrugged. "Like a court shoe?"

"Oh, I've no idea. They'll be in her wardrobe. Don't think they were black either. Pretty sure they're navy."

"And again, this might seem like a strange question. Did Rachel own a top hat or enjoy fancy dress?"

Lou Pearson's eyes narrowed. "No."

"And did she have a pet rabbit?"

"A pet rabbit? No. What's going on? What haven't you told me?"

Cooper lowered her voice. "Mr Pearson, I don't want you to read about this in the papers, so I think it's important I let you know a few details about how Rachel was found."

"Oh, God." He raked his fingers through thinning hair. "Okay, go on."

"When Rachel was found yesterday morning, she wasn't wearing the outfit she'd worn to yoga. She was discovered, dressed in a magician's outfit, with a top hat, black stilettos and a rabbit."

Cooper kept her eyes on Mr Pearson. His face was a picture of pain and confusion.

"I don't understand."

"We think whoever hurt Rachel decided to dress her in a different outfit. We don't know why."

Lou Pearson swallowed and began picking the skin around his fingers. "They said she hadn't been... They told me no one hurt her in that way... But you're telling me someone undressed her and...."

"The pathologist confirmed there's no indication—"

"It makes no sense."

"Mr Pearson, was Rachel interested in magic?"

"No," he shook his head. "Wait, she liked those blokes on the television. The Americans. One of them doesn't talk."

Cooper looked at Tennessee.

"Penn and Teller."

"Aye, that's them," said Lou Pearson. "She liked the stuff they did. Other than that, no, she wasn't into card tricks and that."

Tennessee slowly pushed his chair out from the dining table. "We'd really appreciate it if we could take a look in Rachel's room now."

Lou Pearson lowered his eyes. "All right." Then he turned to Pru. "Would you stay with Sally?"

"Of course," she answered, and she got to her feet and returned to the living room.

Rachel's room was immaculately tidy. The first thing to catch Cooper's attention was the bookcase, where all the books had been turned around so that the pages faced the room and the spines faced the wall.

"Unusual," she said, pointing to the shelves.

"Aye. The latest trend on Insta-whatsit, she told me. Turn all your books around so the colours match and look pretty. Course it means you can never find the book you're after. Style over substance."

Cooper opened Rachel's wardrobe and found her clothes organised by colour. On her desk, make-up was arranged in the order she would use it, and her brushes were arranged by size.

"Most parents have to hassle their kids into tidying their rooms," started Lou Pearson, reading Cooper's mind. "I had to tell her to stop at times. She was always a tidy child, but it got worse after her fall."

"Is this Will?" asked Tennessee, holding up a framed picture of Rachel and a young man."

"Yeah, that's him." Lou Pearson took the photo in his hands and sat down on the edge of Rachel's bed. "This was the end of year awards presentation, before the summer holidays."

Cooper's instinct was to comfort the man, but she was here to do a job. She opened the drawers of Rachel's desk and pulled out a leather-bound notepad. Opening it up, it revealed itself to be a diary. Cooper began to read the latest entry while Tennessee opened a laptop and asked Lou Pearson if he knew the password. He shook his head.

Tennessee closed the laptop again. "We're going to need to let the computer forensics team take a look. We'll check if anyone was communicating with Rachel online."

If Rachel had arranged to meet anyone after class, had been threatened online, or received unwanted advances, the computer forensic analysts would find it.

Lou Pearson stared at the framed photograph and traced his fingertip over Rachel's face. Goodness knows what was going through the poor man's head.

Cooper let out the faintest of coughs. Just enough to get Tennessee's attention. He looked up and saw Cooper motion for him to come and take a look at the diary.

Tennessee drew in a long breath and exchanged a meaningful look with Cooper.

"Mr Pearson," he said. "Did Rachel mention arguing with Will Harper on Tuesday?"

"No. Why?" The man was instantly on his feet.

"It says here that Rachel was annoyed at Will about something that happened at school that day. It reads: *Will was a complete dick to me all day. Making me feel like some sort of slut because Nick said my arse looked good in the skinny jeans I wore at the weekend.*"

Lou Pearson's fingers tightened on the photo frame as Tennessee read.

"He wasn't mad at Nick for not being able to keep his pervy eyeballs in his head. No, he was mad at me for wearing what every girl in our year wears. What does he want? Am I supposed to live my life in joggers and baggy jumpers? Would a burka make him happy? What a dick. If that's how he wants to play it. I'll show him."

Tennessee closed the diary just as Lou Pearson slammed the frame on Rachel's desk, shattering the glass.

"That little... He didn't mention any of that when he was round here this morning with his crocodile tears. Wait till I—"

"Mr Pearson," Cooper cut him off. "Your job is to stay here with Sally. She needs you. This doesn't prove anything. Not yet. We're going to need to take the laptop and the diary."

"Want me to call it in?" asked Tennessee.

"Yes," Cooper picked the diary back up. "We needed to speak to young Will Harper anyway, but this certainly moves him to the front of the queue. Call Sutherland. He and Keaton can pick him up."

"On it, boss."

When Tennessee left the room, Cooper had another glance around Rachel's spotless room. She removed books from the bookcase, read their spines and returned them one by one. None of the books concerned magic, fancy dress or religion. As her father had described, Rachel's shoes were all fashionable flats apart from one pair of navy kitten heels with a glittery finish to the fabric.

"Ma'am," gasped Tennessee. He was running back up the stairs, panting as he spoke. He moved close to Cooper. Close enough to whisper. "We need to go. Another girl's been killed."

-CHAPTER 9-

"ERICA! IT'S SO GOOD to see you."

Bloody hell. That was all she needed.

Detective Inspector Neil Fuller scurried across the lobby of Northumbria Police headquarters. He was a stocky man with a Napoleon complex, a pointed nose, and thick auburn facial hair. Cooper had at one time been quite fond of his beard and how it tickled. It used to look distinguished. Now, he reminded her of a rodent of some kind.

"Neil," she replied, purposely not adding, *it's good to see you too.*

"We'll have to catch up soon. Rushed off my feet at the minute; someone's targeting posh hotels up the coast. Last week two blokes in a white van stormed Langley Castle and Slaley Hall. They arrived at dinner time, held up all the guests, took their money, jewellery, they even nicked the designer heels off the women's feet."

He scratched a scab on his jaw where he must have cut himself shaving.

Cooper's mouth formed into a thin line. "I saw the Slaley case on the news," she said. "The guests were shaken up."

"The bastards are at it again this week. Doxford Hall was done over on Tuesday night. They even nicked a lawn ornament."

Cooper's patience was wearing thin. Neil Fuller wasn't the only one who was busy. She had two murders on her hands. She pinched her nose, but Rat-Face continued.

"Anyway, we don't have much in the way of forensics. The gun they used has been identified as a Smith and Wesson—"

"Really? We're making small talk, Neil?"

Fuller recoiled. He looked genuinely hurt. Cooper might have felt sorry for him had she not remembered how things ended between them.

"I know we're not seeing each other anymore, Erica, but I thought we could be civil, be professional."

Fury flickered in Cooper's eyes. "Okay, have it your way. Let's make small talk. How have you been?" She didn't wait for him to answer. "I'm well. I've been super busy with chemotherapy. That was tonnes of fun. Remember? You were there holding my hand, supporting me, keeping my hair off my face while I vomited. Oh, that's right, you weren't there."

People were beginning to stare, but Cooper didn't care one bit. Fuller, on the other hand, was casting nervous glances left and right.

"You weren't there because you dumped me less than forty-eight hours after I found the lump."

"I... Well... Our relationship was coming to its natural end, Erica." His face was flooding with colour.

"Save it," she said. Cooper turned on her heel and parted the sea of onlookers so she could take the lift to CID. Only when the lift doors closed did she wipe away the tears that formed in the corners of her eyes. Undeterred, Cooper powered into the briefing room just as a wave of nausea swept over her. Grabbing a window ledge, she blinked her eyes a few times and waited for her vision to come back into focus.

Down on the street below, a hunchbacked lady pulled a shopping cart across a zebra crossing. The elderly woman seemed to sense she was being watched and turned her gaze up to the windows of CID.

"Boss?" Keaton's voice made Cooper jump. "Everything all right?"

"Skipped breakfast," replied Cooper by way of an explanation. She turned back to the window, but the woman and her cart had gone.

"I can nip to the vending machine—"

"Thanks, Paula, but we don't have time. Best crack on." Cooper was grateful that Keaton didn't press the matter. She had more important things to worry about than Neil Fuller.

"Right, butts on seats, people," announced Keaton with the authority of someone who used to play fullback. She patted Cooper on the arm and took her own seat beside Sutherland.

A hush fell over the room as all eyes turned to Cooper. She picked a piece of lint from her sleeve and flicked it to the floor before removing a photograph of a smiling, blonde teenager from her file and sticking it to the wall.

"Michelle Smith. Known to friends as Shelly. Fifteen years old, found dead at her home on Belford Terrace just before ten this morning."

Cooper paused and added another photograph to the wall. This time it was of Shelly's body. Horrified murmurs rippled through CID.

"As you can see, we have many reasons to suspect this case is connected to the murder of Rachel Pearson."

Sutherland shifted and rubbed the back of his hand over his mouth. "A serial killer?"

"It's looking that way," said Cooper as more sounds of unease spread through the room. There was no use in denying it. Cooper wasn't one for sugar-coating things.

"We have another case of suffocation," she continued, pointing to the photo. It depicted the blonde with a plastic bag over her head and secured to her neck with duct tape. Cooper stared at the picture silently, allowing the image to burn itself into her memory. She was never going to forget this image so there was no use in trying. The more she looked at it, the more she craved the sweet taste of justice.

"And she's been dressed up," added Sutherland. "Like Rachel was."

Cooper's eyes were still on the photograph. "Yes, as a priest. Or a priestess, to be precise." Her eyes darted over the outfit: black robes, a white dog collar, a purple satin scarf with golden tassels, and a large golden crucifix. "Justin Atkinson has already confirmed that another card was inserted into the victim. This one reads, *The Empress*."

Keaton was on her feet and pacing the length of CID. The sound of her thick-soled boots thudding against the flooring echoed around the room. "The Priestess wasn't the killer? The priestess was the killer's next move? He's telling us what's next."

"That's my understanding," said Cooper.

Disbelief flashed in Keaton's eyes. "What sort of psycho are we dealing with?"

"Believe me, I'm asking myself the same question."

Tennessee took a mouthful of water from a paper cup, crumpled it and tossed it effortlessly into the bin. "Is there any chance this is copycat?"

Cooper perched on her desk. "I doubt it. We kept the card from the press. They knew about the fancy dress, but we didn't tell them about the calling card. Of course, we can't rule out leaks."

Cooper thought of Margot Swanson. Would Margot blab to some handsome journalist who offered his affections or money? No. Margot was many things - a flirt at best and a home-wrecker at worst - but she was no sellout.

"Okay," said Tennessee. "What's the timeline?"

Cooper used her teeth to pull the lid from her pen. She drew a line across the board and began marking times on it as she spoke. "Shelly's mother, Lisa Smith, left for work at six a.m. Shelly would usually get herself ready for school and make her own breakfast. She'd usually leave at eight-thirty and walk to school."

"Which school?" asked Sutherland.

"Tynemouth Academy," answered Tennessee.

Cooper already knew this, but the fact that both girls attended the local secondary made her blood run cold.

"At nine twenty, the school called the mother to enquire about the unauthorised absence. Standard procedure. Lisa Smith picked up her voicemail during her break at nine-thirty a.m. and called her daughter immediately after. When there was no answer, Lisa drove home, assuming her daughter was skiving. When she got to the property, she found Shelly's body posed like this on their front step."

"Christ," said Keaton. She scraped her chair across the floor and sat down again.

Sutherland unbuttoned his blazer and loosened his tie. He looked a little redder in the cheeks than usual. "My girl goes to Tynemouth Academy."

Cooper met his eyes. "I didn't know Caroline had started secondary school?"

"She's twelve now. Started in September."

The last time Cooper had seen Sam Sutherland's daughter, she'd been knee-high to a grasshopper. She had been bawling her eyes out because little Jimmy "Poo-Head" Ashman had spilt cherry cola on her yellow dress at the department barbecue. She couldn't have been more than seven or eight. How time flies.

"If the school's being targeted—"

"We can't jump to conclusions. We need to find out everything that connects these girls. Who did they hang out with? What clubs did they go to? Where did they spend their free time? But Sam," Cooper nervously tapped her pen off the edge of her desk, "my daughter goes there too. It might be worth taking some extra precautions."

"Aye. I'll call the missus and the grandparents. I don't want Caroline left alone for a second. Not until we catch this sicko."

With no parents or extended family in the region, Cooper realised she would have to put some faith in Kenny. She wasn't used to relying on anyone else, especially not him.

"Right," she said. "Where are we with Will Harper, Rachel's boyfriend? Keaton?"

"We called by the school to pick him up. The admin told us he wasn't at school today."

"The Pearsons told us he was taking the day off and had a GP appointment," said Tennessee.

"Yeah," said Keaton. "We assumed something like that. We were on our way to his home address when we got the call about Shelly."

"Okay," said Cooper. "I want you and Sutherland to find him and bring him in. Don't mention Shelly. It's not public knowledge yet. See if he incriminates himself. He'll need a juvenile cell and an appropriate adult."

Keaton tapped her pen to her temple then pointed it at Cooper. "Gotcha."

"Now, back to Rachel Pearson. How are we getting on with the yoga ladies?"

Sutherland opened a spiral-bound notepad. "It's not just women. There were two men at the class on Tuesday."

"Really? New, or regulars?" asked Cooper.

"Regulars. Neither of them even knew Rachel's name, which goes for a fair few of the group. She seemed to keep to herself. Almost everyone in the class parked their cars by the sailing club and drove up the bank and through Tynemouth village to get home. A few reported seeing Rachel walking up the bank, but no one saw anyone else. No one noticed if there were any cars in Haven car park."

"They all went straight home after the class?" asked Cooper.

"Mostly," confirmed Sutherland. "One of the gents stopped for a takeaway in the village, and one of the ladies called by her sister's to pick up her dog. They all have people who can confirm what time they got home."

"Okay. And what about the instructor?"

"She left after the rest of the group. Takes her around fifteen minutes to tidy the mats away and secure the building. CCTV has her leaving the club at nineteen forty-five. All the other cars had left at that point. She didn't see Rachel, but she did see a man walking two Siberian huskies on the Spanish Battery."

Cooper turned to a trainee detective who sat at the back of the room. Oliver Martin was only five-eight, but he added at least three inches to this by gelling his hair into an impressive quiff. Despite his best denials, the team were also convinced he liked to wear make-up. L'Oréal, to be precise. This led to Sutherland and Keaton telling the youngster he was *worth it* whenever they brought him a coffee or helped him on a case.

"Martin, put out an appeal. Our dog walker's a potential witness. Find him."

"I'm on it," he replied. "I've been following the white rabbit," he added, "though that's a line I never thought I'd say. No reports of stolen or missing pets. I've been to the local pet stores and asked them to check their records for sales of white rabbits over the last week or so. I'm keeping an eye out for sales where a customer bought a rabbit without a hutch or much in the way of bedding or food. I figure, why would our man buy the whole kit and caboodle if he knows the rabbit won't be around for long? I'll let you know if anything comes from it."

"Thanks, Martin, and good thinking." Cooper began to pull on her coat. "Keaton, Sutherland, once you've found Will Harper, find out who the FLO with Lisa Smith is and get someone over for a statement. Find out if Shelly was friends with Rachel, touch base with Atkinson, and see what else he's found. Tennessee and I will head to the school. It's time to speak to some of Rachel and Shelly's friends and teachers. Let's find out what or who connects these girls."

-CHAPTER 10-

TYNEMOUTH ACADEMY WAS A modern school having been rebuilt three years ago. The building resembled a giant cube with red brick and black and grey cladding. Surrounded by sports fields, bike sheds and an impressive sports hall, it was clear the students of Tynemouth Academy were keen athletes. The school motto: *in omnia paratus,* was emblazoned across the school gates. Many moons had passed since Cooper had studied Latin, but Tennessee's mumble of, "Ready for anything," confirmed her suspicions. Sadly, she didn't think there was a school in the country that could be ready for losing two students in a manner such as this.

"DCI Erica Cooper and DS Jack Daniel, here to see Linda Webb."

Both detectives held up their warrant cards for inspection by an eagle-eyed school administrator with a pinched face and a sniffly nose. The admin officer sneezed into tissue and led them to a small office just off the foyer.

"Erica," greeted the headteacher, who had never dealt with Cooper in a professional capacity before, only as Tina's mother.

Linda Webb looked like she hadn't slept for a week. Was it the stress of the job? Or, was it Kenny - Tina's father and Cooper's ex - who was keeping her awake until the early hours? Cooper put the thought from her mind. It was none of her business what Kenny Roberts and Linda Webb did behind closed doors.

Cooper and Tennessee sat down opposite Linda's desk. It was piled high with paperwork and management manuals.

"You're here about Rachel," she said, taking deep breaths. Her shoulder pads rose and fell in time with her breath. "Terrible, terrible business."

"Yes," answered Tennessee. He folded one long leg over the other and stared at the headteacher with dark, serious eyes. "And, we're here about Michelle Smith."

Linda's brow lowered. "Shelly? Don't tell me she's somehow caught up in this. She wouldn't hurt a fly."

"No, Ms Webb, that's not what we're saying—"

Cooper cut in. "Linda, I'm sorry to have to tell you this, but Shelly Smith was found dead this morning."

Linda's hand flew to her mouth. "No!"

"She was killed in the same manner as Rachel Pearson. We have reason to believe it was at the hands of the same person, but we're not ruling anything out at this stage."

"I don't... I don't believe this...." Linda's voice trailed off, and she got to her feet to open a window. It was barely above freezing, but Cooper understood how trauma could make you feel as if all the air had been sucked out of the room.

"This is going to be a very stressful time for students and staff," began Cooper.

"Stress? Stress doesn't come close." Linda was shaking her head, causing her long, chestnut bob to swish back and forth across the collar of her blouse. "I've had parents on the phone every five minutes. The press too. Kids asking questions I don't have the answers to. Rumours spreading like wildfire. The governors won't get off my back. The art department are pissed I cut their funding in favour of science; I didn't have a choice given our latest OFSTED inspection. And now Michelle. It's going to be twice as bad."

Cooper shot a sideways glance at Tennessee. He was masking his revulsion well but the way his eyes wrinkled at the corners let her know that he was thinking the same thing as she was. Linda Webb was more concerned about how this affected herself than about the safety of her students.

"I think," said Cooper, bringing Linda's attention back into the room, "that the safety of students should be paramount. I'm going to arrange for a police presence at the school gates to act as a deterrent. We don't know yet if the school is a target, but it certainly connects Rachel and Shelly."

"We'll also arrange for an officer to address the students tomorrow morning," said Tennessee. He uncrossed his legs. "They can speak to the whole school or go class to class, but either way, they'll need access to the entire student body. They'll recommend students walk to and from school in groups, that sort of thing."

"And I can recommend agencies to deliver workshops on online safety," added Cooper. "It's imperative that the children aren't giving any personal details out online. It might also be a good idea to bring in some professional counsellors."

Linda Webb was still pacing and shaking her head, but she'd had the good grace to close her mouth and listen to what the detectives had to say up until that last comment.

"Professional counsellors? We don't have the budget for that. We have an excellent peer-to-peer student counselling system. I set it up last year, and the feedback from the parent and teacher association has been very positive. It'll do for now and then perhaps in the future—"

"No, Linda. It won't do for now." Cooper's voice had hardened. "Two girls have been murdered. There's going to be a lot of grief and a lot of fear. Peer-to-peer is all well and good when someone doesn't get the grade they wanted, or someone's crush hasn't called them back, but this is different. Your counsellors are going to need counselling."

The headteacher took on the look of someone who was used to dishing out scoldings rather than taking them. She pouted - actually pouted - and folded her arms.

"Well, we'll see what we can do."

"Make sure you do," said Cooper, getting to her feet and wishing for the love of God that Linda would close the window again. "For now, we need a room. Somewhere we can chat to Rachel and Shelly's teachers, as well as their friends."

"The staffroom is up the stairs and on the left," said Linda. "There's tea and coffee if you want to help yourselves. I'll send a few of Rachel's friends along once the bell goes for the next class."

Cooper thanked Linda before following her directions to the staffroom. Once out of sight, Tennessee ran his fingers through his curls and shook his head at Cooper.

"Talk about a face like a smacked arse."

"Tell me about it. Two dead girls and she's talking about budgets, and governors, and funding."

"Mum!"

Tina Cooper walked hand-in-hand with a lanky, bespectacled boy who hastily pulled his hand away and tucked it into the pocket of his green school blazer.

"Tina. Nice to see you again, Josh."

Josh turned a deep shade of beetroot. "Ms Cooper," he said with half a bow.

"Are you here because of Rachel?" asked Tina, looking over both shoulders.

"Yes," answered Cooper, though she couldn't tell her daughter about Shelly Smith just yet. "Listen, Tina. I'm going to have your father pick you up from netball tonight."

Tina frowned and then raised an eyebrow. "Why? I'm not supposed to see him until the weekend."

"I just don't want you walking home alone in the dark."

"But..." Tina stopped herself and surveyed her mother's face for a good five seconds. "Fine."

Cooper's insides relaxed. She didn't want to argue with Tina, not with everything else that was going on.

"Thank you," said Cooper. "I'll see you at home. Text me later and let me know what you want for dinner. Right, off to class. You too, Josh."

The two green-clad teenagers walked away, whispering about homework and murder.

The staffroom in Tynemouth Academy felt like a giant corkboard. Every wall was covered in posters and flyers, covering everything from sign up sheets for the next school fundraiser to recognising signs of female genital mutilation.

Under the watch of a few staff members, Cooper found herself a seat and opened a file on her lap. Tennessee made two cups of coffee that looked strong enough to power the next mission to Mars and joined his superior.

"Hello." A man in a paint-flecked shirt held his hand out to Tennessee. He wore beads around his neck and had thick-framed glasses perched on a head of bleached hair. "You're with the police, aren't you? I'm Brian Hutchins," he said by way of introduction.

"And I'm Todd Carpenter," announced another man, one with a hooked nose and possibly the worst posture Cooper had ever seen.

Both men shook Tennessee's hand and seemed surprised when he introduced the skinny woman sitting to his left as the senior investigating officer.

Brian Hutchins took a seat opposite. "I was Rachel's art teacher. I just can't get my head around all of this. It's knocked the faculty for six. Todd here was Rachel's form tutor. If there's anything we can do to help the investigation, please let us know. All the staff feel the same way."

Not *all* the staff, thought Cooper.

"Do you have time for a quick chat, gentlemen? Can you tell me about Rachel?" she asked, turning her eyes to Todd Carpenter.

Todd checked his watch. "She was a popular girl," he replied. "It'll be quiet without her, that's for sure."

"Quiet?" asked Cooper.

Todd sat down next to Brian Hutchins and he nodded in agreement. "Quite the chatterbox was Rachel. She could never chat to the person next to her either; she always had to shout across the room to the person sitting furthest away."

"How did the other students feel about that?"

"I guess it was annoying for the ones who were trying to concentrate," answered Brian. "But those are few and far between. These days, kids are all about their *on-demand* whatnots. Skip this, swipe that, three-second memes and nine-second Vines."

"I can appreciate that," said Cooper, though she didn't know what a Vine was. "Other than being a bit on the noisy side," and noting that it was opposite to how her yoga classmates had described her, "what else can you tell me about Rachel?"

"She was, how's a polite way to say it?" said Todd Carpenter. "Erm... An underachiever? She was bright, but she didn't apply herself."

"I think she did in English, Todd," countered Brian. "I remember Catherine saying she had a talent for poetry."

"Catherine says that about all her students. She's a soft touch."

"And who were her closest friends?" interjected Cooper. "Did she have any enemies?"

"Enemies?" Todd Carpenter's eyes widened. "Goodness, I wouldn't have thought so. All the girls wanted to be friends with her. All the boys... Well, as I said, she was popular."

Brian Hutchins removed his glasses from his head and cleaned them on his shirt. "As for her closest friends... Will Harper was pretty much her shadow. Wherever Rachel went, he wasn't far behind. She was friendly with Tess Livingston as well, and Mackenzie James and Michelle Smith."

Cooper looked to Tennessee. He opened the list of names Lou Pearson, Rachel's father, had given him. The top four names were Will, Mackenzie, Shelly and Tess.

"Brian, and... Todd, was it?" Cooper sat more upright in her seat. "I need you to tell me more about Michelle Smith."

-CHAPTER 11-

COOPER CURSED. SHE WAS utterly useless in the kitchen, and the fact she couldn't even fry an egg without bursting the yolk was testament to that. She scraped up the sorry looking egg, laid it on a slice of sourdough, sprinkled a little salt and handed it to Tina.

"Thanks, Mum."

"You won't be saying that once you've tasted it," said Cooper, her nose wrinkling at her failed attempt at breakfast.

"It's the thought that counts." Tina grabbed her knife and fork and began slicing. "Aren't you having anything?"

"I'll have some toast once I finish getting ready."

"No, you won't," said Tina, pointing her knife at her mother. "You know, you look like a total badass without your wig on. You should go to work like that. Very Mad Max."

Rolling her eyes, Cooper tried to laugh it off. "I don't think so."

The truth was, without hair, Cooper felt like her femininity had been stripped away. Where Tina saw "total badass," Cooper saw prepubescent boy. She felt weak and victim-like whenever she looked at herself without her wig. She was the one who sought justice for victims; she couldn't face being one herself.

"Did you finish your homework?" asked Cooper, changing the subject.

Last night, Tina had asked for help with her maths homework, which was a rarity. Given how gifted Tina was with maths, she couldn't help but think that Tina just wanted her mother's company, and homework was simply an excuse.

Having broken the news of Shelly's death to several teachers and pupils, as well as Tina, Cooper's mind was fuzzy and in need of rest when she'd returned home. Unfortunately, she'd been unable to switch off and was less than incompetent when it came to equations.

"Yeah," replied Tina, taking a bite of egg on toast. "I finished it before my show started."

Cooper kissed her daughter on her head. "You're a bright young thing. No idea where you get it from."

Both ladies swivelled their heads in unison at the sound of knocking on the front door.

"Will you get that, Tina?" asked Cooper, rushing from the room to make herself presentable.

She only took a few moments to change from pyjamas to a suit, pull her wig on and slap on a layer of red lipstick.

"Oh, it's you," she said to Kenny as she re-entered the room.

"Were you expecting the Queen?" grinned the wide-shouldered man whose body had been built through a lifetime in the construction industry.

"No. It's just—"

"Thought I'd swing by and give Tina a lift to school."

"That would actually be—"

Tina's knife and fork clattered off her plate. "I'm walking to school. I'm meeting Josh at the corner."

A vein in Kenny's forehead pulsated at the mention of Josh's name. He turned to Cooper in the hope of backup.

"Coffee?" she offered instead, watching the cogs whirl behind her ex's eyes.

"Please," he answered before turning to his daughter. "Okay. How about we give Josh a lift too? There's plenty of room in The Beast," he said, referring to the monstrosity that was his Ford pick-up.

Tina cleared her plate and tried to bargain for her freedom. "Fine. We'll drive to school, but I'm walking home tonight."

"No, you're not. I'll meet you at the gates."

"But Dad..."

"But nothing. Go get your school bag."

Tina let out an almighty groan and stormed from the room. Cooper counted the seconds until she heard doors slamming. It was six.

Kenny warmed his hands on the coffee mug and leant forward over the table. The steam from the hot drink danced in front of his round, clean-shaven face.

"I spoke to Linda last night," he said with a hint of trepidation in his voice. "Another girl was killed?"

"Yeah. 'Fraid so."

"And there's going to be a police presence at the school? The kids have to attend safety workshops? Erica, is our daughter safe?"

Cooper opened her mouth to give Kenny a well-deserved earful. He'd never wanted a daughter. When Cooper fell pregnant, he'd wanted her to have an abortion. When she'd been unwavering in her decision to keep the baby, he'd promptly ended their relationship by running away to Devon. Being concerned for Tina's welfare now did not make up for twelve years of turning a blind eye to his responsibilities. No wonder Tina spent as little time as possible with him.

Cooper held her venom back long enough to take a sip of coffee and calm her thoughts.

"We're doing our best to find whoever killed those girls, Kenny." Her voice was cold and businesslike. "It's true that both girls went to the same school, but that might not be the connecting factor, if indeed there is one. We need to find out what else the girls have in common."

Tina appeared in the doorway to the kitchen. Her face was still thunderous, but she had her school blazer on, and her backpack was over her shoulders. "You mean, what they have in common other than Will Harper?"

- CHAPTER 12 -

"WHERE'S HARPER?" BARKED COOPER down her phone as she buckled up in the old Mazda.

"We couldn't find the slippery little eel yesterday, boss," answered Paula Keaton. "Picked him up this morning on Front Street. He looked rougher than a badger's arse. We've put him in juvie cell three while we wait for his appropriate adult. Think his uncle's coming in."

"Uncle?" asked Cooper. Usually minors acted all tough until the second the cell door closed, then they'd cry for their mummies like they were still being breastfed.

"Yeah, he was adamant he wanted his uncle and not his mum or dad. Sutherland's doing the Starbucks run on his way in. Want me to tell him to get you owt?"

Cooper started the engine. "An Americano, please."

"Food?"

"A muffin, one of those poppy-seed lemony ones."

"I know what you mean. See you in ten, boss."

Cooper started the engine and headed towards HQ in Wallsend. Ten minutes was wishful thinking. Maybe before they started digging the blasted tunnel for the A19 to pass under the Coast Road, but not now.

When Cooper crossed the threshold of CID, twenty-five minutes later, Sutherland was waiting with coffee and muffin in hand.

"You're an angel," she said, removing her coat and laying it over the back of her chair.

"Will Harper's uncle just arrived. I've put him in interview suite one. Are we still keeping the Smith murder under wraps?"

"No point," Cooper answered. "It's been public knowledge for over twelve hours now."

"Well, let me know when you're ready and I'll move Will from the cells."

Cooper took a deep inhalation of comforting caffeine. "I'll be ready the second I finish this muffin."

THE STENCH OF WEED and cigarettes almost overpowered Cooper as she walked into the interview suite. She brought her coffee to her nose to try to cover it and looked Will Harper up and down.

He was a big lad for his age, a teenage boy in an adult's body. A triangular frame suggested he lifted weights but regularly skipped leg day. A dusting of acne covered his jaw, and he either hadn't washed his hair in a while or he was wearing far too much product. He looked a world away from the photograph Cooper had seen of him in Rachel Pearson's bedroom.

Cooper took a seat and waited for Sutherland to do the same. Pushing a button on an audio recorder, she began the interview.

"Northumbria Police Headquarters, Friday fifteenth November. The time is ten-fifteen a.m. I am DCI Erica Cooper. Also present is DI Sam Sutherland and Walter Harper who is acting in the role of appropriate adult."

"It wasn't my weed."

Will's eyes began to dart around the room; his uncle laid a hand on his shoulder.

"I mean, I wasn't smoking. I don't do drugs. It was a friend. I was next to him while he was smoking. That's what you can smell."

Sutherland placed his hands on the table face up in an attempt at open, non-threatening body language.

"Listen, son. I don't give a monkey's what you smoke, snort or swallow, but this interview is under caution, so I suggest you listen carefully when my colleague speaks."

"Will Harper," continued Cooper, "you are being questioned in relation to the murders of Rachel Pearson and Michelle Smith. You do not have to say anything, but it may harm your defence if you do not mention when questioned something which you later rely on in court. Anything you do say will be given in evidence. Please state your full name, address and date of birth."

The young man looked at his uncle with eyes like saucepans. It took an encouraging nod from the older man for Will to open his mouth.

"William Harper. 162 Knott Memorial Flats, North Shields. May thirtieth 2003."

"Thank you, Will. Can you tell me where you were on Tuesday evening?"

"I was at home."

"All night?"

"Yes. I didn't go out."

"Can anyone verify that, Will?"

Will looked away and pushed his hands under his thighs. "My parents. We had dinner together, then they went—"

He realised too late what he had said.

"Will? Where did your parents go?"

"To the pub. The Lodge."

"What time was that?"

Will swallowed and kept his eyes in his lap. "About seven, I think."

"When did they return?"

"I don't know. I'd gone to bed."

"Will, do your parents often leave you alone to go to the pub?"

He shrugged.

"I need an audible answer for the recording," pressed Cooper.

Will looked up. "I guess so," he said in a quiet huff.

"And where are your parents now?"

"Me da's probably hungover. Ma'll be..." he paused to find the right word. "Working."

Cooper frowned. "What does your mother do?"

Will shuffled and looked to his uncle.

"Will's mother works in the entertainment industry."

There was something in the way Walter Harper said *entertainment* that made Cooper think he didn't mean she was a singer.

"Can you be more specific?" asked Sutherland.

"I don't think it's relevant to your investigation," replied Walter, and he had a point.

"She's a whore." Will's face hardened. "I'm not supposed to know, but I'm not an idiot. She's a smack-head whore."

Cooper made a mental note to contact child services once the interview was over. "Moving on," she said, leaning back in her chair. "So, you were home alone on Tuesday evening?"

"I'm not lying."

"I'm not saying you are." Cooper stopped to take a drink of coffee and to allow a moment of silence. Silence had a way of making people feel uncomfortable.

"I played on my X-box, had a shower and went to bed. I didn't go out."

"Okay," said Cooper. "How about yesterday morning. Where were you then?"

"I... I was in school."

"From nine a.m?"

"Yes."

"That's not true, is it, Will? Our officers went to your school but you hadn't shown up for registration. You told the Pearsons you had a doctors appointment."

"I... I did."

"But you didn't show."

Will's face crumpled.

"We checked," explained Cooper. "Your appointment was at nine but you didn't show."

"Are they allowed to tell you that?" asked Will's uncle. "Isn't that a breach of patient confidentiality?"

"We didn't look at his medical history, Mr Harper. This is a murder investigation, and I'm trying to establish if your nephew has an alibi for the times when Rachel Pearson and Shelly Smith were murdered. So far, he doesn't seem to."

Cooper turned back to Will. "Where were you yesterday morning?"

"I... I couldn't face school. I'd just lost Rachel. I loved her and I..." his voice started to crack as his eyes glassed over. The child in the adult's body was beginning to surface. "I went to the park for a bit. Smoked until I ran out of cigarettes, then I went home and got into bed. Rachel meant the world to me. I still can't believe she's gone."

"Let me guess," said Sutherland. "No one else was home?"

Will said nothing. Cooper decided to change tack.

"Tell me about the argument you and Rachel had on Tuesday?"

"What argument?"

Sutherland slapped his hand on the table. "Don't play innocent with us, boy. We've read Rachel's diary. You're quite the domineering boyfriend, aren't you? Telling Rachel what she can and can't wear. Blaming her when other guys looked at her."

A tear rolled down Will Harper's cheek. Fear? Guilt? Cooper wasn't sure of either.

Sutherland handed the boy a tissue. "Will, we have statements from others in your class who can corroborate Rachel's version of events. You might as well tell us."

Will dabbed his eyes. "She liked the attention. She did it on purpose to wind me up."

"Did what on purpose, Will?" asked Cooper.

"Flirted and shit. She'd rolled her skirt up at the waistband to make it shorter. Then she asked Nick Davies if he thought it suited her, and he said he thought her arse looked better in skinny jeans." Will's face reddened. "She was testing me, trying to make me jealous, and it worked. When we were alone I told her she was making a fool of me."

Cooper leant forward. "And did Shelly ever make a fool of you?"

"Shelly?"

"Michelle Smith. We know you two dated. A bit odd that two girls you dated end up murdered and you don't have an alibi for the time of either of their deaths."

"Very odd," echoed Sutherland.

Panic was etched on the young man's face. He looked back and forth between the detectives and his uncle. "But... No... I didn't do anything, I swear. I'm being set up. I must be." Will's breathing became erratic. "I'm not the only one who had Rachel and Shelly in common. That freak Xander Wright has it in for me. He fancied Shelly, but she only had eyes for me, then he started seeing Rachel. When Shelly and I broke up, Rachel dumped him for me."

Desperate actions, thought Cooper, deflecting the attention on to someone else. She would speak to Xander Wright as soon as she could. In the meantime, Will Harper was headed straight to the cells. No alibi. No bail.

-CHAPTER 13-

"THE SNOW'S BACK," OBSERVED Keaton. She handed Sutherland a biscuit to dunk and moved away from the window.

"The bairn'll be happy. She loves snow," he said before playing a game of chicken between his biscuit and his coffee. A look of regret passed over his face when the biscuit gave way and fell into the drink. "Ah, crud."

Cooper's eyes followed an unusually large snowflake as it fluttered past the window. "Well, I'm sure we all want to get out of here before the snow buggers up the school run traffic. So let's get down to business. Alice in Wonderland," she said, turning to young Oliver Martin, "Did you find the white rabbit?"

"Still stuck in the rabbit hole, ma'am. I've hit a bit of a dead-end with the major pet stores. I've had no sales of rabbits without hutches in the past month. Pets At Home have three white rabbits sold in our timeframe, all with the full set-up. Hutches, hay, food, the works. I've got them all on CCTV. An elderly couple who paid cash, a family with five kids who paid cash and a James King who was alone and used his credit card."

"Have you looked into King?"

"Briefly. He lives in Gosforth with his wife and two sons. No priors, and no connection to Tynemouth Academy from what I can tell. I can look deeper?"

Cooper rested her back against the window. It felt like a sheet of ice, so she pulled away again. "Put it on the back burner for now. Move on to the smaller Mom and Pop pet shops. They might not have as sophisticated cameras as the bigger stores, and they might be cash-only, but hopefully someone will remember something."

"You got it," said Martin.

"How are we getting on with the appeal for the man with his huskies?"

Martin shook his head. "Haven't heard a peep."

"I might have something on that." Sutherland flipped through a notepad until he found the page he wanted. "Earlier today we got a report from Tynemouth Academy of a man walking around the perimeter of the school and staring at some of the girls through the chain-link fence at morning break. Freaked a few of them out, so they fetched a staff member. When approached by a Mr Hutchins, he took off." Sutherland paused to dunk another biscuit. "He was walking two dogs."

"Huskies?" asked Cooper.

"Yellow Labs. The lighting down at the sailing club's a crock of shit. If you ask me, two yellow Labs could be mistaken for two huskies in the moonlight."

Cooper agreed. "Follow it up, Sam. The school has cameras by the main entrance. See if he walked by them. Where's Tennessee?"

Right on cue, Tennessee walked into CID looking out of breath. "Sorry, sorry. Had one of those Lamaze classes."

"What's that when it's at home?" asked Keaton.

"Prenatal classes," answered Cooper while Tennessee got himself settled at his desk. "You practice giving birth."

Keaton's mouth fell open. "How does that work? Actually, never mind, I don't want to know."

Keaton crossed her legs - unconsciously protecting her womb - and addressed DS Jack Daniel. "You finished your reports from the school?"

"Yes. Though there's not much to report. By all accounts, Rachel and Shelly were not the brightest, and they were a little on the disruptive side. However, they were very popular, said to have good hearts, regularly did charity events, that sort of thing. The words that kept cropping up were: funny, sweet, kind, pretty. Everyone thought the world of them."

"Not everyone," said Cooper. Her mind returned to what her daughter had told her. "What about the underclass of kids? The ones who aren't popular. The ones whose lives are made miserable by the cool kids?"

Sutherland tilted his head towards Cooper. As a fellow parent, he picked up on the tension in her voice. "Has Tina said something?"

"She told me she tried her best to avoid Rachel. Said she was manipulative and could turn the whole school against you if she wanted to."

"I spoke to some of Shelly's classmates this morning." Keaton leant back in her chair and propped her feet up on the edge of a waste paper basket. "The name Greg Mason kept popping up. It was his house party where Rachel broke her back. Apparently, he was trying to kiss Rachel on the first-floor landing. Rachel wasn't interested, and when she pulled away from him, she fell down the stairs."

"Jesus," said Cooper.

"Indeed. Shelly saw it all and told the entire school it was his fault. He went from the top of the pecking order to the bottom of the heap in one night."

"That sounds like a motive to me," said Cooper. "Someone find out if he has an alibi for Tuesday night and Thursday morning."

"I'll do it," said Sutherland. "Paula?"

Keaton nodded. "Sure thing, partner."

"Tennessee and I will speak to the Xander kid that Will Harper mentioned. Oliver, can you get in touch with Margot Swanson at the Freeman—" Cooper thought of Margot getting her hooks into the impressionable young man and changed her mind. "Actually, you speak to Atkinson, see if the SOCOs have anything for us. I'll get an update from Margot."

90

Cooper checked the time and watched the snow for a second. It was starting to flurry around the car park beneath them. "You know what to do. Finish your reports and get home to your families. I can think of better places to get snowed in than CID."

-CHAPTER 14-

BY SATURDAY AFTERNOON COOPER was utterly exhausted. Thankfully, her brilliant but stroppy daughter was spending the night at her useless but willing-to-babysit father's.

Tina had been reluctant initially, especially since Josh had asked her to go to the cinema. Kenny had won her over with the promise of Chinese takeaway and the double promise that Linda Webb would not be the centre of his attention for the entire evening. Cooper couldn't blame Tina on that front. What teenager wanted to spend their free time with their headteacher?

After a morning spent catching up on the laundry and housework that had been neglected over the last week, Cooper braved the shops. Predictably, the good people of Tynemouth had panic-bought staples such as bread and milk and now everywhere was out of stock. It was strange how people panic-bought bread - something that goes mouldy in a few days - but not flour. Cooper couldn't talk. The last time she baked bread - when Tina was six - she almost burnt the house down. Domestic goddess, she was not.

Cooper dumped her shopping bags on the kitchen table and tuned into BBC Radio 2. At the first hint of Ed Sheeran she switched to Absolute Classic Rock. Much better. Given her complete lack of aptitude in the kitchen, Cooper's shopping consisted mainly of tinned goods, ready meals to stick in the freezer, and jars of pasta sauces.

Now in her pyjamas, with make-up removed and her wig stored on the mannequin head in her bedroom, Cooper examined her replenished kitchen. What could she cook that even she couldn't balls up? Cheesy beans on toast - easy peasy.

Here's the plan, she told herself, *eat, get in the bath, read a good book, get an early night.* Ten minutes later and her culinary masterpiece was complete. She was about to sit down and eat when someone knocked on the door. *Ignore it.*

"Erica. Open up. It's Justin."

Justin Atkinson, the senior scene of crime officer, peered through the letterbox.

"Come on, Erica. My glasses are frosting over."

Cooper squirmed and ran her palms over her head and looked down at her baggy, faded pyjamas. *Shit.* She unlocked the door and stepped backwards, embarrassment flowing from the top of her head to the tips of her toes.

"Casserole," he announced, stomping his feet on the mat and leaving white snowy prints. "And wine," he added, lifting his elbow to reveal a Waitrose bag, weighed down with a glass bottle.

"I..." Erica was confused. What was he doing here? "I'd just made dinner."

Atkinson looked at the plate of beans on toast and then looked at Cooper over his glasses. "That's not food. That's what students eat when they're thirty grand in debt and have spent their loan on hipster cocktails served in jam jars. You're wasting away. I've seen more body fat on an anorexic whippet."

He strode past Cooper and placed a heavy, white casserole dish on the oven hob. He handed Cooper the carrier bag. "Hope you like lamb."

"I love lamb."

"How about Tina? I know kids can be fussy."

"She's at her dad's stuffing her face with spare ribs."

Cooper opened the wine and poured two glasses. It took every ounce of strength she had not to run upstairs, do her hair and reapply make-up. Atkinson hadn't even done a double-take. He was either very polite or very unobservant. Either way, Cooper appreciated it. But, it didn't stop her from feeling self-conscious.

"Oh well," said Atkinson. "More for us."

He picked up Cooper's plate, opened her pedal bin and slid the beans on toast straight into the rubbish. Grabbing two plates from a shelf, he dished up and handed Cooper a portion that was steaming hot.

"You've cooked enough to feed all of CID," she said.

The smell of lamb was so delightful that Cooper began to salivate.

"Empty nest syndrome," said Atkinson. "I'm so used to cooking for four that I'm incapable of cooking single servings."

Cooper gave the man a supportive smile. It was common knowledge that his wife had run off with a waiter she'd met on a family holiday to Spain. He was twenty years her junior. Atkinson was suddenly a single father to twin boys who had left for Edinburgh University at the start of September.

"It must be quiet at home?"

"Too quiet," he replied. "I've spent two days sifting through the Smith house. That poor girl had been in her home - where she should have felt safe and loved - and some bastard broke that safety and took her life."

He removed his glasses and rubbed his eyes on the back of his wrist.

"She let him in. Did I tell you that?"

She bobbed her head; there'd been no sign of forced entry during the initial walkthrough. The killer had even closed the front gate after himself.

Cooper took a sip of wine and a mouthful of succulent lamb and vegetables. In an instant, she felt the vitamins and nutrients flood her body.

Atkinson let out a long, low sigh and took a sip himself. "Anyway, I couldn't switch off. I went for a run along Longsands but it didn't help, so I busied myself in the kitchen, and before I knew it, I'd cooked up enough food to last me till Christmas. I thought you might be in the same boat. This case is seriously messed up."

"That's an understatement," said Cooper. She took another bite and crossed her legs under the table. "I haven't switched off either. I can't let it go. I won't let it go until I've caught the killer and sent him to Frankland."

HMP Frankland was a maximum-security category-A prison in County Durham. It housed the worst of the worst; Charles Bronson, Harold Shipman and Peter Sutcliffe had all done time there. Cooper had been responsible for sending at least thirty men through their doors on convictions for murder, GBH and rape. Often it was Atkinson's evidence that helped her secure those convictions.

As talk of the case eased off and small talk of Christmas preparations, their children, and TV talent shows took over, Cooper found herself beginning to relax. She was enjoying Atkinson's company. She was also enjoying the wine, which had almost run out.

"I'll open another one," she said, getting to her feet and finding a bottle of red at the bottom of the wine rack. "If you fancy?"

Atkinson's Adam's apple bounced as he swallowed the last of his wine. "Oh? Well yes, of course, if you don't want rid of me, that is?"

Cooper raised her eyebrows. "Don't be ridiculous." She opened the bottle and topped up their drinks. The notion that she liked Atkinson and wanted more than a professional working relationship hit her like a bus. And why not? He was a hundred steps up from Kenny. Or Neil Fuller, now she thought about it. A man who ran away when she fell pregnant and a man who ran away when she got ill. *Wow, Erica, you really can pick 'em.*

Atkinson was ten years older than Cooper. Did that matter? Her mind flooded with questions as she found herself looking at the man through new eyes. They were both single parents, lonely, and came with a tonne of emotional baggage.

The pair retired to the living room, sat a safe distance away from one another and began to swap stories from their youth. It turned out Justin Atkinson was born in the same hospital as Cooper and they'd even attended the same tennis club as kids. Cooper had lessons when she was six but hated it, so her parents gave up forcing the sport upon her after only eight months. Atkinson had played until his mid-twenties. Funny how their paths had crossed without them even realising.

"You don't believe in this nonsense, do you?" asked Atkinson, holding the horoscope section of a newspaper.

The newspaper had probably been down the side of the sofa for weeks, but Cooper was feeling daring – and tipsy.

"Maybe," she said with a playful giggle and a coy tilt of her head. "I'm a Gemini. Does it say a tall, handsome man will deliver cooked food to my door?"

A look of shock passed over Atkinson and he stammered for a moment before reading out, "*As autumn fades into winter, it's time to be your own cheerleader. Venus syncs up with the moon and your sixth house of self-care.* Who writes this stuff? *Numero uno should be your top priority, and Mars...* Yada, yada, yada. Listen to the tall man bearing food—"

"Tall, *handsome* man."

Atkinson's face flushed a few shades lighter than the wine he was sipping. "Listen to the tall, handsome man bearing food."

He shifted closer to Cooper. Close enough for her to smell his aftershave. "He doesn't believe in horoscopes or crystal balls."

His voice was low and soft, and he edged closer still.

"Or tarot cards. Or Ouija boards."

His lips grazed Cooper's. Her heart jolted, but not from lust.

"What did you say?" she gasped, pulling away.

"I... Oh, I'm so sorry, I completely misread the situation. I'm such an idiot."

He was on his feet and moving away.

"No, you didn't," said Cooper. She pulled him back onto the sofa and stared at him. "Tarot cards. You said *tarot cards.*"

"Well, yes I did, but—"

Cooper pulled her phone out and frantically started typing. "Magician, Priestess, Empress. Oh God, they're all tarot cards. Why didn't I see this earlier? They're in order."

The colour drained from Atkinson's face as he realised the scale of what they were facing. He shook his head in disbelief. "How many cards are there?"

Cooper did another quick search, her fingers moving at lightning speed over the keys. "In the major arcana?" Her mouth fell open. She turned to stare at Atkinson. "Twenty-two." She felt sick. "There's twenty-two, and I bet he wants the whole deck."

- CHAPTER 15 -

"THE TAROT CARD KILLER," said Tennessee, taking a look up and down Millview Drive on Monday morning. "Has a ring to it."

Cooper almost choked on her coffee. She was not impressed. "Who came up with that?"

"No idea, but it's caught on throughout the department."

"Well, stop it. It's unprofessional. Besides, the last thing we need is for the press to get hold of it. He'll become some sort of macabre celebrity, an urban legend."

"Roger that."

Tennessee pulled his coat around him and waited for Cooper to finish the Starbucks he'd brought her.

"Nice area," he observed.

Millview Drive backed onto Tynemouth Golf Course; it was lined on either side by large, semi-detached mock-Tudor homes. Audis, BMWs, and Bentleys occupied the driveways. Cooper wondered if any of the cars were worth more than her house.

She drained the last dregs of caffeine and crumpled the cup into her car's drinks holder. "How much do you know about tarot cards?"

"Next to nothing. I know there's a death card, but I don't think it means you're about to pop your clogs. Think it's supposed to mean new beginnings or something. You don't think the killer had their fortune read, got the death card, and thought it meant they should become Death?"

Cooper locked the car behind her and approached number sixteen. The house boasted bay windows and an extension over the garage. A privet bush in the front garden had been trimmed into a perfect rectangle, and someone in the household had taken the trouble to clear the drive of snow and scatter rock salt.

"No idea," she answered as she knocked on the door. "But it's a possibility. If tarot's important to the killer, it's important to us. We need to do some research."

A young man with blue-black hair opened the door. He wasn't much taller than Cooper, and given his age and the green blazer he wore, Cooper assumed him to be Xander.

"Alexander Wright? I'm DCI Erica Cooper, and this is DS Jack Daniel. We're from Northumbria CID."

Xander blinked at the pair while Cooper took in his appearance. He had four earrings in his left ear, expertly applied eyeliner and his nail varnish matched the colour of his hair. His blazer sleeves were rolled up to reveal several woven bracelets around his wrists. Cooper, who knew the school's dress code inside out after Tina fell foul of it a handful of times, could tell Xander Wright was not one to conform.

"I thought it was only a matter of time before you stopped by," he said to Cooper's surprise.

"What makes you say that?"

"Rachel and I used to be a thing. We went out for a while. Aren't something like ninety per cent of female murder victims killed by their partner or their ex?"

Cooper did her best to keep poker-faced. "That's correct," she answered, thinking of how many women were scared of strangers and of walking alone at night. It was a disturbing truth that women who were murdered were most likely to be killed in their own home and at the hands of someone who claimed to love them.

"Suppose you'll want to come in." Xander stepped aside and called for his parents. "MUM. DAD. Told you the police would want to talk to me."

Within thirty seconds Mr and Mrs Wright had joined their son on their impressive leather sofa. Mrs Wright clung to her son's hands in a sign of support as Mr Wright scrutinised the detectives through steely eyes. Three overgrown rats - a Chihuahua, a sausage dog, and a pug - snarled at Cooper and Tennessee from behind a baby gate.

"Was it Will Harper?" asked Xander. "Was it Will who threw my name in the hat?"

Cooper preferred to be the one asking questions. "What makes you ask that?"

"I don't like him. He doesn't like me. He rules the school. You've seen him; he's a right gym monkey. Probably sprinkles steroids on his cornflakes."

"Xander," said his mother with a hushing tone to her voice. "Behave."

"I am. Is it true he was released?"

Cooper leant forward. "I'm not here to talk about Will Harper. But yes, we released him. Tell me about your relationship with Rachel Pearson."

He let out a small snort. "There's not much to tell. We went out a while back, before she hurt her back. She was one of those ridiculously busy girls. Went to the gym before school, had a private tutor some nights, gymnastics the others. At weekends she'd travel to Manchester or Shropshire for competitions. She was nonstop. So, our relationship wasn't much more than handholding at lunchtime. If I was lucky, we'd get to hang out on a Sunday evening after she got back from training or competing."

"How did things end?" asked Cooper.

"She said we'd drifted apart, which was a bit of a joke, I thought. How could we drift apart? We were barely together." He flopped back on the sofa. "A week later, I saw her in Will Harper's arms."

"That must have been difficult for you?"

Xander looked away for a moment. "I wasn't heartbroken or anything. Like I said, we barely had time for each other. My ego was pretty bruised, though."

Cooper realised her leg was twitching. Too much caffeine on an empty stomach. "Thank you, Xander. Now I need to ask you about your movements on Tuesday evening."

Mr Wright folded his arms. "You can't possibly think—"

Tennessee cut him off. "This is a standard line of questioning, Mr Wright. If Xander is to be ruled out of our investigation, we need to establish his alibi."

"I came straight home after school," he started. "I had games last lesson. We played rugby. We're supposed to shower at school, but no one does. So, I showered when I got home at about three forty-five."

"Thank you, Xander," said Cooper, wanting to encourage his honesty. "Then what?"

"Mum was home," he turned to look at his mother; she nodded in agreement.

"I'm a full-time Mum."

Cooper hated that term. As if going to work to provide for her daughter made her... What? A part-time Mum? No, she was as full-time a mother as anyone who had the luxury of staying home. Now, however, was not the time to voice that opinion.

"And you didn't go out again that evening?"

"I walked the dogs," said Xander, nodding his head towards the pack of snarling pups in the kitchen.

Cooper's mind returned to the man with two huskies. Was there any chance someone could mistake those three dogs for two huskies? No, she decided. Definitely not.

"What time was that?"

He puffed out his cheeks and shrugged. "Dunno. About six?"

"Did anyone see you?" she asked.

"Half of Tynemouth. If they didn't see me, they'd have heard me. Well, not me but the dogs. They've all got small dog syndrome, like to bark at every dog we pass. It's annoying."

Xander ran his palms down his thighs and began to tap out a rhythm on his knees. "Oh, I saw the lady from number twenty. She was walking her poodle."

Cooper looked to Tennessee, and he made a note.

"And I called into Gibson's. It's a paper shop. The son was working. I bought a Red Bull."

Mrs Wright shook her head. "No wonder you don't sleep. Those things are poison."

Xander rolled his eyes. "Then I came home and finished my homework."

"What time did you get home?"

Xander shrugged and sighed, then his eyes popped as a lightbulb illuminated in his mind. "Wait," he said, pulling out his phone. "I have it on here. My Fitbit'll know." He opened the app and handed his phone to Cooper.

A red line snaked around a map of Tynemouth but didn't go anywhere near Prior's Haven. The screen read that Xander had walked from ten past six to twenty past seven. There was no way he could have made it back from his house to the sailing club by half seven to meet Rachel as she left her class. Not on foot anyway.

"This is very good, Xander. Do you mind taking a screenshot and forwarding it to this number?" She handed him a card, and he did as she asked. "Now, what about Thursday morning?"

Xander scrunched up his face as he thought. "Ah, that was just a typical morning really. Had breakfast, left about eight forty, met Callum and walked to school."

"Who's Callum?"

"My cousin. Callum Chester. He lives at number forty-three, he's in the year below, but we get on all right. His parents are my Godparents, so we say we're cousins even though we aren't really. Want his number?"

"No, that's okay. We have his address," said Cooper. "And you got to school in time for registration?"

Xander nodded. "Yeah."

Cooper elected to end the questioning there. Xander Wright's movements were accounted for, and she suspected that Will Harper had sent them on a wild goose chase for his own amusement. She thanked the Wrights for their time and turned to Tennessee once they were outside. "What do you think?"

"I think the alibi's solid. I can chase up the poodle lady and the bloke from the paper shop if you like."

"I'll put Martin on to it."

As Cooper got into her car, started the engine and pulled away, her phone vibrated in her pocket. She shifted her weight and handed it to her DS. "Read that, will you?"

"What's your pin?"

"Nine, nine, nine, nine."

"Original." Tennessee unlocked the phone. "It's from Tina. She says she's going to Woods for hot chocolate with Josh after school, and she'll be home by five. Ah, this is interesting. She also says Xander Wright hasn't shown up to school yet."

"That's not interesting. We've just left his house."

"Yes, but Tina says Will Harper is telling everyone that Xander killed Rachel and Shelly and that's why he's not in."

"Little weasel," growled Cooper.

"She goes on. Apparently, the headteacher has - and I quote - done her nut. She's put Will in isolation for spreading rumours."

Cooper chuckled. "Good. We might not have been able to hold him any longer. But Linda Webb can. I'm going to drop you at HQ. Can you type up our report from the Wrights?"

"Sure. You got somewhere else to be?"

Cooper slowed the car to let a cat sprint across the road. "Yeah," she said. "I'm going to gather some intel."

-CHAPTER 16-

COOPER PRESSED THE DOORBELL of a house in the quaint village of Earsdon, but there was no ringing sound. She raised her hand, but before she could knock, the door swung open. A frail, elderly woman in a pink nightdress looked up at her through thick lenses. She blinked twice.

"Hello. I'm DCI Erica Cooper. I'm looking for Charity Mae."

"You found her, dear." Charity Mae's voice had a raspy rattle to it, suggesting anything from the start of tonsillitis to chronic emphysema.

Cooper took in the tiny woman. She was hunchbacked, and her pale skin was flecked with age spots. "Wait," said Cooper, recognising a strong sense of deja vu. "I know you."

"Oh, I doubt that."

"No. I've seen you. You were walking outside police headquarters in Wallsend. You stopped and looked up at the window."

Charity Mae ran her tongue along the edge of her top teeth and chuckled to herself. "To see is not to know. You may have seen me, but you do not know me. How can you know me when you hardly know yourself?"

Taken aback by that comment, Cooper stood quite transfixed.

"Well, don't just stand there, dear. Come in. You'll catch your death." She turned and began to walk along her hallway. "Follow me."

Cooper gathered herself and shut the door behind her. "Mrs Mae," she said to the back of the woman's head as she walked. "I wanted to talk to you about a case I'm working on. I found your address in the Yellow Pages under *psychics and clairvoyants*. I don't know if you caught the news, but two teenagers have been murdered. We think the person we're looking for has some connection to, or fascination with, tarot cards."

Charity Mae's home smelled of cinnamon and cloves, and the chintzy decor took Cooper back in time to a period when she lived with her grandmother. Pastel table cloths covered side tables, floral tiebacks secured heavy curtains. Pictures and figurines of birds decorated every shelf and sideboard.

"Sit," she said, pointing to a comfortable looking armchair. "I'll make tea."

As the woman shuffled towards her kitchen, Cooper called after her. "It's okay, Mrs Mae. I'm not thirsty. I just wanted to find out about tarot cards and what they represent. Especially the major arcana."

Charity took no notice and returned a few moments later with two cups of peppermint tea served in antique china cups. "Now, what can I do for the girl who sees but does not know? You want to know your future? Or, perhaps contact someone who has passed on?"

"No, Mrs Mae." Cooper took the cup of tea and gave a slight nod of appreciation despite explicitly saying she didn't want any. "As I was saying, I'm not after a reading. I'm working on a case involving tarot cards... and I wanted... to..." Cooper's voice slowed as she realised the woman wasn't looking her in the eyes; she was staring at her mouth. For a moment, she considered she had something in her teeth, then it dawned on her. "You're lipreading?"

"Yes, dear. Deaf as a post. Do go on," she said, taking a seat on the other side of a small, round table covered in lace.

"Ah, well. Yes. I work for Northumbria Police. Two teenagers have been murdered, and the perpetrator appears to be working his way through the tarot deck. The first victim was dressed as—"

"A magician. I saw the news. And a priestess, I believe?"

"Yes."

"Truly awful. Are you sure you don't want a reading, dear? The Hanged Man looks down upon you, you know? The sacrifices you have made are written on your face. I can see you work hard to provide for a child, but the harder you work, the less you get to play the mother. Love can not be bought, no matter how hard you work. Nor can time."

Cooper warmed her palms on the cup of tea and considered what Charity had just told her. She'd never given fortune-telling much thought, but she supposed she considered it guesswork; she certainly hated the idea of her life being mapped out or determined by fate. But how did Charity know she was a mother? The comments about working were easy enough. No one got far in the police, let alone CID, without hard work, but she definitely didn't mention Tina in the two minutes since she arrived.

"Moving on," said Cooper, putting the question to one side. "The major arcana. Why is it special?"

"Ah," chuckled Charity, "the big secret."

"What secret?"

"The cards themselves, dear. Major arcana is a Latin term. It means the big secret, and in answer to your question, the cards are not special. They are merely cards, inanimate objects. It is what they represent that is special."

Cooper crossed her legs and tried to keep her expression neutral, but the old lady was frustrating her, and she had places to be. She thought hearing from an expert would be quicker than trawling through Wikipedia, but on second thoughts, she was probably wrong.

Charity opened a wooden box, took out a deck of cards and spread them, face down, over the table. "The tarot is made up of five decks: cups represent love and relationships; swords deal with consciousness and intellect; pentacles are of work and wealth; the wands stand for inspiration and intuition; and finally," she rested her chin on steepled fingers, "the major arcana, which takes our souls on the journey to enlightenment."

Journey to enlightenment. Cooper could imagine Atkinson's face when she no doubt repeated this to him.

"Turn over the card nearest to you, dear."

Cooper did as she was asked and was faced with the Fool. Feeling somewhat insulted, she met Charity's eyes and waited.

"Don't take it personally. The major arcana tells the story of our spirituality as we travel from the naive wonder of the Fool, to..." Charity turned over another card. "To the fulfilment of the World. We are all on a journey, dear. You are, I am, and the man you hunt most certainly is."

Cooper uncrossed her legs. She may be getting somewhere now. "Tell me more."

"He is transforming. With each death, the killer moves closer to his destiny." Charity reached across the table and turned over the king of wands. She smiled to herself as if sharing a private joke. "Energy can not be created, nor can it be destroyed. It can only be transferred or transformed. Am I right in thinking that the man you seek only kills the young?"

"So far, yes."

Charity cocked her head. "And who has more energy than the youth?"

Cooper ran a hand over her face. "You think he kills the young to stay young himself?"

Charity sipped her tea and stared at an embroidered picture of two blue tits. For almost a minute, it was as if Cooper wasn't there. Eventually, she shrugged and turned back to her. "You see but do not know, and I know but do not hear. Perhaps the wise monkey is what we need. Behind you, dear."

Cooper turned. Behind her, on the windowsill, were three jade monkeys. Cooper picked up the one covering his mouth with his hands and handed it to the old lady.

"Speak no evil," said Charity Mae.

"A sentiment people rarely subscribe to these days," said Cooper. She got to her feet and brushed her coat with her palms. The Tarot Card Killer was on a journey. His actions were about more than just dressing up his victims. Although cloaked in some Rosa Lee theatrics, Charity's comments gave her a potential insight into the killer's mind. If she could work out his journey, perhaps she could intercept him along the way.

Cooper extended a hand. "Thank you for your time, Charity Mae. Your ideas about a transformation or the transfer of energy are really quite interesting."

As the pair shook hands, the lights in the room flickered. Cooper's eyes darted to a dusty chandelier above her.

"Oh, that'll be the postman." Charity let out another rattle of a laugh. A second later, Cooper heard the sound of letters dropping through the letterbox.

Astonished, Cooper's mouth fell open. "NO!" she gasped. "There's no way."

Psychics aren't real, she told herself. They're actors, aren't they?

"Relax, dear. Did you not consider how I knew you were at my door when I can't hear the doorbell? There's a pressure pad under my doorstep. It makes the lights flicker when someone stands on it. My son installed it."

Cooper relaxed, but only a touch. Something about the little old lady made her feel strangely on edge. She might not have predicted the postman, but it still didn't explain how she knew Cooper was a mother.

Charity interlaced her fingers and rested them over her small round stomach. "Allow me to read for you."

"Thank you, but no. I just wanted a better understanding of the cards."

"You're not a believer. That's okay. Not many are. But did you know the FBI have often turned to clairvoyants? Desperate times push people to expand their horizons."

Cooper checked the time on a gold clock on the mantelpiece. It was stuck on five past four.

"Indulge an old lady."

Cooper sighed and wondered what the harm would be. The old lady was right about the FBI; their most well-known psychic, Troy Griffin, worked on over a hundred cases. Although, it was usually as a last resort and his success rate was under twenty per cent. "All right," said Cooper. "But let's keep it snappy."

The smile on Charity's face pushed her glasses up an inch. She collected the cards, shuffled them and placed them on the table. "Cut the deck, dearest."

Cooper halved the deck and placed the top half under the bottom half. Charity dealt the top three cards and laid them face down on the lace. She pointed to each card in turn.

"The past, the present, the future." She motioned to Cooper to turn over the first card. "Ah, the nine of wands. Look here, dear. You see the old man carrying the wand? You see the eight wands stuck in the ground around him? The wands in the ground represent the battles he has faced. The wand in his hand is the battle to come. If you look closely, you'll see the man looks weak and injured, but his face is determined. There is still fight in the old man, and he still desires the win."

Turning her eyes to admire a collection of decorative plates, Cooper thought about Charity's interpretation of the card. According to Margot, the person who strangled Rachel and Shelly had to be a man or a large female, given the size of the bruise marks on Rachel's neck. Could a weak or injured man have overpowered the girls? Perhaps he could, especially in the case of Rachel, who was herself weak from injury.

Charity blinked her magnified eyes at Cooper. "The present?"

Cooper turned the card; it read *Strength* and depicted a woman battling a lion.

"Interesting." Charity leant forward in her armchair. "The lion is strong, but the woman in the card is stronger. Her face looks calm and collected despite the terrifying act she is engaged in."

Two options popped into Cooper's mind. "Is the killer the woman? Or, is he the lion?"

"If he were the lion, who would be the woman?"

"Well, me, I suppose." Cooper tensed. "I'm the one battling him."

"See how the card is rotated towards me rather than you?" asked Charity. "The lion is a symbol of courage and passion. But reversed it depicts a lack of inner strength, fear, and a lack of conviction and confidence in one's own abilities. Perhaps he is questioning how far he can continue on his journey? Maybe he has forgotten the fulfilment he feels from doing what he loves?"

"No," said Cooper. "I don't think he'll stop after two. I think he plans on seeing this through. He'll not stop until he has the full set or I put him behind bars. Right. Last card." She turned over the final card. "Two of swords. What does that mean?"

"This card depicts the future in our spread. There is a woman, blindfolded, holding a sword in each hand. In the background, you can see a sea filled with crags and rocks. The rocks are obstacles to ships; they stall progression."

Cooper's mind went straight to the Black Middens, a reef in the mouth of the Tyne that had claimed several boats and hundreds of lives before the days of lighthouses and radar.

"Are the rocks the police? Are we stalling the killer?"

"Or?"

Cooper sighed. Did Charity Mae have to be this exhausting, or was it all part of her act? "Or he could be the rock, hindering my investigation?"

Charity merely smiled. After a few seconds she added, "The blindfold signifies a situation which prevents the woman from seeing clearly, and the swords show two choices that lead in different directions. It may seem like an impossible choice, but choose she must."

Scepticism flowed through Cooper, and she wondered how much money the FBI had spent on psychics over the years. "So," she said to humour Charity, "the murderer had a troubled youth. He's faced adversity, and his killings are his way of taking back control? He's lying low until he can harness his strength, and in the future, he has to make a choice. A choice between two victims?"

"Very good," said Charity. She pointed an arthritic finger at Cooper. "Did you ever hear the story of Esmerelda Day?"

Cooper stood up and shook her head.

"Once, there was a young man in York who visited a travelling fair. He wanted to fool the fortune teller, so he put on a wig, a dress and a pair of women's shoes, and he knocked on the door of Esmerelda's wagon. Esmerelda looked into her crystal ball and told him he would marry a fair man with dark eyes. The young man laughed and removed his wig. He handed her the sixpence that he owed and called her a fraud. Guess what happened to that young man?"

Hoping to find a polite moment to make her escape, Cooper had begun to edge herself towards the door. "I don't know," she answered. "She put a curse on him?"

"No, dear," laughed Charity. "Curses aren't real."

Nor are psychics and clairvoyants, thought Cooper, *and yet here we are.*

"The next year, he met a beautiful woman, fell in love and married her. Her name was Lucy Fairman, and she had eyes as black as night. You see, child, there are always two sides to every prediction. You thought we were talking about the killer, but it was you who cut the deck and you who turned the cards. It is you who is weak from battle, you who questions her abilities and you, my dear, who will need to make a choice."

- CHAPTER 17 -

COOPER PACED BACK AND forth in the glass-fronted lobby of Northumbria Police headquarters. Charity Mae's words wouldn't leave her head. For a hunchbacked wannabe gypsy, she'd really gotten under Cooper's skin. Had Cooper forgotten the fulfilment she should feel from doing what she loved? Was she suffering from a lack of confidence and conviction? Yes. As much as she hated to admit it, Cooper still hadn't settled back into her role as Chief Inspector.

"Screw her," muttered Cooper. She turned and paced in the opposite direction. Cooper wasn't just going through the motions. She loved her chosen career; she was sure she did. This role wasn't for someone who didn't care. Cooper cared. Her pacing and tormented inner monologue stopped dead when she spotted a blue Citron Cl pull up in the car park and watched as Lisa Smith, Shelley's mother, got out. Cooper greeted the petite, fragile woman at the door. Unlike her daughter - who was blonde and fair-skinned - Lisa Smith had dark features with almost black hair, brown, bloodshot eyes, and a ruddy complexion.

"Thank you for coming in, Mrs Smith. We could have come to you, you know?"

She replied by shaking her head. "No. I needed to get out. Sitting around doing nothing's tormenting me. It's torture. I'd much rather come here. At least this way, I feel like I'm doing something."

Cooper placed a hand on the lady's upper arm and guided her towards one of the family rooms. She felt it would be less intimidating and more appropriate than an interview suite.

Cooper got Lisa Smith settled and had Oliver Martin bring her a cup of camomile tea. She gripped the mug between her palms. Her whole body was shaking. It wasn't cold in the family room, the temperature was centrally controlled to twenty degrees, but Cooper knew from her own experience that trauma and stress could make you shiver even with the heating set to maximum. She thought back to a time when she hadn't been able to warm up for two days straight, no matter how many blankets she wrapped around herself.

"I understand you're staying with friends, Mrs Smith."

The small woman looked up from her tea. "Please," she said, "call me Lisa. And yes, I'm staying with Isabella Lopez, a colleague of mine. I can't go home. I'm going to get the house on the market as soon as possible. I don't think I'll ever be able to step through that front door again."

Cooper was sympathetic. She couldn't imagine living in her home if something like that happened to Tina.

"Lisa, the gentleman in charge of the forensics team has informed me that there's no sign of forced entry at your home. I'm led to believe that Shelley either let her killer in, or he had a key. Would Shelly be likely to open the door to someone she didn't know?"

Lisa shook her head. "Absolutely not. She hated answering the door to anyone; she was always convinced it would be Jehovah's Witnesses or someone trying to sell us something. Rachel was her best friend. She cried all night after we heard the news about her. And I mean, all night. We had a big chat about safety. I just can't believe she's gone," her voice cracked. "Why my Shelly? My baby. Someone killed my baby girl."

She placed her tea on a small side table and buried her head in her hands. "I told Shelly I'd meet her after school that day. I'd booked for her to speak to a therapist because of what happened to Rachel. But..." Her voice trailed away because they'd never kept the appointment.

"We were quite open with each other," continued Lisa. "She didn't keep secrets from me. She wasn't the best behaved child, I know that, but she was always honest with me. For instance, she went to a party a little while back, and she told me about being asked out by this boy that she liked. She was so happy. She also told me that one or two of the kids there were doing coke. She said she had nothing to do with it. But she wanted me to know that it was there in case I heard it from someone else."

"It sounds like you two had a good relationship."

"We did."

Lisa took out a hanky and blew her nose.

According to Atkinson and the team of SOCOs, Shelly had been killed in her living room. The perpetrator then changed her clothes and posed her on the doorstep before leaving and closing the gate behind him. Officers had spoken to several residents on the street, but so far, no one reported seeing anything unusual.

"Who has a key to your home, Lisa?"

"Just myself, Shelly, her grandparents and my ex-boyfriend."

"Is that Shelly's father?"

"No. He died when she was just an infant. He was killed in combat. Iraq."

"I'm sorry to hear that," said Cooper, and she was. Lisa Smith had faced more than her fair share of sorrow. "I'd like someone to contact your parents and make sure that they still have their key, check that it hasn't been stolen."

Lisa nodded. "Of course. I'll give you the number."

"Your ex-boyfriend. Can you tell me his name?"

"It's Ralf. Ralf Bennett."

Cooper felt the tiniest of tingles in the base of her skull.

"Is he local?" asked Cooper.

"Yes. He lives in Tynemouth."

"And have you been separated long?"

"About six months. I never got around to getting my key back. I was putting off seeing him. I should have just told him to put it through the letterbox."

"Can you tell me how things ended between you?"

"He hit me," said Lisa. She picked her tea back up and took a sip. "Only the once. It only needed to be the once. I was knocked out cold and unconscious for over a minute. Shelly saw the whole thing. I'm no idiot." She sniffed. "I wasn't going to stay in that relationship, no matter how many times he said he was sorry and promised to change. I grabbed Shelly, left for my parents, and told him I wanted him gone before I got back. You don't think he could have—?"

Cooper had misjudged Lisa Smith. She might be small, but she was far from fragile. Cooper spent a further twenty minutes with the grieving mother, trying to gather all she could about Shelly's personality, friends, routine, and the things she did every week. Afterwards, she found Tennessee as quickly as she could.

"I need you to get on to the tech team. Find any connection between Shelly, Rachel, and a Ralf Bennett. He was in a relationship with Lisa Smith, and he has a violent streak. He hit her; that's why they broke up."

"Piece of shit," grumbled Tennessee. "They should lock men like that in a room with men like me. See how they like it when someone their own size hits them back."

"He still has a key to their house. I recognised the name as soon as she said it, but it took me a while to place where I'd seen it before. It was on Rachel's Facebook page. He was one of the people who liked her photo in her gymnastics leotard. Why would a grown man befriend his girlfriend's daughter's friends on social media? That doesn't sound right to me."

Tennessee lowered his eyebrows. "That doesn't sound right to me either. Not in the slightest. Do you have an address?"

"I do. Rodney Street."

Tennessee's eyes widened. "That's literally around the corner from the Pearsons. This is promising. Right, I'll speak to tech, then I'll get us some vests and we'll get over there."

"We could do with some backup," said Cooper. "I'll get Paula and Sam. Meet me back here in ten."

RALF BENNETT LIVED IN a standard red-brick two-up-two-down semi-detached. A dirty white van was parked in the driveway; someone had smudged the words *clean me* in the muck. Through the front window, a fifty-inch flat-screen was playing The Jeremy Kyle Show.

Cooper and Tennessee approached the house while Keaton and Sutherland waited in an unmarked car at the end of the street. Tennessee rapped his knuckles on the front door, when there was no answer, he did it again.

Cooper heard huffing and grumbling and the sound of heavy feet shuffling towards the door. It opened ajar, and a man with shaggy blond hair and a stubbly jaw peered out behind the chain.

"What?" he asked in a thick Geordie accent.

Tennessee held up his warrant card. "Mr Bennett? I'm DS Daniel from—"

He didn't get to finish. Bennett slammed the door in Tennessee's face. The detective's nose exploded with thick, scarlet blood. He swore at the top of his lungs before throwing his weight into the door and knocking it off its hinges.

Bennett dashed along the corridor. He wore a dressing gown, black pyjama pants and a pair of slippers.

"He's going out the back," yelled Tennessee, his voice muffled with pain.

Cooper darted along the narrow alleyway that divided the sets of semi-detached houses. She scrambled over a wooden gate and landed in the back garden in time to see Bennett scaling his back wall.

"Stop! Police!" she called out. Cooper grabbed her hand-held radio and directed Sutherland and Keaton towards the main road. "Stop where you are!" she shouted again.

Bennett dropped over the wall and disappeared from sight. Cooper wasn't going to give in that easily. She might be small, but she was agile. It was how she got through all those bleep-tests when she first joined the force. She was never the fastest in the sprints, but she could turn on a sixpence. She grabbed the top of the wall and heaved herself up. Tennessee emerged from the back door and sprinted across the wet grass. The wall grazed Cooper's hands and tore at the fabric of her trousers but she managed to swing her body over it. Being light had its advantages. She landed like a cat and went in pursuit.

As adrenaline surged through Cooper's body, she realised these were the moments she lived for. Thoughts of cancer and chemotherapy faded away to nothing. The title and pay increase that came with being DCI was all well and good, but she loved the chase. She loved the pursuit. This is what she was meant to do. Insecurities about returning to work after four months seemed a distant memory. That upside-down Strength card could bugger off. Erica Cooper was back.

The unmarked car screeched around the corner. Bennett narrowly dodged a speeding Audi as he weaved his way across Tynemouth Road. His dressing gown billowed behind him like the cape of the worst superhero imaginable. Cooper was hot on his heels, and Tennessee wasn't far behind her. Bennett turned into a bridle path that cut away from the main road and headed to Tynemouth Metro station.

"Take Station Terrace," she shouted into her radio.

With only two strides separating her and her target, Cooper launched herself at the back of the man's legs. She wrapped her arms around his calf and pulled him off balance. He hit the ground with a bang and a string of swear words. There was no way Cooper could control him by herself, but Tennessee arrived in the nick of time. He flattened his weight on top of Bennett - drips of blood falling from his face - and secured his arms behind his back with handcuffs. Cooper took a second to get her breath and check that her wig was still in place. Boy, she had missed this.

"Ralf Bennett, I'm arresting you on suspicion of the murders of Rachel Pearson and Michelle Smith," started Tennessee.

"No. Let me up, ya bastard. I didn't do anything."

"You do not have to say anything—"

"Dirty pigs! Let me up. Now."

"As you wish." Tennessee yanked on the handcuffs as hard as he could and roughly pulled the man to his feet. Bennett squirmed and pulled against the cuffs like a dog fighting his leash. He was covered in a mixture of mud and Tennessee's blood.

The unmarked car pulled up at the end of the bridle path. Keaton got out and opened the door to the back seat. She gave Cooper a searching look and Cooper responded with a subtle thumbs up. She was fine. No need to worry over her.

"I'll leave this one in your capable hands, DS Daniel," she said. "Mr Bennett, your chariot awaits."

COOPER LET BENNETT STEW in his cell while she took a shower and changed into a clean suit. She treated her palms with antiseptic and threw her old trousers away. She doubted even an experienced seamstress could disguise the fact both knees had been shredded.

"How's your nose?" she asked when she emerged from the shower room.

Tennessee lightly pressed his face with his fingers. "Tender, but it's all right. I'd have been miffed if he'd broken it. Paid five grand for this nose."

Cooper laughed. "I knew that bone structure was too good to be true." She searched his face. "What else have you had done?"

A delicate flush formed over Tennessee's cheeks. "Just the nose," he said, and then, much quieter, "and maybe the ears."

"I knew it. I bloody knew it. Where is he anyway? Still in the cells?"

"Sutherland has him in interview suite two. He's refusing a lawyer."

Cooper frowned. "Really? Not the brightest move."

"He's not the brightest of bulbs, that's for sure."

"Did Sutherland find any evidence in Bennett's home? Anything relating to the occult?"

Tennessee shook his head. "A team's still raking through the place, but from what I last heard, it's just a typical bachelor pad."

A few minutes later and Cooper was dragging her chair across the floor of the interview suite. The action created a nails-on-chalkboard sound, causing Bennett to wince.

"I'm sorry, Mr Bennett. Was that annoying?" asked Cooper. "Not nearly as annoying as ruining a good suit by having to drag myself over your garden wall, I bet."

He scowled and bore icy blue eyes into her. "No one made you chase me."

"No one made you run."

Cooper turned on the audio recorder and stated the date, time and venue of the interview. She introduced herself and DS Jack Daniel and began her questioning.

"Tell me how you knew Shelly Smith."

"I was seeing her mother, Lisa." His voice was low and gravelly.

"Did you get on with Shelly?" asked Cooper.

"I guess so. She was a good kid. A bit lippy at times."

"A bit lippy, you say? She was cheeky? Answered back a lot?"

"Yeah, that was Shelly."

"Did you ever hit her for her cheek?"

"What? No, course not." He folded his arms.

"But you hit Lisa."

"No. I never."

Cooper leant back in her chair and waited.

"Well, just the once," he mumbled after thirty seconds of silence. "That doesn't mean I killed Shelly. I was as shocked as anyone by the news."

Cooper blanked him. "Do you have a key to Lisa and Shelly Smith's home?"

He shuffled his weight around on the cheap plastic chair. "Might have. I'm not sure, can't really remember to be honest."

Tennessee turned his eyes to the ceiling and tutted. "Listen, Mr Bennett, we pulled a set of keys off you when we brought you in here. They're currently bagged and in evidence. There are six keys on that keyring. Two for your front door, one for your back door, and one for your van. What are the other two keys for?"

He shrugged.

Tennessee leant forward and rested his elbows on the table. "Think hard Mr Bennett, because if that key fits the lock at Lisa Smith's home, you will be in a world of trouble."

"That still wouldn't prove anything."

"It would prove that you like lying to the police. And I can tell you now that's not a very good look."

Bennett chewed the inside of his mouth but said nothing. Cooper decided to move the conversation forward. She tapped her finger on the table four times and asked, "Have you ever had your fortune read?"

The change in topic confused Bennett. "No," he said with a questioning tone. "I'm not into that shit."

"Do you believe in a higher power?"

Bennett frowned. "No, not really."

"What about a lower power? Satan, perhaps?"

He looked from Cooper to Tennessee and back to Cooper. "What are you on about? No, I'm not a Satan worshipper. And I didn't kill Shelly. Are you going to let me out of here or what?"

Cooper narrowed her eyes and decided to switch topics again. "Tell me about your relationship with Rachel Pearson."

"What relationship?"

"Well, you knew her. You were close."

"No, we weren't." A line formed between his eyebrows. "Who told you that?"

"You're Facebook friends with her. Isn't that right?"

"Yeah. So what? I'm friends with loads of people on there. I've got like six hundred friends."

Cooper wanted to make air quotes with her fingers when he used the word *friends*. "And how many of those six hundred friends are fifteen-year-old girls?"

"Woah! Hang on a minute! First, you try and pin these murders on me. Now you're making me out to look like some kind of nonce. I'm no murderer, and I'm no paedo."

Cooper opened a file and spread a selection of photographs over the desk. "For the record," she stated, "I am showing Mr Bennett photographs of Rachel Pearson taken from her Facebook page. They include a picture of her in a gymnastics leotard and two pictures of her in bikinis. Do you recognise these photos, Mr Bennett?"

"Should I?" His tone was angry now. He was struggling to control his temper.

"Yes," replied Cooper. "You liked all three of them. And on this one," she tapped the photograph to her right, "you left the comment: *Looking good, Rach.*"

Bennett jumped to his feet. Tennessee matched his speed and stood between him and the door. "Don't even think about it."

"Sit down," snapped Cooper. "Or we'll cuff you to the chair."

Bennett clenched his jaw and reluctantly sat back down. "Liking photos isn't a crime," he grumbled. "I didn't kill Shelly, and I didn't kill Rachel."

"Then prove it," said Cooper. "Tell us where you were at the time of the murders. Let's start with Tuesday evening when Rachel was killed. What were you doing then?"

Silence.

"Okay," said Cooper with a sigh. "And Thursday morning?"

More silence.

"Mr Bennett, you don't need me to remind you that you have been arrested on suspicion of murder. When we came to your home, you ran. When questioned about—"

"I didn't kill those girls," he growled through gritted teeth.

"So, where were you?" Cooper sat back in her chair. "I'll wait."

Bennett rested his head in his hands then ran his fingers through his messy hair before folding his arms again. "I was at home."

"With?"

"No one. I was alone."

"Can anyone confirm that? Did anyone pop round? Did you make any phone calls?"

Bennett shook his head.

"For the record", started Cooper, "the suspect is shaking his head. And we will check your phone records, by the way. We'll know if your phone was on Rodney Street."

Across the table, Cooper saw Bennett swallow.

"Right, so when Rachel Pearson was being strangled to death, you were in your house, alone?"

His lips pursed as he looked to his right. "Yes."

"And what about Thursday morning? Where were you when Shelly Smith, your ex-girlfriend's daughter, was suffocated?"

Bennett's gaze darted around the room before finally coming to rest on Cooper. "I was home alone."

Cooper took a long, slow breath, placed the photographs back in the file and got to her feet. Bennett may be an expert in playing the fool, but Cooper was far from convinced he was on a journey to enlightenment. "Have it your way," she said, thinking she'd at least give the forensics team some more time to sweep his house for traces of the murdered girls. "A good night's sleep in your cell might help jog your memory. I'll speak with you again tomorrow."

- CHAPTER 18 -

COOPER YAWNED. HER AFTERNOON had been spent speaking to the owners of fancy dress stores. She and Keaton had called every store within a ten-mile radius of Tynemouth. They'd asked the owners and managers if they had sold any outfits that matched up with the cards from the major arcana. Almost all of them had priest, magician, death and devil outfits, and a fair few of them had sold costumes matching those descriptions in the past month. Cooper requested any credit card information and any CCTV footage that the stores had. It would take a while for Martin to sort through it all, but needs must. She also sent Bennett's image to all the stores in case the owners recognised him. It wasn't exactly scintillating work and it in no way compared to the thrill of chasing a bad guy down a lane and dragging him to the mud in a tackle Keaton had described as "gnarly."

"Ten quid says he got his outfits online," Keaton put the phone down on the latest shop owner and swigged from a can of full-fat cola.

"That's a safe bet. He'll have used a VPN, paid in bitcoin and had it delivered to an InPost locker." Cooper balanced her chair on its back two legs. "But he's flat out denying any involvement, and frankly, we need more evidence than we have if we're going to charge him. So, until then, we're not leaving a single stone unturned."

"What's your gut saying?" asked Keaton. "Did Bennett do it?"

"All my gut's telling me is that last night's ready meal was a bad idea. As for Bennett, I think he's fishier than North Shields Fish Quay. Whether he's a murderer or not remains to be seen."

"And you think the killer's obsession with tarot means he's on some sort of journey?"

Cooper let out another yawn and covered her mouth with her hand. "Apparently that's the point of the picture cards; a journey from cluelessness to knowledge. The psychic thinks he might be harvesting the kids' energy in some sort of bid for immortality."

Coke spluttered from Keaton's lips. "That's messed up. Sounds like this guy's more than your average bed-wetter with an Oedipus complex. So, what was the psychic like? She give you the lottery numbers?"

"Creepy," Cooper answered, "and I forgot to ask." She checked her watch. It was almost half three, and she was due at Tynemouth Academy to conduct additional interviews with Rachel and Shelly's teachers and to check in with the two uniforms who had been watching the school.

"I can take over here if you need to get off," said Keaton. She shifted her chair back so she could rest her ginormous feet on the standard-issue desk. Cooper should tell her to sit up straight and respect her surroundings, but the posture rather suited Keaton. The woman had an air about her; she exuded the sort of confidence that didn't come easily to those under five-foot-five.

"Thanks, Paula." Cooper pulled on her coat and grabbed her files. She walked past Tennessee's desk where he was furiously scrolling through the database for any previous crimes related to the occult. "Come on. We'll go via the burger van."

Tennessee's eyes lit up, and he practically flew out of his seat and out the doors of CID.

Five minutes later and the detective sergeant was stuffing a greasy burger down his throat.

"Brilliant. Thanks, Coop. Hayley never lets me eat junk food."

Cooper held back a snort. Her sergeant shouldn't be worrying about what he ate. He was at that age where he could eat anything.

"Well, I'm not your wife, and I'm not your mother. I'm your chief. And I don't care how much junk you eat as long as you pass your physical."

"The bleep test?" he said with his mouth full. "I can do it walking on my hands."

"Now that I'd like to see."

Cooper pulled into the only parking space available at Tynemouth Academy. It happened to be the space furthest from the front doors.

Tennessee stuffed the last few bites of his burger into his mouth, swallowed and gave himself the hiccoughs.

"Looks like a - hic - bit of trouble at the gates there." He slapped his hand against his chest a few times in an effort to make his diaphragm cut it out.

Cooper followed his gaze. A small group had gathered to watch an argument between two students and an adult. One of the girls was gesticulating wildly.

"Oh, for crying out loud," muttered Cooper as she got closer. The students were Tina and her boyfriend, Josh. The adult, if she could call him that, was Kenny.

"I'm walking."

"No, you're not."

"We agreed. We're going to Woods café, then Josh will walk me home."

Kenny folded his arms, making his upper body seem even bigger. "You expect this little dweeb to keep you safe?"

"Hey!" Josh's shoulders rounded and his jaw tightened.

"Give over, lad. You couldn't punch your way out of a wet paper bag."

Josh shoved a hand into Kenny's chest. It was probably akin to trying to push over a house and judging by the way Josh staggered backwards, it was a move he instantly regretted. Luckily Cooper, who had hurried over, was now only two steps away. From the opposite direction, Linda Webb was also hightailing it towards the melee.

"Kenny," they both snapped in unison.

Linda was first to say her piece. "Lower your voice. You're scaring some of the children."

"I'm just trying to get my daughter home in one piece, Linda," he grumbled, his lip protruding.

Several students began to giggle when they realised there was something between the head-teacher and Tina Cooper's father.

"Then compromise," hissed Cooper, lowering her voice so the crowd couldn't continue to eaves-drop. "Let her go to the café and pick her up from there. I shouldn't say anything yet, but we have someone in custody. The danger might be over."

"Might?"

"We're still gathering evidence."

Kenny shook his head, but Tina burst into tears before he could say anything. Half her year group had watched the scene play out. The poor thing must be mortified.

"I wish you'd stayed in Qatar," Tina spat. She turned and walked away, her head lowered, allow-ing her hair to fall over her face and hide her tears. Josh took off after her.

Kenny turned on Linda. "Look what you did."

"Nice try, Kenny." Cooper wasn't Linda's biggest fan, but she wasn't letting Kenny pin this on her. "This is your doing. If you want to keep your daughter safe, maybe start by not pushing her away. She never met you until she was twelve, and you expect her to hug you and call you 'Daddy?' I don't think so. She's known Josh longer than she's known you. That girl barely knows you, let alone respects you."

Kenny bristled, unfolded his arms and shoved his hands in his pockets. He looked back and forth between Cooper and Linda before stomping off himself.

Like father, like daughter, thought Cooper. Sometimes nature well and truly trumped nurture.

"Right." Cooper straightened her posture and plastered a fake smile on her face. "Linda, let's head indoors. I'd like to speak to the teachers who taught Rachel on Tuesday afternoon and those who taught Shelly on Wednesday afternoon. Sergeant Daniel," she turned to Tennessee. "Clear the rubberneckers and speak to the patrol officers. I want to know if the man with the dogs has been back. Show them Bennett's photo while you're at it. When you're done, come find me."

"Roger."

LINDA SHOWED COOPER INTO the staffroom.

"Brian," she called. "You remember Erica Cooper? She needs to speak to you again if you have five minutes."

Brian Hutchins turned around from the sink where he'd been washing a coffee mug. He removed his glasses, tucked them over the collar of his t-shirt and checked his watch. "Five minutes is all I have, I'm afraid. Culture club starts at quarter to."

"Culture club?" He couldn't possibly mean the band.

"Catchy name, isn't it?" He motioned to the chairs, and Cooper took a seat. "I run the group with Phillip Dunn, the music teacher and Catherine Grainger, who teaches English literature. Each week we do something different: pottery, poetry, a new song, that sort of thing. Last term we took the group to the Theatre Royal to watch an opera. I was worried they'd misbehave, but they were enthralled. Some of the girls loved seeing a larger female as the star of the show. They said it was refreshing. The club's becoming rather popular, and tonight's activity is sculpting, so I'll be leading the group."

Cooper thought back to the after-school options she'd had as a teenager. If you weren't into hockey, netball or choir, your options were limited. She folded her hands in her lap and lifted her eyes to meet Brian Hutchins's. "I understand you taught Rachel last Monday afternoon?"

"Yes, that's correct." He sat opposite Cooper.

"How did she seem that day?"

"What do you mean?" asked Brian.

"Did she seem worried about anything?"

Brian sat back in his chair and brought a finger to his lips. "No, not really. There was tension between her and William Harper, but you've already ruled Will out of the investigation, haven't you?"

Will Harper was still a person of interest. Cooper, however, didn't feel the need to share that information with a member of the public - she'd already shared too much by mentioning Bennett to Kenny - so she moved on.

"Did Rachel talk about her routine during class? Can you recall if she mentioned where she'd be going after school?"

He thought for a second. "I don't think so. Not that I remember. She used to. I mean she used to talk about gymnastics at length, how hard she'd trained and where she was off to next. Since she stopped competing she became more of a girlie girl." He paused to pick some paint from his watch strap. "Oh my, that's not very politically correct, is it? What I mean is, lately, she was always chatting about boys and make-up and parties. She started to gossip more. But knowing Rachel and how she conducted herself in class, if she'd told anyone she was going to yoga that night, the whole class would have heard. I mentioned before that she could be a bit of a foghorn, didn't I?"

Cooper nodded. "So, just to confirm. She didn't seem anxious or stressed?"

"Not at all. She was more angry than anxious. Like I said, she was a bit short with Will."

Cooper got to her feet. "Thank you, Brian. I won't keep you any longer. Could you tell me where I'd find Pete Parke?"

"Are my ears burning?"

Cooper turned to the door to see a rotund man in head-to-toe Adidas approaching.

"You must be Detective Erica Cooper? Linda sent me to talk to you about Shelly Smith."

Cooper thanked Brian Hutchins again and shook the newcomer's hand.

"I've been told you taught Shelly on Wednesday afternoon." Cooper's eyes flicked to the door as

Tennessee entered the room. He introduced him-self to Pete Parke and sat next to Cooper.

"Yes," he confirmed. "She was in my PE class. Dreadful thing to happen to her and Rachel. Just dreadful. Please tell me you're closing in on who-ever did this?"

"I can't comment on that just yet, but I can tell you we're doing all we can."

"I couldn't believe it when Terry called me. In a right state he was."

"Terry?" asked Cooper.

"My brother, Terrance. He was the one who found poor Rachel. He and his wife, Gwen. They're torn up. Gwen's refusing to go back to the beach and she loves the sea. It's not the kind of thing you can un-see though, is it?"

Cooper gave him a sympathetic look. It was true. She'd seen countless dead bodies since joining the force, and she'd yet to forget a single one of them.

"Mr Parke—"

"Pete, please."

"Pete, tell me about that PE class on Wednesday afternoon. How did Shelly seem?"

Pete tugged at the hem of his sweatshirt. It was slightly fraying and in need of a trip to the washing machine.

"She... she seemed her usual self, I guess."

"And what was her usual self?" asked Cooper.

Pete's lips folded inward while he thought. "Bub-bly," he said once he found the word. "She was bubbly with her friends. She was a bit annoyed at me, like."

Tennessee wiggled out of his coat. "Why was that?" he asked.

The PE teacher took a deep breath. "She didn't want to do PE that day. Told me she had her period. She hoped I'd be, I don't know, grossed out, tell her to sit and rest, send her home, who knows. Anyway, I told her if she needed sanitary products, she should pop to the school medical room and be back in the shed within ten minutes. I don't think she was impressed."

Cooper could empathise. She'd used that old chestnut once or twice in her day. What girl hadn't?

"The shed?" she asked.

"That's what we call the sports hall," answered Pete. "The big wooden building across the other side of the field. The kids started calling it the shed and it stuck."

Tennessee removed the lid to his biro and held it between his lips. "You said Shelly had been bubbly with her friends. How was she with the other children in the class, the ones she wasn't close with?"

Pete pulled his lips in again and let out a low hum. "She could be a little..."

"You can say it, Pete," said Tennessee. "I understand people don't wish to speak ill of the dead, but it's important we get a clear picture of Shelly and how she was in the days leading up to her death."

He hummed again. "Okay. She was a little bitchy. That's such a terrible way to describe it, but I can't think of a better way."

"Bitchy in what way?" asked Tennessee.

"Well, she'd make fun of some kids if she didn't approve of their clothes or hair. You know what I mean?"

"She was a bully?" asked Cooper, thinking about how Tina had almost sounded scared of Rachel Pearson. Shelly was beginning to sound the same.

"Sometimes," replied Pete, his lip curling in disgust at himself for talking about his former student that way.

"Please think carefully," urged Cooper. "Did she bully anyone the last time you saw her?"

He shrugged. "It's a big class. Thirty-two unruly teenagers, one teacher and a load of shuttlecocks flying about. Sorry. If she did, I didn't notice."

BACK IN THE WARM serenity of her Tynemouth terrace, Cooper frowned at the empty casserole dish. She'd have to return it to Atkinson at some point. Social etiquette would dictate that she should cook something for him in return, but there was more chance of pigs flying over the Tyne Bridge than her subjecting someone she liked to her feeble excuse for cooking. She'd take him to a restaurant. She'd wait for this awful case to be out of the way and for her hair to grow into something resembling a cute pixie cut, then she'd ask him to join her for dinner.

Upstairs, Tina was still not speaking to either parent, and loud music had been blasting from her room for hours. She'd hung up on Kenny and refused to open her bedroom door to Cooper. An offer of takeaway pizza couldn't even tempt her out.

She doesn't even like music, thought Cooper. She never listened to the radio and rarely watched music videos on YouTube. The only reason for Tina's sudden interest in Slipknot was to annoy Cooper by making the house too loud for her to watch television.

It had been a productive day, so Cooper smiled as she sat down on the sofa. The joke was on Tina. Little did her daughter know, Erica Cooper had been quite the metalhead in her youth. That's how she'd met Kenny. Cooper hadn't been able to see a damn thing from the back row of the Metallica concert, but after a third beer, she'd had the bright idea to crowd surf to the front. Hundreds of hands guided her towards the band, and when she finally dropped, she landed straight into Kenny's arms. He'd been broad and strong and his aftershave had sent her into a blushing mess.

Cooper kicked off her shoes and bobbed her head back and forth to the music while she thought back to her younger years. It took her three songs before she realised she had eight missed calls from Chief Superintendent Howard Nixon.

-CHAPTER 19 -

SUPERINTENDENT HOWARD NIXON'S VOICE was twenty decibels higher than usual. "Cooper," he barked, "where the bloody hell have you been? Two kids never made it home from school."

Cooper got straight to her feet and plugged a finger in her free ear to dull the music coming from Tina's room. "From Tynemouth Academy?"

"Yes. Jasmine Lee, fifteen, and Reuben Jones, sixteen."

"Fucking hell." Cooper's heart was already racing. "But we have Bennett in the cells."

"Calm down, Cooper. I need you focused. We know fine well the evidence against Bennett is sketchy at best. The killer might still be out there."

"Or Bennett has an accomplice?"

"That's a possibility. Now chances are these kids are fine. Just two kids arsing about and giving their parents the runabout, after some attention, you know."

"We can't take that chance, sir, not if the killer's still on the loose. Not if there's a chance he's targeting the school."

"Exactly, but we're not going to panic. I've approved the chopper. It should be airborne within ten minutes."

Cooper pulled on her boots. "I need numbers, sir. As many uniforms as you can spare."

"I'll do what I can, Cooper. There's been a major disturbance in town. A pub brawl's got out of hand and knives have been drawn. It's a blood bath. West Yorkshire and Cumbria have offered support, but it'll take an hour at least for their units to arrive—"

"Dogs?"

"Already prepped. Handlers are at the homes getting items of clothing so the dogs know the scent. They'll then follow any trail from the school." Nixon paused for breath. "Cooper, you know how I feel about relying on neighbouring forces. It's embarrassing. It makes us look weak and ill-prepared."

"There's no shame in asking for help, sir."

"I beg to differ. Commissioner Begum's breathing down CC Davison's neck and he, in turn, is breathing down my neck. Davison's requested a meeting with me tomorrow. We need to find those kids tonight, Cooper, or someone's head'll be on the chopping block, and it won't be mine. Do I make myself clear?"

"Crystal." Cooper checked her watch. "We should notify the media. We've missed the six o'clock news, but I want those kids' faces all over the local press's social media. I want the news channels ready to run an appeal at ten o'clock if we haven't found them by then. I want everyone north of Durham and south of the border out looking."

Nixon coughed. "I'll get the guys in the press office onto it; they'll want a press conference. You know the tabloids are going to want a face to go with the story, and you're the SIO."

"There's no time for that." Cooper grabbed her keys. "If they want me, they can come and find me. I'm joining the search."

"Cooper—"

It is you who will have to make a choice. Was this what Charity Mae had warned her about? Cooper was not interested in playing the media darling to appease her boss, even if it would be a sign of strength for the department. She could drum up more publicity by speaking to the press, but she preferred to be more hands-on. Surely her time was better spent doing what she did best.

"Sir, I live in Tynemouth. I grew up in Tynemouth. These are my streets. These people are my people, and if two kids are missing, I'm going be out there helping to find them. Potts can handle the press. Now, where's my team?"

There was a moment of silence from Nixon. Cooper assumed he was biting his tongue after his DCI cut him off. She heard a sigh, and then, "Daniel's with Martin. They've just left the Lee household in Cullercoats and are on their way to the Jones's on King Edward's Road. Keaton and Sutherland are briefing a search party on Front Street."

"I'll meet them there," Cooper said before hanging up. She spun on her heels. Her instinct as a member of the force was to get out there as soon as possible, her instinct as a mother was to protect her child. She stormed upstairs and walked into Tina's room without knocking and pulled the stereo's plug from the wall.

"Hey!"

"Hey, nothing," snapped Cooper.

Tina was sitting crossed-legged on her bed with textbooks fanned out around her. Her hair was a mess and she'd clearly been crying, but Cooper would have to put the parenting on hold.

"Listen. Two kids from your school have gone missing. It'll be on the news soon enough. I need to join the search—"

Tina sat up and straightened her posture. Her brows knitted together, and her eyes scanned back and forth over Cooper's face. "Can I help?"

"No. Absolutely not. I need you to make a choice and make it quick. I can drop you at your dad's, or you can lock the doors from the inside and promise to not let anyone in other than me."

Tina wiped her eyes and left a trail of mascara across her face. "I'll stay here... If you're sure I can't help."

Cooper wrapped her daughter up in a bear hug and spoke into her birds-nest-hair. "I'm sure. I love you so much, Tina."

She released her and quickly checked the latches on all the upstairs windows and motioned for Tina to follow her downstairs where she double-locked the backdoor and checked the kitchen window.

"Here," said Cooper, handing Tina a paring knife. "Take this. Lock the door behind me and secure the chain and bolts. I want you to text me every fifteen minutes, no exceptions. Do you understand me?"

Tina nodded. Her face had tightened and she suddenly looked five years older. "Yes, I do. But, Mum, the knife...."

"Just in case," Cooper said. She gave Tina a meaningful look. "If you need to use it, don't hold back. Okay?"

Tina swallowed and let the thought mull around her mind for a moment. "Okay," she replied in less than a whisper.

"Every fifteen minutes?"

"Every fifteen minutes."

Cooper closed the front door behind her and waited until she heard all the locks click into place before running in the direction of Front Street. As she ran, she pulled her phone out and called Kenny. The call went straight to voicemail.

"Kenny. It's Erica. I might be wrong about that suspect. Two kids from the academy have gone missing; I'm joining the search party. Tina's at home, the house is secure, and she has strict instructions to only answer the door to me. Can you call her every half hour? Text me when you get this. Oh, and don't go round there unless she asks you to; you might get stabbed."

Cooper found Sutherland and Keaton outside Marshall's fish and chip shop. A row of men and women in reflective gear were fanning out across the street, torch lights sweeping back and forth.

Front Street was the centre of Tynemouth village. At its western end, a village green sported a statue of Queen Victoria, and at its eastern end, you'd find the North Sea. In between, the street played host to wine shops, pubs, bars, seafood restaurants and quaint B&Bs.

"What's the score?" Cooper asked, clutching her chest. She hadn't expected to need to run twice in one day. Sutherland watched the search party split in two, half heading north onto Hotspur Street and half heading south through an alleyway between two bars. He guided Cooper inside the fish and chip shop where the warmth from the heaters and the friers helped restore feeling to her extremities. They took a seat at one of the tables near the door.

He opened his notes. "Jang-Mi Lee - known as Jasmine - and Reuben Jones stayed late at school for something called culture club."

"Yes," said Cooper with a nod. "Artsy stuff?"

"Aye," confirmed Sutherland. He slid two photographs across the formica tabletop. "The club finished at four-thirty, and the teachers who run the club walked the students to the front gates. From there, they were in sight of the officers stationed at the front of the school. Some of them were met by parents, others walked off. The officers at the school this afternoon were Andrews and Kowalski; they haven't reported anything unusual."

Cooper looked down at the photographs. Jasmine Lee was of far-eastern descent, with poker-straight black hair, a heart-shaped face and ears - that unfortunately - could rival those of Prince Charles. Reuben Jones was a slim boy with pale skin, grey eyes and a trendy sculpted hairstyle that Oliver Martin would approve of.

"Jasmine and Reuben left on foot?" Cooper asked.

"Yes, with Freya White," said Sutherland. "Jasmine suggested fish and chips, so the three of them cleared it with their parents and came here. I've spoken to the staff and they have confirmed the three arrived here at around four forty. Freya tells us that Jasmin and Reuben were courting, and she felt like a third wheel."

Keaton rolled her eyes. "Courting? All right, grandad."

"Less of your cheek," he retorted. "Courting, dating, gannin' oot, an item, whatever you call it. They were a couple. Anyhoo, this Freya lass was feeling awkward 'cause Jasmine and Reuben spent more time snogging than talking to her. So she left."

Keaton had tipped a small pile of salt onto the table and used her fingers to swirl it around. "No one says snogging anymore either."

Sutherland scowled but remained on task. "Freya got home at ten past five. They'd all agreed to be home by six, so when Jasmine didn't show by six twenty, her mother called her. Jasmin's phone is either turned off or out of battery. Same for Reuben's parents. His phone's off as well. They got hold of Freya at six-thirty and by seven they'd called the police."

Cooper checked her watch; it was gone eight. "What time did Jasmine and Reuben leave here?" she asked.

Keaton broke free from her daydream. "Best estimate they could give us was half five."

"And no one's seen them since?"

Keaton shook her head. "Not that we've been able to ascertain. We have people checking with everyone who went to the culture club - a lot of them are out looking - and we've shown their pictures to all the businesses on Front Street."

At that moment, a canine unit entered Marshall's. An older woman with platinum hair shouted from behind the counter, "Sorry love, no dogs allowed apart from guide... Oh."

She blushed realising the dogs were here on business and not pleasure.

One dog sniffed the air; the other had his nose glued to the ground. They headed straight to the third table on the right and let out yelp-like barks. It was amazing; the dogs could still pick out Jasmine and Reuben's scents over the smell of vinegar and batter. A handler fed them both a treat as they turned out the shop and headed west up Front Street.

"I take it, that's where the kids were sat?" asked Cooper.

Sutherland nodded. "Aye. Let's hope they find those kids safe and sound."

"If anyone can, the dogs can." Cooper stood. "But that being said, let's get out of here and help. Where are the volunteers?"

Keaton opened her phone. "They're in groups of about ten to fifteen and spread out over Tynemouth as well as Shields and Cullercoats," she said, referencing the town to the south and the village to the north. "They're using *hashtag find Jasmine and Reuben* on Twitter to organise themselves. Let me see, ah yes, here we are. A group just finished combing Longsands beach and are moving onto King Edward's Bay. Another group are zigzagging up and down the back lanes around Preston Grange. They have a WhatsApp group too, they've added me, so I'll know straight away if anything comes up."

Cooper was impressed. "What about the teachers?"

"The three who taught the club are with a bunch of other staff members and were scouring the Fish Quay last I heard."

"Right, let's start with them. Then I want to meet Freya."

THE FISH QUAY ON the north shore of the River Tyne was the industrial hub of North Shields, a proud fishing town famous for its crab shacks and smokehouses. Cooper, Sutherland and Keaton jogged down Ropery Stairs - 120 steep steps that connected the old lower and upper towns - and found the search party on the quay.

Cooper discreetly checked her phone and was relieved to find three messages from Tina. The most recent read, *I'm fine, or I would be if Dad stopped calling.*

Brian Hutchins was on his knees, shining a torch under parked cars. "Oh, thank goodness you're here," he said when he spotted Cooper and company. His glasses were perched on his head, and he was wrapped up as if ready to trek to the North Pole. He shook Cooper's hand and introduced himself to Sutherland and Keaton.

"I can't believe it. I just can't," he said, his voice trembling. He drew the attention of two other teachers who came over to flank him on either side.

"I'm Phillip Dunn, this is Catherine Grainger," said a short man in a flat cap. Catherine Grainger had wild, red curls and was as small and thin as Cooper.

"I feel awful," said the slight redhead. "Just awful. We should never have let them walk home. It's all our fault."

"Don't say that," said Brian, a hand coming to rest on his colleague's shoulder.

Phillip agreed. "We walked them to the gates, Catherine. The police were there. We can't very well drive them home ourselves. You know the rules."

"Yes..." she sniffed and began to wring her hands together, "but the rules shouldn't apply now. These are special circumstances."

"Child protection rules are in place for a reason," started Brian, but Catherine cut him off.

"Well, they haven't done an outstanding job tonight, have they? The rules haven't kept them safe tonight. Oh lord, what if something's happened? What if they've been killed?"

"Let's not get ahead of ourselves," said Cooper, though she felt the same way. Her gut churned round and round and filled her with the over-whelming feeling that they were already too late. "Please take a moment and then talk me through this afternoon. Tell me about Jasmine, Reuben and Freya."

Cooper waited a few seconds whilst the troubled teachers gathered their thoughts. Around her, other staff members were checking behind bins, shining their torches over the side of the dock to look into the fishing boats, and were popping in and out of the establishments that lined the quay. As someone entered an Italian restaurant, the smell of garlic temporarily overpowered the scent of the river, and a surge of laughter erupted from a pub named the Salty Sea Dog. All around them, people were going about their business and enjoying their evening, unaware that something diabolical could be happening at this very moment.

"Let's walk and talk," suggested Keaton, an idea which seemed to please Brian, Phillip and Catherine. It helped them feel useful.

Brian turned his torch back on and scanned the ground. "We were sculpting in class this afternoon."

"I remember you telling me," said Cooper, taking a second to count how many people were in the search party. There must have been at least twenty-five of them.

"They did well. The whole group, I mean. They seemed to enjoy it," he continued.

"Well, Freya enjoyed it," said Phillip Dunn. "She was very keen on culture club. Jasmine was, I mean is, her best friend. They're inseparable. Reuben isn't exactly a natural at music or art. I think he feels he's a bit on the cool side to be there. He comes to the club because Jasmine does, and Jasmine comes because Freya does. You get the idea."

Sutherland and Cooper gave each other a look. As parents of secondary school pupils, they most certainly did understand.

"But they tried their best," said Catherine. "Jasmine's sculpture turned out rather well tonight. We were recreating Henri Moore pieces. In miniature, obviously."

"How did the three of them seem tonight?" asked Cooper.

"Happy," answered Brian. He strode away for a moment to check in with another member of the search team and returned.

"Yes," said Catherine, "happy, giggly, the usual. Some clay was thrown about at one point, but it was in good jest."

"Who threw it? And at whom?" asked Cooper.

"Reuben threw it at a young chap named Greg."

"Greg Mason?" asked Cooper.

Catherine nodded. "Yes, that's the one."

Cooper's face betrayed nothing, but she could see Keaton making a note and showing it to Sutherland. This wasn't the first time they'd heard that name.

"Did Greg walk home?"

Catherine looked down as she thought. "Hmm. I think so." She looked to Phillip.

"I can't remember, sorry."

"What time did the club finish?" Cooper said, moving on.

"Just before four-thirty," answered Brian. "As Phillip said, we walked the children to the gates. Then we returned to the art studio to tidy up. That took about ten, maybe fifteen minutes."

"Then what?"

"We said our goodbyes, signed out at reception and headed home ourselves. I was halfway through making dinner when I heard. There was no way I could sit down and eat a meal knowing two of our flock were missing. I called Brian, and he called Catherine."

"Yes, and before long we were all searching. The caretaker is here," she pointed further down the quay towards a vast, white cuboid of a lighthouse that jutted up into the dark sky. "So is Pete from the PE department and some of the admin staff."

"What's really interesting," started Brian, turning to look at his two colleagues. "Is who *isn't* here." He raised his eyebrows at Cooper.

Keaton's radio crackled; she moved away from the group.

"Now, now, Brian. This isn't the time to question—"

Brian cut Phillip off. "This is precisely the time to question her leadership... Or lack of it."

"Boss." Keaton bobbed her head to the left, drawing Cooper away from the bickering teachers.

"What you got, Keaton? Tell me it's good news."

"A hotline's been set up. Calls have been coming thick and fast. Mostly anonymous time wasters."

"Yeah, yeah, it's the same every time."

"Two stand out, though. First, a pretty foul call came in earlier from someone claiming to be the killer. Described what he was doing to Jasmine in horrific detail."

Cooper's heart jolted. "Have they traced it?"

"A payphone in Sunderland. A local unit's following it up. My gut says it's a fake. For one, he didn't mention suffocation or strangulation. Two, he didn't say anything about fancy dress or costumes, nothing about cards. And three, the things he was saying he was doing weren't done to Rachel or Shelly, if you catch my drift."

"I do," said Cooper, hoping Keaton didn't feel the need to elaborate. "What was the second?"

"A possible sighting. A lady who works at the estate agents at the top of Front Street called the hotline to say she saw a boy and girl in green school blazers getting into a car shortly after five-thirty while she was locking up."

"Any further details?"

"She reported the girl as having long dark hair. That's all I've been told."

Cooper sucked her lips in; they were becoming chapped from the cold. Over the smell of the Tyne, Cooper could sense the subtle aroma of imminent snowfall. "Right. Here's the plan. You and Sutherland find Greg Mason."

"You got it. But Mason's just a boy. Aren't we looking for an older geezer who thinks he'll become immortal from killing kids?"

"Perhaps," Cooper answered. "Or, perhaps we don't put too much stock in a walking fortune cookie. I'm inclined to say the perp's older, but I'm not chancing it. I don't want a hiding from Nixon, or Davison for that matter, because we didn't follow up on a lead."

"The CC?" Keaton's face was etched with concern.

Cooper sighed. "Nixon's feeling the pressure. It's nothing for you to worry about. It'll be me they come after if we can't stop this guy. Anyway, I'll meet up with Tennessee and have a quick chat with Freya White and the woman from the estate agents. I need a better description of the car before the additional units arrive. Let's meet at HQ in an hour."

Keaton brought her hand to the side of her head and saluted. "I'm on it."

- CHAPTER 20 -

ETHAN REED TRAILED AT least five paces behind his classmates as they walked to school the following day. Hassan and Miles talked about football – as usual – and if Ethan tried to join in, they would remind him that he was a soft southerner who should stick to rugby. Ethan had, on more than one occasion, tried to tell them that rugby players were tougher than football players, but they'd given a wedgie and pushed into a pile of dog shit for his efforts. He'd learned his lesson after that.

Ethan bowed his head to the wind and let his thoughts drift to Phoebe-May Corrigan, his eighteen-year-old neighbour who, praise the lord, had forgotten to close her curtains before changing last night. He knew he shouldn't have watched, but he was only human, and he'd never seen you-know-whats before. Not in the flesh, anyway, only in the dirty pictures Miles forwarded from his big brother's WhatsApp group.

"My money's on the caretaker," said Hassan, kicking a rock along the dirt road that led out the back of Northumberland Park.

"Ol' Pickett?" laughed Miles.

"It's always the caretaker. Haven't you seen Nightmare on Elm Street?"

Ethan's brain kicked back into gear when he realised his friends had given up discussing the missed penalty at last weekend's game.

Miles shook his head. "It's rated eighteen."

"I've seen it," said Ethan. "It's proper ancient. But I doubt Ol' Pickett killed those girls."

"Yeah," echoed Miles. "He's like a hundred and five. He hasn't got the strength to wring out his mop, let alone wring someone's neck."

Ethan wrinkled his nose. "Miles!"

"What? I'm just sayin'. It'll be that Will Harper anyway. My brother says he was arrested."

"And released," said Hassan.

"Whatever. It'll be him. Mark my words."

Ethan stifled a shriek as he walked through a spider's web. "Eugh. Gross." He dusted his blazer and tried to change the subject. "Did you finish the physics homework?"

"Yeah. And what a waste of time that was. What am I going to need physics for? I'm going into the army like me da and his da before him."

Miles finished a can of soda and tossed it into the bushes. Ethan wanted to say something, but he didn't want another wedgie. Instead, he promised himself he'd come back after school, pick it up and bin it.

The trail out the back of Northumberland Park connected the park with Tynemouth metro station. It didn't see much footfall, not in the winter anyway. Each side of the track was lined by grassy verges, nettle bushes and bare sycamore trees. As the three boys approached a dog turd the size of a cow pat, Hassan shoved Miles in the back. The youngster stumbled but managed to avoid getting his feet dirty.

"Tosser," said Miles before the pair began to play fight.

"Guys," said Ethan, trying to get their attention.

Miles and Hassan's play fight descended into some elaborate, choreographed kung-fu scene that incorporated all the cheesy lines they loved from action films.

"Guys," Ethan tried again.

Hassan repeatedly punched the air. "Yippee ki-yay!"

Miles removed his backpack and swung it around before flinging it at Hassan. "Hulk smash!"

Hassan grabbed the backpack and bellowed, "Do you feel lucky? Well, do ya, punk?" before hurling it towards the nettle bushes.

The boys watched the backpack fly through the air and land at the base of a tree, where the bodies of a boy and girl they recognised were propped up against the trunk.

- CHAPTER 21 -

THE TRACK BETWEEN NORTHUMBERLAND Park and the metro station was closed at both ends. Cooper met Tennessee at the station end and was shepherded under the police tape by a uniform who noted her arrival in the scene log. They were both handed covers for their shoes and asked to walk on thin boards that had been placed on one of the grass verges so they wouldn't disturb any prints on the track.

"Did you sleep?" asked Tennessee.

"Not really," said Cooper. "I joined the search again at around eleven after we'd finished at Freya White's house. Must have been about half two when I got to bed. Even then, I don't think I really slept."

"Same here. Hayley wasn't impressed at how late I got home. Said I'd take her out at the weekend to make up for it. There's some new vegan place she wants to try. It's not my cup of tea but if eating rabbit food gets me back in her good books, then just call me Bugs." He stifled a yawn and rubbed his eyes. "I could do with a jug of coffee and a cold shower."

As the pair followed the track, the white forensics tent came into view. "Well, Bugs, both of those will have to wait."

"Do you know what to expect?"

Cooper stopped for a moment and looked to the ground. "Only what Nixon relayed. Three year-nines found two bodies on their walk to school."

"Fancy dress?"

Cooper's eyes had glazed over. She wasn't looking at the ground, more through it. Her vision was unfocused, and she had the same feeling of dread in her stomach that she'd felt last night. She nodded. "Yes, an empress and an emperor." She could hear her voice quiver.

Tennessee placed a hand on her back and let out a long breath. "It's not your fault."

Cooper straightened up. "I know." Her eyes were red, and her stomach turned over as if she were on a roller coaster. "But I wish we'd saved them. I mean, the whole town was out looking for Christ's sake. We had the chopper. We had the dogs..."

Tennessee ran his fingers through his short blond curls. "We did our best."

"It wasn't good enough." Cooper fastened the top button on her coat and mentally counted to three. "Sorry. I don't mean to snap. I'll pull myself together."

165

Tennessee shrugged and watched a seagull fly overhead. "No need to apologise, Coop."

The seagull cawed loudly and soared to the chimney of one of the terrace homes that backed onto the park. Cooper wondered what she had done in a past life to be assigned such an understanding DS. She patted Tennessee the way he had done to her, and together they approached the tent.

Paula Keaton was standing sentry. "Morning, boss."

"Paula."

"Here's what I've pieced together so far. Three boys were walking through here on their way from Linskill Terrace when they found the bodies propped up against a tree. A male and female matching the description of Jasmine and Reuben."

Cooper's eyes darted over the tent. It was actually two tents, fashioned around a tall tree.

"Where are the boys now?" asked Tennessee.

"A couple of uniforms took them back along the track and into the park. They're waiting in the café for their parents to arrive. We found some blankets for the little tykes. They were pretty shaken up. Trying to act tough, but I could tell. I've got three little brothers, I know when a boy is struggling to keep it together."

A train rumbled past; Cooper waited for the noise to finish before she continued.

"Did they recognise the victims?"

"Yeah. They're adamant that it's Jasmine and Reuben."

"Did they see anything suspicious? Anyone hanging around?"

"Negative. They'll give full statements once their parents arrive."

"Who's breaking the news to victims' families?" asked Cooper.

"Sutherland and Martin are on it."

Cooper ground her teeth together. "How did we miss this? The park was checked."

"Tell me about it," said Keaton. "A volunteer group came through at about nine or half nine last night, and I was here with the police team at eleven-ish."

Tennessee snorted. "Right under our effing noses. Could we have missed it?"

"I doubt it," said Cooper. "My guess would be they were brought down here after the searches finished for the night."

Keaton blew into her palms. "Do we let Bennett go?"

"Not a chance," said Cooper. "He can stay there until he tells us where he really was during the other two murders. He had a key to Shelly's, and he had an unhealthy obsession with Rachel."

"Tech called me," said Tennessee. "It wasn't just Rachel's Facebook pictures. He followed her on Instagram too and had saved over twenty of her pictures to his phone."

Keaton's nose wrinkled. "Urgh," she grunted. "That's disgusting."

Cooper stifled a yawn and turned back to Keaton. "You been in yet?" she asked, pointing to the forensics tent.

Keaton swallowed. "It's not pretty."

"It never is." Cooper took a small tub of Tiger Balm from her coat pocket and rubbed a little under her nose. It was a trick Atkinson taught her over five years ago; it would help, but it wouldn't completely mask the smell. She offered the tub to Tennessee, and he gratefully accepted.

"After you," said Tennessee with an extended arm.

Cooper jutted her chin towards the tent. "Nice try. Get in there."

"Ladies first?"

"Get in, or I swear to Kevin Keegan, I'll transfer you to Sunderland."

The corners of Tennessee's mouth turned down; he bowed his head before slipping beyond the white fabric. Cooper followed. Her eyes widened and her mouth fell open as she took in the scene.

The girl was slumped against the trunk of the sycamore tree. She wore a full-length dress of red silk, with golden embroidery and an elaborate headdress decorated with gold flowers, red beads and red tassels. Under different circumstances, the dress would have looked beautiful. As it was, it looked horrendous. Mud and blood covered the delicate fabric, and a trail of blood ran down her arm. Cooper's eyes followed the trail to the source and found a deep wound to the girl's bicep; poking out of it was the corner of a laminated card. She could make out the *eror* of *emperor*.

Cooper brought the back of her hand to her mouth and suppressed her need to vomit.

A slain Roman emperor lay with his head on the Chinese empress's lap. There was nothing delicate or elaborate about how he was dressed. The boy was clothed in a cheap polyester costume consisting of a white tunic and red sash. The tunic was gathered in the middle by a plastic gold belt. The same plastic formed a laurel wreath around his head. Brown sandals with long straps that snaked up his calves completed the look. At least eight patches of red blood had seeped into the white fabric of the boy's tunic.

The magician, the high priestess, the empress and the emperor. The killer was progressing through the tarot deck at an alarming pace. Four down, and unless Cooper could do anything about it, eighteen to go.

Justin Atkinson approached Cooper. "He changed his MO. The boy was stabbed."

Cooper met his eyes and looked away again. She desperately wanted to talk to him about Saturday night, but it would have to wait. "What about the girl?"

"I think she was strangled." His tone was low; he spoke slowly. "There's bruising around her neck. We'll get them both to the Freeman as soon as possible so Margot can confirm it."

"Any sign of a murder weapon?"

Atkinson shook his head. "We'll go over this place with a fine-tooth comb, but I'd be surprised if we find a weapon down here. There isn't enough blood." He pointed to the boy's chest. "He has multiple wounds to the torso," then his hand moved towards the thigh, "but this one, this would have made him bleed out. The ground's frozen solid. If that had happened here, there'd be more blood. A lot more."

Cooper shuffled her feet and silently mulled over the information. "What else?"

"He messed up. In choosing that Roman outfit, I mean."

"In what way?"

"I couldn't find a shred of evidence at Shelly Smith's house, which suggests our guy wore gloves. With Rachel, there was a tonne of different prints because who knows how many people had touched that boat. We're still running them through the lab to see if anything matches the database, but it'll take a while to sift through them all. But with this young man, we have some beautiful prints on the plastic belt."

Tennessee folded his arms and turned to face Atkinson. "No chance they're the boy's?"

"Unlikely. I'm no pathologist, but I'm fairly certain the boy was killed before he was dressed this way. Besides, the prints are quite large, and the victim is on the slender side."

Cooper agreed. "Do you have any idea how the bodies were brought down here?"

"There's no access for cars," said Atkinson. He looked around as if looking for somewhere to sit. With no chair available, he sighed and squatted down, removed his gloves and hid his face behind his palms for a moment. "There are several footprints and animal prints in the mud, but they're not fresh. The ground was too hard last night to leave prints. Under the bridge was more sheltered.

Hong found some wide tyre tracks under there. An off-road bike, perhaps?"

The pressure was getting to Atkinson. His eyes were sunken, and he looked to be shaking. Cooper tilted her head towards the tent entrance, a signal to Tennessee to step outside. Alone with Atkinson, she extended her hands and pulled the much taller man back to standing.

"I thought I'd seen it all, Erica. I've worked on child murders before, but this is something else."

"Yeah." She let go of his hands and looked back at the bodies of Jasmine Lee and Reuben Jones. "This is new territory for all of us."

"Listen, Erica..." Atkinson's voice wavered. "I'm sorry again. About Saturday. If I misread the situation, or I made you feel uncomfortable—"

"Jesus, no," she hushed. "I like you, Justin. You didn't misread anything. It's just..."

"It's just we both have a lot of baggage?"

"A lot of baggage and..." Cooper swept her arm outwards. "And a child killer to hunt down."

"I understand."

Cooper sucked her lips in for a moment. "I don't think you do," she said quietly. "I think we need to escape this for a while. We all need to switch off." She thought of Tennessee returning home to his pregnant wife and Keaton returning home to her partner and their three cats. She loved Tina, but she wanted companionship too. "Tomorrow night. Do you want to have dinner? No work talk?"

His face lit up. "I would like nothing better than dinner and no work talk."

"I'll text you," said Cooper. She couldn't bring herself to smile. Not in her current surroundings.

Back outside the tent and pleased to have fresh air in her lungs and sunlight on her face, Cooper found Tennessee and Keaton under a stone bridge watching a bunch of SOCOs conduct their business. There was a rumble of a car passing over the bridge and a rustling in the bushes. Cooper's eyes moved fast enough to see a rat disappear into a shrub.

"Oi, you two!"

Tennessee and Keaton approached. They both looked older. This case was ageing them all.

"Right, this is our timeline: Jasmine Lee and Reuben Jones left school at half four with Freya White, and they arrived at the chippy at four forty. Freya left shortly after five, and from what we can gather, Jasmine and Reuben stayed until around half past."

Cooper took a deep breath. "At around the same time, a woman named Sandra Pickering reported seeing two kids in green blazers getting into a car at the top end of Front Street. One male, one female. She couldn't confirm if it was Jasmine and Reuben, but she described the girl as having long, straight, brown or black hair, and she described the boy as slim and pale."

"Did you get a make of car?" asked Tennessee.

"Not quite. It's an estate car. Dark blue or black and had a round logo on the front grill. She thought it was probably a Vauxhall or a VW."

"Well, that narrows it down," he said with a sarcastic drawl.

172

Keaton adjusted her ponytail and smoothed her palms over her hair. "A volunteer search party came through here at around nine last night, and we covered the same area at eleven."

"The search was called off at two," said Cooper, stomping her feet in the hope of bringing some feeling back to her toes, "and the boys found the bodies at ten past seven."

"Ten past seven's pretty early for kids to be heading to school," said Tennessee.

"They were going to the school's breakfast club," said Keaton. "I've called the school to check, and they were all registered. The three of them go every day."

"So, the bodies were transferred here at some point between two and seven this morning. Margot should be able to narrow it down."

"They locked the gates to the park after the search," said Keaton. "How'd he get them in here? I can't see the perp carting two bodies in fancy-dress down here at six when the gates are reopened. This track might be quiet, but the main park would have dog walkers coming through as soon as the gates opened. He must have done it in the dead of night."

Cooper nodded. "You're probably right. Okay, Tennessee, you're up. How'd he get in here when the gates were locked?"

Cooper liked to test her detectives. She had no desire for a flock of yes-men. She wanted independent thinkers who could forge their own theories and come to their own conclusions.

Tennessee glanced around the scene. "I doubt he abseiled off the bridge. There's allotments up that way, though." He gestured up the steep bank. "They back on to the park. He could've broken into an allotment, or..."

"Or, he has an allotment," said Keaton. "I'll check who the leaseholders are when we get back to HQ, and I'll get a team up there to inspect every square centimetre."

"Good," said Cooper. "See if there's any sign of breaking and entering, trampled cabbage patches, damaged fences, you get the idea. If anyone objects to you poking around, get a warrant and get back in there. We're not going to be pissed about by a bunch of green-fingered old-fogies, especially if there's a chance one of them's our man. He could've stashed the bodies in one of the allotment sheds and moved them after the search was called off. I want every shed and storage box inspected."

She turned to Tennessee. "What else?"

"There's the change in MO." He shrugged. "Something changed last night. I don't think it all went to plan. Something makes me think he saw an opportunity to get Jasmine, but she was with Reuben, so he took them both."

Impressed, Cooper urged him on. "Good. Keep going."

"Or vice versa," he said. "They must know the killer, or one of them does at least. Teenagers aren't complete idiots. They'll have known not to get in a stranger's car. You're taught that from the minute you're out of nappies."

His eyes darkened, and Cooper wondered if the younger man was thinking about his soon-to-be son and how he'd have to warn him about the dangers of this world.

"Anyway," he continued. "He wouldn't have been able to strangle them both because while he strangled one, he'd have to fight off the other. I don't want to be sexist here," he looked at Keaton, "but he was probably safer killing the lad first."

Keaton's shoulders lifted for a second or two. "You're right. He probably stabbed Reuben to get him out of the way. He did it quickly and violently. Even if Jasmine leapt to his defence, it would be too little, too late. Then, he would have easily overpowered her."

The three stepped aside as Hong, Atkinson's assistant, shuffled past with potential trace evidence in sealed tubes.

"Which means," continued Keaton, "he either killed them in the car then took the bodies somewhere and hid them. Or, he took them somewhere and killed them wherever that somewhere is. Then he dressed the poor kids up and somehow brought them down here."

Cooper looked behind her. "They've found tracks in the mud. Justin suggested an off-road bike of some kind, but I'm thinking—"

"Wheelbarrow?" asked Tennessee, eyebrows raised.

"Bingo. It wouldn't have been easy to move two teenage bodies. Not over this terrain. Given the allotments up there, it would make sense. So, what's next, Paula?"

"I'm going to put out an appeal for further witnesses. Someone else must have seen them getting into the car. Let's see if we can get a better description."

"Good. Tennessee?"

"There's not a lot around here, but there's a few shops near the back of the park and some industrial units across the road from the front entrance. I'll have a word and see what they have CCTV-wise. I'll check in with the incident room too and see if any other calls have been made to the hotline."

Cooper sighed. "There's always the possibility he was caught on camera at the metro station. But one, I don't think this guy's that daft, and two, we're not that lucky. I'm going to get a team together and start the door-to-doors. Hopefully, some of the locals have door cameras. If not, I'm certain someone must have seen, or more likely, heard something."

"He might come back," said Tennessee. "They often do. I'll have the guys guarding the entrances watch out for anyone who cranes their neck a little too much."

"Coop," Keaton had folded her arms; they looked thicker than Cooper's legs.

"Yes, Paula?"

"That's four kids. All from Tynemouth Academy. Do we close the school?"

Cooper turned to walk back up the track towards the station. Keaton and Tennessee followed her. "I don't know." She let out another long sigh and felt anxiety flood her stomach. "I just don't know. I'll talk to Nixon, but I think the kids are safer in school than home alone while their parents are out at work. I mean, look at Shelly Smith. She was at home. I'll tell the officers stationed at the school to be on the lookout for dark estates, and," she paused, "I'll have young Oliver find out what type of car every member of staff drives. From Linda Webb to the admin staff, to the caretakers, cleaners and God-damned dinner ladies."

- CHAPTER 22 -

AFTER A FEW HOURS of conducting door-to-doors with the team, Cooper decided to head west towards the Freeman Hospital to see if Margot Swanson had any initial findings for her. Chatting to the locals who lived near Northumberland Park had produced some positive results. Cooper looked forward to discussing them when she got back to CID.

Margot was waiting for Cooper at a bus stop just outside the grounds of the Freeman hospital. She was wrapped up in a glamorous red duffle coat that accentuated her curves and perfectly matched the heeled boots and expensive-looking lipstick she was wearing. For someone who worked predominantly with dead people, she was remarkably stylish.

"Morning, Erica," greeted Margot in her soft Scottish accent. "Thought I'd meet you out here. I haven't had a smoke all morning. Where's that lovely Jack Daniel? Did you not bring him with you today?"

The corner of Cooper's mouth twitched. "DS Daniel is busy following leads."

Margot lit a cigarette and blew a billowing plume of smoke around her. "Pity," she proclaimed before extending an arm and indicating that Cooper and she should walk towards the park across the road.

Freeman Park was a popular area in Newcastle. It housed football pitches, a basketball court, a pond filled with mallards and sticklebacks, and a children's play area. The park was quiet at this time of the day; there was no one around save for a man with a black Labrador puppy and a woman pushing twin babies in a stroller.

"Shall we start with the girl?" asked Margot.

Cooper nodded.

"Cause of death was strangulation. There was bruising around her neck and damage to her larynx. She also had some nasty cuts to the palms of her hands. They look like defensive wounds. I suspect she tried to grab the knife as it was being used on the male. There's evidence that she's had sexual intercourse in the last twenty-four to thirty-six hours. However, there's nothing to suggest that it was non-consensual, no bruising or damage to the genital area."

"And Reuben?"

"The boy died from cardiac arrest following massive blood loss. He received twelve major incisions in total, nine of which were in the torso, including a puncture to his liver and his left lung. He has a slashing wound to his lower abdomen and another on his right thigh. There's a deep wound to the left thigh which went straight through the femoral artery."

Cooper winced. The bastard hadn't held back. Not one bit.

"There's slight fish-tailing to the entry wounds," continued Margot, "that suggests a single-edged blade. The depth of penetration indicates a blade of around twenty centimetres in length and three to four centimetres in width."

Cooper watched the black Lab jump into the pond and send the mallards skywards. The owner shook his head and shouted for the dog to get out of the water.

"A kitchen knife, perhaps?" asked Cooper.

Margot shrugged. "Something like that. He put up a fight, mind you. He has bruising to his knuckles and defensive wounds on his arms."

Cooper stopped by a bench and took a seat. The cold of the wood seeped through her trousers and made her shiver.

"Good," she said. "Hopefully, he hit the bastard hard enough to leave a mark. What about the cards?

Margot took a long draw on her cigarette. "The cuts were made by something very short and sharp. It was an extremely straight blade, like a scalpel or an exceptionally sharp Stanley knife. I'm more inclined to say a scalpel. Whoever did this had a steady hand; the cuts were perfectly straight. Jasmine's card was in her upper arm next to her bicep muscle. The killer inserted the emperor card but didn't stitch the wound back up."

Cooper looked sideways. "In a hurry?" she asked.

Margot shrugged. "Could have been, but the precision of the wound would suggest he wasn't. Reuben's card was inserted into his right forearm. I've removed the card, and it's bagged, ready for you to take. Forensics might be able to lift a print from it. You never know."

Cooper folded her legs. "We have a print from his belt. Hopefully, we can get another from the card, and fingers crossed, they match. How about the stitching?"

Margot stared ahead. "Reuben was stitched back up very neatly. And again, just like with Rachel, it appears to be regular thread that you could buy anywhere."

"What did the card say?"

"Heirophant."

"That fits the pattern. Do you know the time of death?"

"It's harder to tell with Reuben due to the lack of blood. However, extensive livor mortis on the back of Jasmine's legs and torso suggests she was laid supine after her death. The rigor mortis in her upper body indicates a time of death of between five and eight last night."

Cooper pursed her lips. "We believe they were taken shortly after five-thirty."

Margot took another drag on her cigarette. "Poor bairns didn't have very long. Additionally," she continued, "there was very little animal interference with the bodies. I'd estimate they were placed outdoors a maximum of three hours before they were discovered."

Cooper slid her hands into her pockets. "That ties in with what I suspected. Thank you, Margot. Do you have anything else for me?"

Margot shook her head and got to her feet. "Not at this time. Obviously, I've only just scratched the surface with these two. I'll run toxicology and some other tests, and I'll get back to you as soon as I can."

Cooper got to her feet and shook Margot's hand. Margot turned and walked away, following the path around the duck pond. Her bright red coat shone out on the bleak winter's day and made Cooper think of a lighthouse for some reason. She looked down at the grey coat and black boots she had opted for and felt dowdy in comparison.

Get a grip, she told herself. *You're a detective, not a fashion model.*

Cooper turned and walked in the opposite direction. She hoped that the little café would be open so she could grab some caffeine. She had a feeling she would need it.

-CHAPTER 23-

THE INCIDENT ROOM AT CID headquarters had the distinct aroma of Nando's chicken. Tennessee had brought a boatload of the stuff in from the nearby retail park having said he was *hangry* and ready to hulk out at the next person that wound him up.

Cooper could hardly imagine her mild-mannered, baby-faced sergeant hulking out at anyone. He was always professional, a real gentle giant. Although, to someone Cooper's size, most people were giants. Thank goodness the days when the British police had a minimum height requirement were long gone.

Keaton unfolded a napkin and laid it across her lap. "Thank the lord for flame-grilled chicken," she said with a smile on her face.

"Hear, hear," agreed Cooper. "I feel like I haven't eaten in a month."

"And you look like it too," said Sutherland.

Cooper raised an eyebrow. The man could do with losing a few kilos.

He patted his belly. "Yeah, yeah. I know what you're thinking."

Cooper picked up a chicken piece using a napkin and tore a section off with her teeth.

"Have you heard from Tina?" asked Sutherland.

"Yeah. Kenny dropped her at school this morning, and she sent me a text during morning break. How about Caroline?"

"The missus and I decided to keep her off school. Sue had to go into work today, so the grandparents have come down from the farm to stay with her. Her grandad – Sue's pop – gave me the fright of my life when he pulled his hunting rifle out the backseat of their Land Rover. I started reciting the Firearms Act, but it was like talkin' to a brick wall. I made him lock it in the garage in the end. Caroline thought she would have a day of sitting on her arse watching Netflix, but her grandmother has other plans. She's printed off a bunch of GCSE sample papers for her to work through today.

"Oh, Caroline's going to love that."

"She'll be begging to go back to school tomorrow, mark my words."

Cooper pulled her phone from her pocket; she had another message from Tina. "Listen to this," she said to Sutherland. "Tina says OFSTED inspectors have shown up. Linda Webb's flipped out and done a runner leaving Hutchins as acting head. Apparently, over a hundred parents turned up to take their kids home and the ones who are left are being forced to do tree-hugging-hippy exercises."

"Tree-hugging-hippy exercises?"

"Bonding. Share your feelings stuff."

Sutherland pulled a face and let out a harrumph.

Just then, Oliver Martin walked in carrying a bunch of files. He dumped them on the nearest desk when he spotted the haul from Nando's.

"Brilliant," he declared, scooping up a box of chicken and a portion of fries. "Who brought this in?"

Cooper pointed to Tennessee.

"Thanks, big man."

"No bother," replied Tennessee. "You're worth it," he added with a wink.

Martin stuck two fingers up at him and cleared his desk of empty soda cans, a tub of hair wax, and half a dozen notepads, and sat down with his lunch.

Cooper considered telling the guys to grow up, but a little banter and some lightheartedness wouldn't do them any harm. She gave the team ten minutes to complete their meals and get themselves ready for the briefing. Turning to face the murder wall, Cooper pinned photos of Jasmine and Reuben next to those of Rachel Pearson and Shelly Smith. She felt her heart split in two when she thought of the four lives that had been cut short. Who would these kids have grown up to be? What would have become of them if some psycho hadn't killed them? Doctor? Sports star? Banker? Journalist? Mothers? Fathers? Grandparents? Who knows where their lives could have taken them.

After ten minutes, Cooper threw her rubbish in the bin and waited for the rest of the team to do the same. Keaton announced her approval of the meal by burping loud enough for the whole building to hear.

"Charming. Let's get on with things, shall we?" asked Cooper. "The good news is we have a fingerprint from the belt Reuben was wearing. It also matches a partial print that Justin Atkinson pulled from the boat that Rachel was found in. The bad news is, it doesn't match anything in the system."

"So, we don't have a name?" asked Keaton.

"We don't have a name," Cooper replied, before adding, "yet."

"And Bennett is still snug as a bug in custody?"

"That he is, and making a right song and dance about the quality of food he's getting by all accounts."

Keaton stuck out her lower lip. "Aww, poor baby."

Tennessee let out a little chuckle. "He might not have wanted to give us an alibi, but I've got the ANPR results for his van for the times of Rachel and Shelly's murders."

Cooper met his eyes. ANPR stood for automatic number plate recognition. "Let's have it then."

"He was pinged headed north on the A1 last Tuesday evening. He passed Alnwick at seven-fifty and came off the A1 somewhere before Brownieside. He pinged again when he headed back south shortly after nine. He made the same journey on Thursday morning."

Cooper picked at her nails while she mulled over the information Tennessee had given her. "Why wouldn't he want us to know he was driving around Northumberland?" she muttered to herself. "This puts him forty miles in the clear." Her mouth fell open, and she clapped her hands together, not caring that she looked like a circus sea lion. "Oh, that little shit! A white van, A1 north, came off before Brownieside? Tuesday evening? That's when Doxford Hall was done over."

"The hotel heists! What else was going on at the time of Shelly Smith's murder?" asked Tennessee.

Sutherland did a quick search on his computer, but it didn't take him long to check the records. "The robbery at Newton Hall."

Tennessee slapped his hand on his desk and laughed at the ceiling. "Ha! We've only gone and solved Fuller's case for him. I can't wait to see his weaselly little face when you tell him."

The thought of telling Neil Fuller that not only did she have a plausible suspect for him but that she already had said suspect in custody made Cooper want to break out the dance moves.

A slow smile crept over her face as she imagined the scene. "I can't bloody wait, either. In the meantime, let's find out who's killing the teens of Tynemouth Academy. We have a number of statements from locals who reported noise at around half four this morning. One lady said her dog started barking at four thirty-seven after something activated her security light. We also have a gentleman with a motion-activated door cam that recorded a car rolling by very slowly with only its sidelights on. That was at four thirty-eight. The car looks to be an estate, but the footage is dark and grainy. Tech are going to see if they can work some magic with it."

"Did Margot give you anything useful?" asked Tennessee.

"Her timings fit with ours. Time of death between five and eight last night but not moved outdoors until at least four a.m."

Tennessee nodded and made a note.

"She also says the weapon used on Reuben was a single-edged blade, around twenty centimetres long and four centimetres wide. He fought back, so our guy might have a couple of wounds of his own. As suspected, Jasmine was strangled. The same scalpel style blade used on Rachel and Shelly was used for the calling cards. The card in Reuben read: *Heirophant.*"

"What's one of those when it's at home?" asked Keaton.

"It's like a pope," answered Cooper. "Tennessee, what do you have?"

"He definitely came into the park via the allotments. There're signs of disturbance including a broken lock on one of the gates and a tyre track going through a vegetable patch. It looks the same as the track we saw under the bridge. Justin's team are taking impressions to compare, but they looked identical to me. There's a hole in the fence at the back of the allotment and a partial trail coming through the bushes."

Cooper was pleased. They were getting somewhere. "Brilliant. Paula, did you find out who the allotments were leased to?"

"Sure did, boss. There are a few worth noting. First, there's a Frederick Webb."

"Related to Linda Webb?"

"That's what I wondered. Haven't checked yet, but I'll get right on it. Second, there's Victor Pickett. You recognise his name?"

"Yes," answered Cooper, "But I can't place it."

"He's the caretaker at Tynemouth Academy," said Keaton.

"Interesting."

"I thought so," said Keaton. "The last one we should look closer at is Isabella Lopez."

"I know that name too."

"When we arrived at the scene of the Smith murder, it was Lopez who Lisa Smith requested we call. She's a friend and colleague of Smith's."

"Whose allotment was damaged the worst?" asked Cooper.

"That would be an Alistair Goodwin. He's out of the country. On holiday in France for two weeks. I've spoken to him and he was very cooperative, had no problem with us poking about. Wanted us to catch whoever broke his gate."

"Not bothered about us catching a murderer, though?"

Keaton laughed. "Not so much. I heard from Hong earlier. He had some updates from the forensics team. Justin got a good set of footprints from the bushes behind the allotments; they match some from under the bridge. They haven't identified the specific brand of shoe, but they're size tens. There was a very small amount of clay under Jasmine's nails and some trace amounts of something called poly... polyvinyl...poly-vinyl-pyro-something. I can't pronounce it, but it's usually shortened to PVP."

"What's that?" asked Oliver.

"I looked it up and it's used in a tonne of stuff. It's a binding agent. It's in medicines, foods, make-up. The shit you put in your hair? That'll be full of it."

Martin's hands went to his head, and he checked that his style hadn't budged.

"We can probably assume the clay under her nails was leftover from the sculpting class," said Cooper. "But we should ask for some samples from the school to compare. Anything else?"

"Grey denim fibres," said Keaton. "On both Jasmine and Reuben's clothing."

Tennessee lifted his pen in the air. "That Xander kid had a grey denim bracelet around his wrist when we went to see him."

Cooper nodded. "Yes, I remember. But he had a solid alibi. Besides, so many people wear denim, it'll be tough to follow that one up. We'll bear it in mind, though. You have the floor, Tennessee. What have you got?"

"I have sweet FA. The lumber yards near the park have CCTV, but they only cover their front gates. I've taken a look and there's no activity in the early hours. Same story at the car wash. There's a Chinese takeaway around the back of the park with cameras on their door. It's closed now, but I've left a message asking the owner to get in touch as soon as they can. It opens at five. If I haven't heard by then, I'll go round myself."

"I've had more luck with the car," said Martin, flipping open a spiral-bound notepad.

"Go ahead," Cooper replied.

"Well, you asked me to find out what car every member of staff at the school drove. There's four that I would call dark-coloured estate cars, and all four are driven by people whose names we'll recognise."

Keaton sat up a little taller. "The plot thickens."

"Parke, the PE teacher. He was the last staff member to see Shelly alive and was part of the search party for Jasmine and Reuben. He drives an old grey Skoda. Phillip Dunn: music teacher, part of the group who run the culture club, and also out searching last night. He has a black Volvo V60. There's a blue VW Passat driven by Victor Pickett, school caretaker and allotment owner."

Ears pricked up and eyes darted about CID as everyone read each other's faces.

"And the fourth?" asked Cooper.

"A grey Mercedes E class, driven by a Ms Linda Webb."

Cooper raised her eyebrows. "Bloody hell."

"And Webb was notably absent from the search," said Sutherland. "The other teachers were miffed about it."

"I think we have enough to seize the cars. Oliver, make the arrangements. Paula, go with him. Give Justin's team a call and have them conduct a sweep for any forensics."

Martin picked up his phone. "Right away, Coop."

"Last but not least," she turned to Sutherland. "Tell me tech came back with something?"

"They're still working through the laptops and phones from the four kids. One thing they did mention was that all three girls had secret Instagram accounts."

"What do you mean by secret?"

"They had two accounts each. A nice, polite one for their families to follow. Wholesome pictures of family gatherings, cute pictures of pets, you get the idea. Their second accounts were followed by school friends and the pictures were not so wholesome. Drinking, smoking weed, less clothing, more skin."

Cooper knew the second she got home, she'd check Tina's phone for secret social media accounts.

"There's some private messages between Shelly and Jasmine regarding a 'Dunk the Hunk', whoever he is."

Cooper shook her head and wracked her brains. "I can't recall a Duncan from the lists of classmates and friends."

"Me neither. There's also some text messages between Reuben and Xander about Rachel and Shelly. They were sent after the girls were killed and they weren't exactly kind. I've printed them off."

Sutherland handed out the copies and Cooper watched faces wrinkle as they read. She took a deep breath and tried to keep her thoughts under control. They were supposed to be eliminating suspects, but the list seemed to keep on growing. Right now, it felt like everyone was a suspect.

"I want alibis for everyone," she told the team. "I want to know where our four estate drivers were between five and eight. While we're at it, I want to know where they were at half four in the morning. According to my daughter, Linda Webb has done a runner from the school."

"Will Kenny know where she is?" asked Sutherland.

"Hopefully. I'll pay her a visit. As for Xander Wright and Will Harper, let's find out what they were up to last night and early this morning. If they have alibis, they'd better be airtight."

Tennessee stood up and smoothed his hands over his shirt. "But first?"

"First, you and I need to practice our smug faces. Neil Fuller awaits."

***

"Right, you time-wasting piece of dirt." Cooper marched into the interview suite where Ralf Bennett sat. He'd been handcuffed to his chair and an officer with a sense of humour had placed a chocolate bar and a can of coke just out of his reach.

Bennett's eyes flicked to Cooper's. "Let me go. I didn't kill them," he spat. "And what have I got to do to get a toothbrush around here? My mouth tastes like rabid badger vomited in it."

"Delightful imagery." Cooper leant against the door frame and folded her arms. "Mr Bennett, the good news is I am releasing you without charge."

"Ha!" His eyes lit up. "I told you I didn't do nothin'. Daft cow trying to pin—"

Tennessee slammed his hand on the table and pointed a finger in Bennett's face. The sad, bitter man shut his mouth and he swallowed anxiously.

"As I was saying," continued Cooper, "before you rudely interrupted me. The good news is that I'm releasing you. You are no longer a suspect for the murders of Rachel Pearson and Michelle Smith."

A satisfied look passed over his face, closely followed by a look of confusion as Detective Neil Fuller shuffled into the room and took a seat opposite him.

"The bad news," said Fuller, "is that I'm arresting you for illegal possession of a firearm and the robberies of six Northumbrian hotels. You do not have to say anything, but it may harm your defence if you do not mention when questioned something which you later rely on in court. Anything you do say may be given in evidence."

"This is bullshit."

"No," said Cooper. "This is justice." She turned to Fuller and placed her hand on his shoulder. "I'll leave you to it. Pleasure doing business with you, Neil."

Cooper maintained her professional composure as far as the double doors at the end of the corridor. When they closed behind her, she turned to Tennessee and they slapped each other's palms in triumphant high-fives.

- CHAPTER 24 -

IT HAD BEEN A long day, but it was far from over. Cooper took a window seat in The Lock café at Royal Quays Marina and watched Themis, an impressive thirty-five-foot yacht, manoeuvre from the Tyne towards the jetties. A slender woman with long, dark hair dropped anchor while a dashing man at the helm guided her in. He leapt from the mid-ship and secured the warps to a cleat.

Must be nice, thought Cooper, to have the freedom of sailing. Another day, another bay. She ordered a bacon and sausage sandwich that appeared big enough to feed a small nation. It took Cooper almost twenty minutes to eat it, and when she was finished, she felt bloated, a little nauseous, and in need of a nap. Sadly, she had work to do. She paid the bill and began walking around Royal Quays towards a modern apartment block where she understood Linda Webb rented a penthouse.

A gaggle of reporters lurked around the entrance to the building. Cooper thought she recognised one or two of them from press conferences, but before she could say 'excuse me,' she had a dictaphone shoved in her face.

"Do you live in the building, madam?"

"Do you know Linda Webb?"

"Do you think she killed those kids?"

The questions came thick and fast before a man with a bushy, auburn beard bellowed over the hubbub. "That's Erica Cooper, you daft shite." He held a microphone with one hand, and with the other, he held an ice pack over his temple. "She put Eddie Blackburn in Frankland. I'm Vince Shepard, Evening Chronicle. Is Webb a suspect? Is Webb the Tarot Card Killer?"

Cooper groaned inwardly. Did someone from the department leak the nickname, or did the press come up with it on their own? She pinched her nose for a moment and took a deep breath.

"The investigation is still ongoing," she said. "Any questions can be directed towards the press desk. Now, please let me through. And if I hear of you pestering anyone else who's trying to access this building, I'll have you arrested faster than you can say *extra, extra, read all about it.*"

Cooper pressed the intercom and waited.

"I told you to bugger off," came the reply.

"Kenny, it's me. Erica."

In less than a second the intercom buzzed and the door clicked open. Cooper turned and gave the reporters a stern look before making her way to the lifts.

"Are those vultures still down there?" asked Kenny as he opened the door to the penthouse. He pulled her in for a quick hug. The stress must be getting to him; Kenny Roberts was not usually the hugging type.

"They are," said Cooper, breaking free. "And one of them's holding an ice pack over his face. Did you have something to do with that, by any chance?"

Kenny didn't say a word, but he briefly glanced at his knuckles; it was the only answer Cooper needed.

Cooper stared at him and looked aghast. "For goodness sake, Kenny." She sighed before continuing, "How's Linda doing?"

"About as well as you can imagine. Come on through to the kitchen. She's making some horrendous looking health drink. Says she needs the vitamins."

Linda's kitchen was vast and sported sweeping views over the marina and the Tyne. White gloss doors were accented with copper trim and the appliances were all top of the range. The room screamed *high-end*.

"They think I did it," said Linda as she peeled a banana and threw it into an expensive blender. She was dressed in a silk dressing gown and fluffy slippers. "I heard them muttering in the staffroom. How dare they," she rambled to herself.

Linda opened a cupboard and pulled out a bunch of plastic tubs containing vitamins and supplements. She took a scoop of spirulina and added it to the blender along with a multivitamin, a calcium tablet, some activated charcoal, and a pinch of wheatgrass powder.

"Me? Me? That school was rated inadequate before I turned up." She pointed at her chest before hitting the button on the blender and whizzing its contents into a dark green sludge. She poured the contents into a glass and then held her nose as she drank. She rinsed the blender and popped it into the dishwasher before announcing, "I'm going back to bed."

Cooper let Linda get as far as the kitchen door before she said, "Your absence was noted last night, Linda. I'm sorry to do this, but I need you to tell me where you were. We can do it here or at the station."

Linda stopped in her tracks and placed her hand on the doorframe. She stayed motionless for a good ten seconds before slowly turning and looking back and forth between Kenny and Cooper. She folded her arms and stuck out her lower lip. "This is unbelievable," she hissed.

Cooper opened her notepad and poised her pen above the paper in a posture that suggested she would wait all night if she had to.

With a noise that reminded Cooper of Tina's teenage tantrums, Linda began pacing back and forth in front of her floor-to-ceiling window. "Fine. I, I left school at around three forty-five yesterday."

"That's rather early," remarked Cooper.

"I had a salon appointment. I got a haircut, not that anyone noticed." She flashed Kenny an annoyed look.

"Which salon? And how long were you there for?"

"Serenity Lounge. I was there about an hour, maybe an hour and a half."

Assuming that the appointment was at four o'clock, that took Linda's alibi up to around the half five mark, the same time Jasmine and Reuben went missing.

"Did you drive?" Asked Cooper.

Linda turned to face her. "Yes," she said with a clenched jaw.

"And can you confirm that you drive a dark grey Mercedes E class?"

"I do. How do you know that?"

Cooper ignored the question. "And what did you do after your hair appointment?"

"I came home and did some paperwork until Kenny came over at about nine. Was it nine?"

Kenny nodded.

"I didn't have the TV on, so it was a shock when Kenny told me about the kids."

Television or not, Cooper knew the news had been all over the internet and social media sites. What were the odds that none of her colleagues sent her a text message or picked up the phone?

"Did you speak to anyone when you arrived home? A neighbour? A doorman?"

"We don't have a doorman. And no, I don't think I saw the neighbours. You'll have to ask them."

"What did you do after Kenny told you about Jasmine and Reuben?"

Linda thought for a moment. "We had dinner. Thai food. Then we," she paused, "went to bed."

Cooper got the idea. She thanked Linda and asked Kenny to walk her out. Once they were alone, she lowered her voice and turned to Kenny.

"How did Linda seem when you told her about the missing kids?"

He shrugged his broad shoulders. "Dunno. She was shocked. She didn't cry or owt. Think she was stressed more than anything. That's understandable, right?"

Cooper did her coat up, ready to face the November winds. "I know on a personal level it's none of my business, but I'm here on business. Did you spend the night?"

"No." His brows furrowed, and a deep line appeared between them. "I left at midnight, or thereabouts. I didn't have a change of clothes with me so I went back to mine. Why? Is there something I should know, Erica?"

"I'm doing my best to eliminate her from the enquiries, Kenny, but she is a person of interest." Cooper saw concern etched on Kenny's face. "I'll keep you posted if that changes."

Kenny opened the door. "Do you still need me to pick Tina up?"

"Please. That would be great. But Kenny," she lowered her voice to a whisper, "no Linda, okay? Just you."

He nodded and gave her another quick hug. Two in one day. Wasn't Cooper a lucky girl?

"I think Tina wanted to spend time with Josh," said Cooper. "If you could pick them both up and bring them to mine, they can hang out there until I get home."

Kenny's mouth thinned.

"Come on, give the girl a break. No Josh bashing. They're allowed in Tina's room as long as the door stays open. I should be back by five."

"You're killing me here, Erica. But okay, I'll see you at yours at five. Stay safe."

"Same to you," said Cooper.

IT WAS A PLEASANT surprise to be home at the time she'd promised to be. Such days were a rarity since Cooper had returned to work. But, she'd done all she could for one day and her pyjamas were calling. After a warm shower and a full exfoliation, Cooper changed into her favourite PJs and joined Tina in the kitchen, where she found her reading the case file on the Tynemouth murders.

"Tina, you know you shouldn't be looking through that."

Tina didn't even look up. "Why not? It's interesting."

"For a start, there are details in there that haven't been released to the public. And second, it'll give you nightmares."

Tina rolled her eyes.

"How are you coping with all of this?" asked Cooper, aware that she hadn't checked in with Tina other than a few text messages here and there.

Tina finally looked up. "I'm fine, I guess."

"You guess?"

She shuffled into a seat at the dining table. "Well, it's a bit weird, isn't it? Having four people you go to school with murdered."

Weird wasn't the word Cooper would have chosen.

"But I wasn't close to any of them," she continued. "It's still horrific, mind you. No one deserves to die like that. I don't think anyone has the right to take someone else's life."

Cooper reached across the table and took Tina's hands. "Are you worried?"

Tina averted her eyes. "Hmm. Not really. I keep looking over my shoulder, but the only one following me about is Dad."

"It won't be forever, T. We will catch whoever's doing this. Anyway, I wanted to talk to you about something. I invited a colleague over for dinner tomorrow night. I wanted to check that it was okay with you."

Tina brought her eyes back to her mother's but removed her hands from hers. It was either eye contact or physical contact, never both.

"A man?"

"Yes. If that's all right?"

"Oh, not Neil?"

Cooper laughed. "No, not Neil."

"Good, because he was a total wanker."

"Tina!"

Tina raised an eyebrow. "He was. Admit it."

"You might have a point," conceded Cooper. "Well, this guy isn't a *total wanker*, as you put it. His name is Justin, and he works in forensics. He's a few years older than me—"

"Do you like him?"

Cooper thought back to all the interactions she'd had with Atkinson. "He's a nice guy. Yeah, I like him."

Tina shrugged and got to her feet. "Then I like him too. You deserve a little romance after everything you've been through this year."

Tears formed in Cooper's eyes. It was a struggle to hold them back. She got to her feet, pulled Tina in for a hug and spoke into her hair. "You're brilliant, you know that?"

Once she released Tina, she removed a cookbook from the kitchen shelf. Until that moment the book's only use had been to act as an occasional doorstop. "Right, come on then. Help me choose what I'm going to make."

Tina froze for a moment. "Oh no," she said, her eyes widening. "No, no, no, no, no. You said you like this guy."

"I do."

Tina snatched the book from her mother's hands. "Then there's no way in good conscience that I can let you cook for him. He's not going to stick around if you give him salmonella."

Cooper scrutinised her daughter. "Nice to know you have so much faith in me."

"I have faith in *you*," said Tina, "just not your cooking. Look, I got an A in food tech. Leave it to me; I'll make something. All you'll have to do is serve it up when he gets here. He'll never know."

Grateful, but perplexed at how her daughter could out *adult* her, Cooper agreed. It wasn't that long ago that she'd described her daughter as a 'sneaky little genius.' She'd been right.

-CHAPTER 25 -

AFTER WHAT HAPPENED AT the school gates with her father, Tina asked to be dropped off two streets away when Cooper drove her to school on Wednesday morning. Cooper couldn't blame her; the poor thing had been thoroughly humiliated. Josh was waiting on the corner as Cooper pulled up. He was playing keepie-up with an empty can of Pepsi. He threw the can into the nearest bin when he saw the car approach.

"Morning, Josh."

"Morning, Ms Cooper."

"Are you ever going to call me Erica?"

He looked at his feet and then broke into a huge grin when Tina jumped out of the car and took his hand.

"I might see you at school," called Cooper as Tina and Josh began to walk away. "I need to speak to a few people. Otherwise, I'll see you back home tonight. Your Dad's picking you up. Tina? Are you listening?"

Tina looked over her shoulders and hissed. "Yes. Be cool."

"Be cool?" muttered Cooper under her breath. "I wouldn't recognise what passes for cool these days if it slapped me in the face." She restarted the engine, tuned into Absolute Radio Rock and was pleasantly surprised to hear Guns and Roses playing. "Now this is what I call cool."

Cooper easily found a parking space on the road outside Tynemouth Academy. She was reluctant to turn off the radio until Sweet Child O' Mine finished, but duty called.

"Drew," she said as she approached PC Andrew Underwood, who was one of the uniforms stationed at the school gates.

"Ma'am," he replied, "the man with the two yellow Labs was back yesterday."

"Oh, really?" asked Cooper, letting the *ma'am* go, for now.

"We got the name and address. The bloke's called Nate Douglass. Lives in the village. I called Oliver Martin with the details so he can run a background check."

"What was your impression of Douglass?"

He scrunched up his face. "Told me he was only talking to those girls because his dog's ball had gone over the fence, and he was asking them to throw it back to him. He certainly didn't seem shifty."

"They never do."

"Yes, ma'am."

Cooper winced. There was something about that word that was like nails on a chalkboard to her. "Anything else to report?"

Drew Underwood shook his head. "To be honest, it's pretty quiet. A lot of the parents are keeping their kids at home."

"So I heard," said Cooper. "Thanks, Drew. I'll check in again with you later."

The glass doors to Tynemouth Comp slid open and Cooper entered the lobby. The atrium seemed sterile, cold and clinical. It was as if the cleaning staff had worked overtime to scrub away the horrors of the last week.

"Chief Inspector. Good morning." Brian Hutchins approached and took Cooper's hand in both of his. The art teacher stood with impeccable posture, he fixed a welcoming smile on his face, but his eyes were red and gave away the stress he and the other staff must be feeling.

"How are you this morning, Mr Hutchins?"

"It's Brian, please, and we're coping the best we can. I've brought in a team of eight counsellors, but we have around twelve hundred students today. If we're lucky, they'll make it round all the most vulnerable by the end of the day."

"What's the usual attendance?" asked Cooper.

"Almost two thousand," said Brian. "Did you hear we have OFSTED inspectors in?" He glanced at an antique clock that hung over the reception area. "Due at any moment. Talk about timing. I don't think it's a coincidence."

At that moment, a group of surly-looking men in business suits arrived.

"Oh, speak of the devils," said Brian. He removed his glasses from his pocket and popped them onto his face. His eyes appeared to double in size. He took a deep inhalation and held it for several seconds before finally breathing out. He turned to Cooper, "I'll assist you in any way that I can. The rest of the staff feel the same. Just let us know what you need."

"I need to speak to someone from the culture club. I understand you're busy so I won't keep you. Perhaps you can direct me to Phillip Dunn or Catherine Grainger?"

Brian raised his hand in greeting to the inspectors. "Of course. Catherine is on the third floor so it will probably be easier for you to find Phillip. I believe he has a free period first thing. If you follow this corridor," he motioned to his left, "right to the end, it's the last office on the right."

Cooper nodded her thanks and set off down the corridor, leaving Brian Hutchins to turn on the charm offensive for the box-ticking, paperwork-loving henchmen of the Department of Education.

When she found Phillip Dunn, he was slumped over his desk. His head rested on his forearms and his back rose and fell in a slow rhythm that suggested he was asleep. His flat cap and coat had fallen off the peg on the back of his door and lay in a heap on the floor.

"Mr Dunn?"

He didn't stir so Cooper gave a loud cough, jolting him back into consciousness. "Huh? What?"

"Mr Dunn. It's DCI Erica Cooper. We met—"

"At the search. Yes." He ran his hands over his face. His cheeks had the permanent flush of a man who consumed too much alcohol and he had two days' worth of stubble on his jaw. "Tell me, detective. Why was my car taken as evidence last night?"

Phillip sat back in his chair, his eyes running up and down Cooper in a manner that made her skin crawl.

"Jasmine and Reuben were seen getting into a dark-coloured estate car on the evening of their disappearance. A number of cars have been—"

"I helped try to find those kids and now I'm being treated like a suspect!" His voice took on an aggressive tone and his fingertips turned white where they gripped the wooden arms of his chair.

"They came to my house," he continued. "My wife was home. My kids were home. My daughter goes to this school. You know that? You should have seen the way she looked at me. Like she didn't know who I was anymore."

"Mr Dunn, it's important that we—"

"We're a one-car family. I had to take three buses to get here this morning. My wife had to get a taxi."

"Mr Dunn," Cooper's voice hardened. "I'm sorry that our quadruple murder investigation is an inconvenience to you, but if you're quite finished interrupting me, I need you to take me to the art department so I can collect some samples of the clay used during Monday's culture club."

"Why?" he asked with lowered brows.

Cooper didn't answer. "Then I need you to show me where I can find," she checked her notes, "Leroy

MacDonald. He was Jasmine and Reuben's form tutor. Correct?"

Phillip nodded and got to his feet with a number of groans. "This way," he said. There was still no warmth to his voice. "So, who else had their car seized?"

Cooper followed but said nothing.

"Victor drives a blue Passat. He arrived on foot this morning. In here." He opened the door to a large open space that smelled of white spirit and body odour. Wooden desks were splattered with bright paint and covered in ink doodles, making each table a work of art in its own right. Paintings hung to dry on lengths of string that zigzagged across the ceiling like a clothesline.

A handful of children who looked to be twelve or thirteen removed their green blazers and donned coveralls. They rummaged through drawers and collected their materials for the lesson. A woman with thick, postbox-red curls and heavy jowls took a seat at the teacher's desk.

"This is Henrietta Winters. Substitute teacher. Stepping in while Brian is acting head," explained Phillip. "Henrietta, this is DCI Cooper. We'll be out of your hair in a moment; we just need some clay."

Eyes followed Cooper and hushed whispers flitted around the room as the students recognised Cooper as a detective.

Phillip entered a store cupboard at the back of the room. Cooper declined to enter the confined space with a man as grumpy as Phillip, so she waited by the door. He emerged after a few seconds of annoyed searching.

210

"Here. This is the clay we used."

He dropped a brick-sized lump of clay wrapped in clingfilm into Cooper's hands."

"Thank you, Mr Dunn. You've been very helpful." The temptation to use a sarcastic tone was strong, but Cooper's professionalism held it at bay. "Now, where will I find Mr MacDonald?"

"Upstairs. He shares an office with Pete Parke. Room thirty-eight." And with that, Phillip Dunn walked away with his arms folded over his chest. He didn't seem like the same man Cooper had met during the search for Jasmine and Reuben. His mood was understandable if she considered his daughter's reaction to his car being searched by forensics. Tina had called Cooper many names over the years but she'd never suspected her of violence, or worse.

Once upstairs, Cooper knocked on the door to room thirty-eight. A prompt reply told her to "Enter."

Leroy MacDonald and Pete Parke's office was a cramped affair with two desks that were too big for the room squashed in with filing cabinets and piles of textbooks. One half of the room was cluttered: papers, half-drunk cups of coffee, a newspaper, and at least six pens littered the desk. This was the side of the office where Leroy MacDonald sat. He pushed himself to his feet when he saw Cooper was not a student.

"How can I help you?"

"DCI Erica Cooper. I'm investigating the murders of Rachel Pearson, Michelle Smith, Jasmine Lee and Reuben Jones."

"Of course. Come in, come in. Please, take Pete's chair. He's in the shed teaching basketball to the year tens."

By contrast, Pete Parke's half of the room was sparse and tidy. His desk was clear save for two framed photographs and a bottle of Evian water.

Leroy MacDonald was a portly man with a thick beard and a bald head. He wore a crisp white shirt tucked into faded black jeans.

"Awful times. Just horrific." His voice was quiet and soft with hints of an Irish accent. "Do you have children, detective?"

"Just the one," said Cooper. "She goes here. Tina Cooper."

"Oh, of course. I thought I recognised you. I only ask because I have two myself and I'm finding the whole thing just so..." His voice trailed off. "I keep having nightmares."

"I can imagine," said Cooper, and she could. Only last night she dreamt someone was taking a scalpel to her chest as someone had done to Rachel.

"My two are younger. In the primary school in Monkseaton. Ben's nine and Julia's eight. I've enrolled them at the boxing club. Not sure what good it'll do against an adult but I want them to be able to throw a punch if needed." He turned and stared out of the window.

"You were Jasmine's form tutor?"

"Yes," he answered without turning back to Cooper. "And Reuben's. Joined at the hip, they were. Freya too. Poor lass hasn't returned to school yet. Can't say I blame her."

Cooper swallowed. The situation was horrible for everyone involved. "Can you tell me about Jasmine and Reuben?"

Leroy turned his back to the window and pushed his thumbs into the belt loops on his jeans. "They were sweet kids. Rebellious, yes, sometimes, but they weren't bad kids."

"Rebellious in what way?"

"Hmm." He mulled over his words. "Well, Jasmine acted like the rules didn't apply to her. She was put in isolation more times than I can count for uniform violations. Make-up, skirt too short, heels too high."

"Lots of girls like to dress older than their age."

"Oh, I know. I'm not trying to shame her, or whatever they call it. I'm just saying she didn't like following the rules. Reuben was the same. He liked to wear trainers, wouldn't tuck his shirt in or tie his tie correctly. What I'm saying is they liked to test their boundaries, see what they could and could not get away with. Then they were suspended for two weeks each last term."

"What for?"

Leroy sat back at his desk and began to run a biro between his thumb and forefinger. "Smoking marijuana on school premises."

Cooper's brow lifted. "Weed? In school?" Never in her metal-head youth of underage drinking and fooling around with boys would she have ever taken drugs during the school day.

"Yes. Caused rather a stir."

"Leroy. Can I call you Leroy? Shelly Smith's mother mentioned Shelly had been to a party recently where coke was available." Her mind also turned to Will Harper, who had reeked of weed whilst he was being questioned. "Is there a drug problem at this school?"

Leroy considered the question. "Yes and no," he said. "Yes. Some of the student body definitely use drugs. But, no, I wouldn't say the school has a problem. We're doing well in the league tables. It's incredibly rare something like that happens on school grounds. With Jasmine and Reuben it was a one-off, and as awful as it sounds, I think Jasmine was the instigator. I always got the impression that Reuben just went along with anything Jasmine suggested."

Cooper leant back in Pete Parke's chair. "It does make me wonder, who's dealing to these kids? Are drugs, or drug money, part of this?"

Leroy closed his eyes for a moment and pressed the heels of his hairy hands into his sockets. When he opened his eyes again he said, "If I find anyone trying to sell anything like that to my kids..."

"It's probably best you don't finish that sentence," said Cooper, though she felt the same way. "Can you recall if Jasmine or Reuben seemed worried about anything, or anyone, lately?"

"Not at all." Leroy shook his head. "They appeared not to have a care in the world. Very *que sera sera* kids."

"And their attitude didn't change in the last few days?"

"Not that I noticed. Not even with everything that's been going on. But to be honest, I'm only their form tutor. I only saw Jasmine at registration or if there was a problem. I saw Reuben a little more as I had him for biology three hours a week."

"Okay," said Cooper. "I won't keep you much longer. You said Jasmine and Reuben weren't bad kids. Tell me about their positive attributes."

"Well, by all accounts, Reuben could be a very sweet young man. Despite his rule-breaking, he'd often help teachers carry things, or he would hold the door open for others, that sort of thing. He was raised to have good manners. I could tell. He had decent grades in most subjects. He actually had a bit of a gift for biology. He told me he wanted to go into marine biology when he finished school."

Cooper had wondered where the lives of the four victims would have taken them. The world was now down a marine biologist. Perhaps he would have rid the oceans of plastic or brought a species back from the verge of extinction. She'd never know because Reuben Jones never got to follow the path he'd chosen.

"Jasmine wasn't academic, despite pressure from her parents. Mrs Lee was a bit of a tiger mum. Tried to push Jasmine into piano and violin. She had private tutors for maths and science, but it didn't help. Her heart was never in it. She loved sport, though. Pete thought the world of her."

"Pete Parke?"

"Yes. He said she was a born runner. Said she was like a gazelle on the track."

Cooper spun on her chair and faced Pete Parke's desk. Neither of the framed photographs was of his family. The first was a picture of the school's athletics team. Jasmine Lee was front and centre in a fitted running vest and tiny shorts. She was gripping a trophy and smiling from sticky-out-ear to sticky-out-ear. The second framed photograph featured the netball team. The seven first-team players sat on a bench with the seven reserves standing behind. The girls wore short netball dresses in the same shade of green as their school blazers. Cooper recognised two faces: Michelle Smith, wearing a captain's armband and cradling a netball under her arm, and fresh-faced, bare-legged Tina Cooper.

- CHAPTER 26 -

AN UNEASY FEELING SETTLED in the pit of Cooper's stomach. What sort of teacher had photos of his teenage students, rather than his family - or at least a pet - on his office desk? She put her concerns to one side so she could make a quick phone call to Tennessee.

"DS Daniel."

"It's Cooper. How are things at your end?"

There was unusual silence from Tennessee.

"Talk to me, Jack."

He sighed. "I'm not sure how to say this, ma'am. Shit. Sorry. I'm not sure how to say this, Cooper, but the Chief Constable's shown up. Looks a right flashy git in a designer suit and Rolex. He's been holed up in Nixon's office for an hour."

Cooper had to steady herself against a wall in a corridor of Tynemouth Academy; she felt as if she was falling. She knew Nixon was under pressure; she just hoped he wasn't throwing her under the

217

bus. She felt small and feeble and vulnerable. She had to move quickly and solve this bloody case before it was taken off her.

"Coop?"

"Just processing everything. Do you have any good news?"

"Justin's been on the blower. He's finished with some of the cars."

"And?"

"And Dunn can collect his car later today. There're five sets of prints in the car, but none of them match Jasmine or Reuben. No blood or sign of a struggle. There's also no sign of the car being cleaned recently to rid it of evidence. No bleach or anything like that. There were green fibres. The same green as the school blazers but we know his daughter attends Tynemouth so they probably came from her."

Cooper walked along the school corridor, occasionally glancing through a classroom door and seeing a number of empty chairs. The school had an eerie silence to it.

"What about Pickett?"

"Only one set of recent prints. There's plenty of mud and soil in the driver's footwell, which ties in with him leasing an allotment. There's a muddy print as well, a size twelve."

"Too big. Unless he squashed his feet into a smaller shoe before dumping the bodies."

"Is that likely?"

Cooper puffed her cheeks. "Anything goes with this case."

"Have forensics started on Webb's car? Or Parke's?"

"Parke's car was immaculate. Must have had a full valet within a few hours of us picking it up."

"Hmm," said Cooper.

"Hmm, indeed. Anyway, Justin says they need to run more thorough tests to get to the microscopic level. It will take a little longer, but if there's evidence, they'll find it."

"Webb?" asked Cooper. She paused outside the girls' toilets.

"Well..."

"Spit it out, Tennessee."

"Linda Webb hasn't surrendered her car yet."

Cooper rested her back on the wall. "So go seize it."

"I wish we could. She wasn't home, so we called her to find out her whereabouts. She said she'd gone out for the day and didn't tell us where."

Cooper was astounded. Linda Webb was the most unhelpful, selfish, self-obsessed...

"Tech are tracing her phone signal, and we have ANPR requests for her plates. We'll have the car by the end of today, Coop. I promise."

She believed him. Her team could be like a dog with a bone at times. They did not take kindly to being messed about.

Cooper pushed open the door to the girls' toilets. There was a smell of bleach and cheap perfume. "Does Paula have any news?"

"Err, yeah. She mentioned some news from a couple of fancy-dress retailers. Want me to get her to call you? She's at the allotments with Hong."

"No, that's all right, Tennessee. I'll call her in five. I'll see you at HQ."

"Roger."

Cooper hung up and stared around the girls' toilets. She had a hunch the secrets of Tynemouth Academy could be found in here, and she wasn't disappointed. The walls of each cubicle were a maze of graffiti. Every ounce of gossip, every accusation, and every rumour was scrawled in marker pen. Cooper walked the length of the toilets, letting her eyes wander up and down the walls before dialling Keaton's number.

"Hey, boss." Keaton's voice was muffled.

"Are you eating?"

"One of the gardeners down here at the allotments, he grows the best apples I've ever tasted. The last of the season. Gave me a bunch to make a pie with. A bag full of quince too. He's helping us with our enquiries. Says the hole in the fence was definitely not there at the start of the week."

Cooper listened whilst she read the graffiti in the first cubicle. It didn't take long to spot the first musings that concerned the murdered girls: *Shelly deserved it.* Cooper put Keaton on hold and used her phone to take a photograph.

"Tennessee mentioned you had news from a fancy-dress store."

Will Harper is the hottest, was written in red pen. *Baby killer. Jasmin Lee had an abortion,* was written in black.

"Yes, boss." There were more chewing noises before Keaton swallowed. "A decent lead. An online retailer called the hotline. They received an order for three pope outfits to be delivered to a locker at Morrisons in Tynemouth. The buyer used PayPal."

"Do we have a name?"

Written in blue biro: *Xander is gay.* Scratched into the tiled floor: *Webb is a bitch.*

Cooper smiled at the last one. Then she saw *Hands off Dunk the Hunk. He's mine,* and worryingly, another line of graffiti that she couldn't turn her eyes away from.

"Just an email address," answered Keaton. "Tech have it. They'll see if they can get anything from it. Martin's working with the Royal Mail to coordinate when the costumes will be delivered. We'll get the locker number, and then we can post someone to keep watch. Intercept when he collects the parcel."

"Good work, Paula."

Cooper felt sick when she hung up the phone. She knew fine well that teenage girls were prone to gossip and spreading lies - she'd been one herself - but there was also a nagging doubt. Where there's smoke, there's fire. On the back of a toilet door, written in Tip-Ex was: *Rachel lifts her skirt for Paedo Pete.*

- CHAPTER 27 -

COOPER PRACTICALLY RAN ALONG the corridor. When she reached the school lobby she urgently banged her fist on the door to the school office. Behind the glass panel, the school administrator looked up from her keyboard. She had the office phone tucked between her ear and her shoulder and her fingertips moved at lightning speed over the keys. Cooper banged her fist again. The administrator looked around; she was red-nosed and angry-browed. She held up a finger in Cooper's direction, a signal for her to wait. Cooper was in no mood for whatever first-come-first-served system the administrator was operating, she marched into the office and pressed the phone's hold button.

"Brian Hutchins. I want to speak to him now."

A look of pure indignation formed on the woman's face. "He's in with the OFSTED inspectors, you'll have to wait," she said with a prim and put out voice.

Cooper took a step closer to the woman and invaded her personal space. She stared down at her, fury coursing through her. Around the woman's neck, hung a security pass bearing the name Norma Medford.

"Norma, I don't give a shit about the inspectors. He could be having tea with the queen for all I care. Go and fetch him."

Norma Medford huffed through her nose and got to her feet. "Well I never," she mumbled as she left the room. "Manners cost nothing, you know?"

It didn't take long for Brian Hutchins to appear. He was flustered, glancing back over his shoulder at the men in suits who had followed him out of his office.

"Norma," he whispered as he approached the administrator. "Could you take our guests to the staff room, please? see if they'd like a coffee and perhaps a tour of the science wing."

The school administrator bowed her head. "Yes, Mr Hutchins."

"Detective?" he turned to Cooper, shifting his weight from one foot to the other. "What's going on? Has someone else gone missing? Please tell me no one else has been hurt. I don't think I could bear it, I don't think any of the staff could, and as for the students—"

"Calm down, Brian." Cooper patted him on the arm and offered him Norma's seat but he shook his head. "What's going on?" he repeated.

"As acting head, you're now the senior child protection officer for the school, correct?"

He nodded.

"Have any complaints ever been made about Pete Parke?"

"Pete? Oh, I wouldn't have thought so. I've known him since I joined the school. Ten years ago now."

Cooper's mouth thinned. "That's not what I asked. I don't want to know if you think anyone has raised concerns about Pete Parke. I want to know for definite. Where do you store the school's welfare concern reports?"

"They're locked in a filing cabinet in my office, detective, but they're confidential. I can't just let you go through them. I think you'd need a warrant or—"

"Brian!" Cooper's voice was tense. She was doing all she could to hold herself together. She didn't have time to go back to Nixon and request a warrant. It would waste time she just didn't have. Who knew when the killer would strike again and if Parke was involved she had to find grounds to arrest him and get him out of the school and away from these kids as soon as possible. Every second counted. Letting out the tiniest of grunts, Cooper grabbed Hutchins by the elbow and frog-marched him along the corridor and into the girls' toilets.

"Staff aren't supposed to enter the student toilets," said Hutchins. "It's a safeguarding issue."

Safeguarding issue, thought Cooper, staff entering the student toilets is the least of these girls' concerns when it came to safeguarding. Cooper grabbed the door to the first cubicle and swung the door open with enough force that it bounced back on its hinges. She didn't need to say anything, she simply pointed at the accusation scrawled on the back of the door in Tip-Ex.

"Think we can take a look at that filing cabinet now, Brian?"

HUTCHINS PULLED A KEY from his desk drawer and unlocked the bottom drawer of a filing cabinet.

"Here. This is where we store any reports." He pulled out a plain brown box file. "This file is for the current school year, and this one is for last year." He handed Cooper the two files.

"How far do your records go back? she asked.

"Five years. Then we move them to storage." Hutchins added three more files to the pile Cooper held in her arms and she watched his face crease.

"I seriously doubt there's anything about Pete in there. Most of the pink slips concern children with unexplained bruises, kids turning up to school hungry or in dirty clothing, that sort of thing."

Cooper dumped the box files on Hutchins's desk and took a seat in his chair. She opened the uppermost file and began to sift through the pieces of paper. Cooper was careful to keep the files in order, laying each pink slip face down on top of its predecessor so she could return them to the box in the exact order as they had been. Hutchins had been right about the contents of the slips; most were completed by teachers who were concerned about their pupils' home lives and it didn't take Cooper long to find a slip concerning Rachel Pearson. Catherine Grainger had completed a form after asking Rachel about the number of bruises on her arms one day. According to the slip, Rachel had told her the bruises were from playing with her neighbour's dog. Cooper handed the sheet of paper to Hutchins. "Was this ever followed up?"

The new headteacher adjusted his glasses and held the sheet at arm's length. He frowned and shook his head. "I'm not sure. It was reported to Linda Webb. If it was a one-off, she'd be inclined to believe Rachel, if not, it may have been reported to Child Protection Services."

Cooper made a note of the slip's number and placed it on the pile to her left and continued making her way through the pile on her right. A number of slips expressed concern over William Harper and comments that were overheard by teachers about his mother. And a student named Lola Greens confided in Todd Carpenter about Jasmine Lee and the pressure she was under from home to achieve good grades in her GCSEs. Greens had suggested Lee had developed anorexia from the stress. Again, Cooper noted the slip number and continued. Eventually, she stopped, stared at one of the pink slips for a long while and slid it across the desk to Hutchins.

"Were you aware of this?"

Hutchins propped his elbows on the table and Cooper watched his eyes shift left and right as he read.

"It says," started Cooper, "that on the eighth of September, two students complained about Pete Parke entering the boys' changing rooms after football practice and that he was carrying his smartphone. I'm guessing that if staff aren't supposed to enter the student toilets, they're also not supposed to enter the changing rooms?"

Hutchins nodded. "That's right, not unless we think bullying is occurring or a student is in need of first aid."

"And is it normal practice for staff members to have their mobiles on them?"

"Definitely not. We leave our phones in the school office during lessons and can check them at lunchtime and at breaks. Also," he rubbed his brow, "the changing rooms are classified as no phone zones. All the students know they can't take their phones out of their bags in the changing rooms. It's an instant detention. Not that we can really enforce it."

"And as a staff member, Pete Parke would be well aware of this?"

"Of course, look, these boys that complained, they were probably miffed that a teacher broke the no phone rule when they'd get disciplined for it."

"Or, they were rightly concerned that someone who should know better, entered the changing room when they were getting undressed and that he was carrying a device that can take images and record film." Cooper got to her feet. "Please excuse me for a moment."

Alone in the corridor, Cooper placed a call to Superintendent Nixon.

"Cooper?"

"Sir, I'm at Tynemouth Academy. I'm going to bring one of the teachers in for questioning. A man named Pete Parke. His car's currently at the lab. I heard it was very recently valeted, which is suspicious enough, but I found graffiti concerning him and Rachel Pearson in the girls' toilets here as well as a report about a safeguarding violation."

"Be more specific, Cooper."

"Yes, sir. The graffiti implied Parke and Rachel had a sexual relationship, and a report made by two boys accused Parke of bringing his smartphone into the changing rooms. I think this, combined with the fact he drives an estate car, is enough—"

"Bring him in," said Nixon. "Do you need assistance?"

"Kowalski and Andrews are stationed here. I'll have them escort him to HQ."

"Okay. But Cooper, don't arrest him unless it's necessary. Try to get him to come in voluntarily. That way, we can run some background and give the lab time to work on the car without eating into the twenty-four hours we'll get if we arrest him."

"Good shout, sir. I'll see what I can do." Cooper knew she might not have a choice. If Parke refused to leave the school or suspected something was up, he'd be unlikely to come to the station voluntarily. It was worth a shot, though. She hung up and dialled Sam Sutherland's number.

"Boss?"

"Hey, Sam. You got a minute?"

"For you, I have two. Keaton and I are putting together a plan for tomorrow. We're going to find out who ordered the three pope outfits."

"Great, let me know what you decide. Anyway, you spent the most time with Rachel Pearson's diary, didn't you? Did you find anything about the school's PE teacher in there?"

"Parke? Not that I can recall. Want me to go back through it?"

"Please. Can you ask tech about her phone, too? See if there was any romantic communication between her and anyone other than Will Harper."

"Aye, no worries. What's going on? You suspect the PE teacher?"

Cooper sneezed and hoped she hadn't caught something. "Yeah. I'll have him in HQ within half an hour. Can you do me a favour and ask Tennessee to run a background check on him and have him pull up the guy's latest DBS check?"

DBS stood for the disclosure and barring service and was the standard check used in the UK for individuals working in schools and organisations where children and vulnerable adults were present.

"Aye. Anything else I can do you for?"

"No, that's it. I'll see you in a bit."

She hung up and re-entered Hutchins's office. "Brian, I'm going to ask Mr Parke to accompany me to the station."

"Good God. Are you arresting him?"

"Not yet. I understand he's teaching at the moment. Can you take me to him?"

A look of worry passed over the man's face. Having a member of his staff escorted off the premises while OFSTED were present was all he needed right now. He nodded, got to his feet and silently guided Cooper out a side door and across the school field to the sports hall known as the shed.

A basketball lesson was in full swing with rows of teenage boys and girls taking turns to dribble their balls up to the various hoops fastened to the walls and take their shots.

"Mr Parke," said Cooper as she approached. The man's eyes narrowed, and he wiped his palms on his Adidas joggers. Cooper spoke quietly so as to not attract too much attention from the class. "I'd like to ask you a few questions. Would you please accompany me to the station?"

"Now? I'm teaching a class."

"Mr Hutchins will have someone cover for you."

"But... Wait, am I...?" He looked around nervously. "Am I...?"

"You're helping us with our enquiries," suggested Cooper. "You want to help us, don't you?"

"Well, yes, of course."

"Then follow me."

The sound of basketballs being bounced off the wooden floor came to an abrupt stop, and thirty pairs of eyes followed Pete Parke as he shuffled out of the shed.

Cooper walked ahead and had a quick word with PC Kowalski before turning back to Parke. "This is Mr Parke; he's kindly agreed to help us with our enquiries. Could you drive him to HQ?"

Kowalski nodded and held the door to his squad car open. Parke's posture shifted, he swallowed nervously. Cooper wanted to keep him onside as long as she could so she adopted a softer voice and tried to put the man at ease, even though every instinct she had told her to cuff him.

"Mr Parke, this is PC Kowalski and PC Andrews. There'll give you a lift to the station and make sure you're comfortable. If you want tea, coffee or anything while you wait for me, just ask. We really appreciate your help. She laid a hand on his arm and the gentle gesture was enough to persuade Parke to get in the squad car.

COOPER KEPT PARKE PLIED with tea and chocolate digestives for over an hour while Tennessee worked his magic trawling various databases. The first thing he noticed was that Parke's latest DBS check should have been renewed two and a half years ago but it hadn't.

"What else can you tell me?" asked Cooper.

"Peter James Parke, aged fifty-two, married to Heather Parke, three children, two girls and a boy, youngest is sixteen, eldest is twenty-four. He left school at sixteen and played cricket professionally for Durham and Yorkshire, has two caps for England."

Cooper pulled a mildly impressed expression. "Go on."

"He retired from cricket at twenty-one after a rotator cuff injury - I got that from Wikipedia - before going back to college to train to become a teacher and has been at Tynemouth Academy for the last fifteen years. No criminal record, couple of speeding fines and police have been called to his home in Cullercoats a number of times over an ongoing dispute with his neighbour."

"What's the dispute about?"

"Anti-social behaviour. Loud music, keeping a Shetland pony in the back garden and letting it shit everywhere, throwing fag ends over the garden fence—"

"You're talking about the neighbour, right? Not Parke."

Tennessee laughed. "Yeah, the neighbour. Have you heard from Atkinson about the car yet?"

Cooper's chest warmed at the sound of Atkinson's name. She checked her phone and shook her head. "They're doing their best, but it takes time. Shall we pay our guest a visit then?"

Cooper and Tennessee headed to interview suite four where they found Parke dunking a chocolate biscuit into his tea. Around his mouth was a thin circle of dark chocolate. Cooper handed him a tissue and sat down opposite him.

"Thanks again for coming in and helping us, Mr Parke. This is DS Daniel. I hear you were quite the cricketing wiz? Played for England no less."

Parke studied Cooper. "Have you been running some sort of background check on me?"

"Not at all," she lied. "Leroy MacDonald mentioned it earlier while I was chatting to him."

The answer seemed to placate him and he returned to his packet of biscuits.

"What was it like teaching Rachel Pearson?"

Parke sighed. "It could be challenging. I mean, you know about her accident, right? I had to adapt a lot of the lesson plans so that she could still join in. We'd play walking football sometimes and I'd give her easier alternatives for some of the exercises."

"That's very inclusive of you."

"Well, I didn't want her to feel left out, you know."

"Did you ever give Rachel one-on-one training?"

He shook his head, the circle of chocolate was back around his lips.

"I saw on your desk that you have pictures of the netball and athletics teams. You must be very proud of their achievements."

"Oh yes." The man's eyes lit up. "Very proud. Well, you'll know how well the netball team are doing. Tina's one of the best wing attacks I've ever had the pleasure of coaching. So quiet off the court and so aggressive on it."

Cooper wanted to slap the man and tell him to keep her daughter's name out of his mouth. Tennessee must have sensed a change in Cooper because he took over the questioning.

"Shelly Smith was also on the netball team, wasn't she?"

"Yes, she was. Poor soul. Very talented girl, very talented. She was the team captain. Really understood tactics."

"The last time I spoke to you, you called her bitchy."

The corners of Parke's mouth turned down, and he lowered his eyes. "Yes, I did, didn't I? I'm not proud of that. Even if she could be that way inclined, it's no way to speak about a student, especially after what happened to her."

"And what about Jasmine Lee?" continued Tennessee. "You must have spent a lot of time with her?"

Again, his face lit up. Parke clearly loved talking about his prize athletes. Was he living vicariously through their achievements or did he enjoy talking about these girls for other reasons?

"Jasmine didn't run. She flew. She was like a comet. I called her The Bullet. She was devastated to only place second in the county trials. A real perfectionist, she was. Second was just never good enough for that one. I know she didn't apply herself as well as she could in some of her other subjects but she was an angel when it came to PE and games."

Cooper crossed her legs and smiled as if she was sharing the memories with Parke. "You must be very proud of what Jasmine and Shelly achieved?"

"Yes, of course I am. When Shelly joined Tynemouth she couldn't catch a ball to save her life, but by year ten she was captaining the school team."

"Is that why the photos are on your desk?"

Parke met her eyes and scrutinised her as if he wasn't sure if she was accusing him of something or not. Cooper kept her face neutral and waited to see how he would react.

"Yes," he answered with a questioning look. "I am extremely proud of the kids on the sports teams. Some of these kids, they're not good at academic stuff, struggle with maths and science and the like. If I can help them excel in sports, it gives them a sense of achievement that they're otherwise lacking. A purpose, if you will."

Cooper nodded in agreement and slid her phone across the desk. "I took this photograph earlier today. It's from the girls' toilets on the ground floor corridor."

Parke's face flushed beyond red. His cheeks turned to a purplish-blue. "I... I..." He swallowed. "I heard I was this year's punching bag, but I'd... I'd never..."

"What do you mean by punching bag, Mr Parke?" asked Tennessee.

"It's just kids being kids. You know what teenagers are like; there's always one teacher who gets more than their fair share of rumours being spread about them. It's obviously my turn."

"Obviously," repeated Tennessee, not letting an ounce of sarcasm slip into his voice.

"It was Catherine they went after last year. The rumour was that she was a lesbian. She's not, but she's not homophobic either, so when she brushed off the rumours and showed she wasn't bothered the kids must have got bored and moved on to me."

"Paedo Pete," said Cooper. "Not a good nickname to find yourself with. Do you think these rumours started after you took your smartphone into the boy's changing rooms?"

Parke slid his chair back a few inches and shoved his mug of tea away. "That was dealt with internally. How do you know about that?"

"Why did you have your phone on you, Pete? The changing rooms are designated no phone zones, correct?"

Parke looked from Cooper to Tennessee and back again. "Do I need a lawyer?"

"You're not under arrest."

"Well, it feels like I am." Parke stood up and took a step towards the door but found his exit blocked by Tennessee. Cooper now had no choice. If an individual helping police with their inquiries wanted to leave at any point they must be allowed to. If the police tried to stop said person from leaving, they must arrest him or her and let them know their rights.

"Mr Parke, I am arresting you on suspicion of four counts of murder. You do not have to say anything. But, it may harm your defence if you do not mention when questioned something which you later rely on in court. Anything you do say may be given in evidence."

Parke's mouth hung open, and he made a futile attempt to manoeuvre around Tennessee. Before Parke even knew what had happened, his hands had been cuffed behind his back.

"I want a lawyer!" His voice quivered between a snarl and a sob.

"And you are entitled to one, Mr Parke," said Tennessee. "I'll take you to the custody officer, who will brief you on your rights."

IT TOOK PARKE'S LAWYER two hours to arrive and a further hour to be fully briefed by his client. Cooper used the time to check in with Sutherland

and Keaton about their plan to intercept a delivery of pope outfits the next day. They'd been assigned a handful of PCs, had been in communication with the Royal Mail and seemed to have the whole thing under control. She grabbed a sorry-looking sandwich and a packet of salt and vinegar crisps from the canteen and called Atkinson from a quiet corner of the incident room.

"Erica."

"Hey, Justin. I'm just calling to keep you in the loop. We've arrested Pete Parke. I'm hoping you have some news regarding his car."

"I do, actually."

Cooper's heart raced.

"The car was thoroughly cleaned. I'd say it underwent two back-to-back valets given the amount of cleaning solution we found. Anyway, I can tell you that the tyre prints don't match any of the ones we found at Priors Haven."

"Shit."

"But," he continued, "I did find a long dark hair trapped between the cushions on the back seat."

"Jasmine Lee had long dark hair, so did Rachel Pearson."

"We're checking against the DNA samples we took from Jasmine and Rachel to see if they match."

"Any chance we can get those results in the next twenty hours?"

Atkinson made a sound as if stifling a laugh.

"It was worth a try," said Cooper. "Keep doing what you do and call me if you find anything else. Okay?"

"Naturally. Oh, and Erica?"

"Yes?"

"I'm really looking forward to this evening."

Cooper's heart raced again and she glanced around the room to make sure no one had noticed her Cheshire Cat grin.

"Me too."

Across the room, Keaton waved to her and called out, "Boss, the lawyer wants you."

Cooper picked up her files and made her way back to the interview suite, making sure to sweep the crisp crumbs from her suit jacket. She recognised Zach Hodge at once. He was a squat, mousy-haired man who spoke with a lisp and walked with a cane.

"I'm afraid this has been a waste of both of our times, DCI Cooper. Had you asked the most important question first, you'd know my client's alibi is airtight and you must release him at once."

Cooper felt as if she'd been sucker punched. She rested her back against the wall and cursed at her feet. "Go on then," she said, inviting Hodge to pass over the information he had gleaned. He was probably going to relish it as well.

"At the time of Rachel Pearson's murder on Tuesday the thirteenth, my client was at home with his wife and three kids. At the time of Michelle Smith's murder, he was, as you can probably guess, already at work. The school operate an electronic signing-in system. His time of arrival will be logged on the system."

"And on Monday night? I know he was involved in the search party. What about before and after?"

"My client was coaching an inter-school football match when he heard Jasmine and Reuben had gone missing. He went straight from the game to the search, where he helped until ten p.m. Afterwards, he had a drink in the Salutation Inn on Front Street. He's confident the barman will remember him as not many men drink rosé wine. He was back with his wife by ten fifty."

A string of expletives exploded in Cooper's head. The lawyer was right, this had been a massive waste of time and instead of bumbling on about photographs and graffiti, her first port of call should have been to establish any alibi. Zach Hodge's cane tapped against the floor as he waited for Cooper's response. No doubt his lawyer buddies would get a good laugh out of the stupid female detective who was letting her standards slip.

"He's not leaving until I can confirm his version of events with his wife, the school and the Salutation Inn. You're welcome to wait."

Hodge scoffed. "I have better things to do, detective. However, I will be calling to check up on my client. If he hasn't been released by four p.m. I will be back, and I will be very annoyed."

Cooper turned so he couldn't see her rolling her eyes.

- CHAPTER 28 -

AFTER A REFRESHING SHOWER and a liberal application of aromatherapy oils, Cooper joined Tina in the dining room where she found her daughter stirring a pot of massaman curry whilst simultaneously flicking through the Tarot Card Killer's case file.

The scent of lemongrass and coriander crashed over Cooper. "It smells like heaven in here," she said, taking the file from Tina. She stopped short of chastising her or even giving her a reproachful look. Tina was inquisitive by nature and telling her off for reading the file whilst she was cooking up a storm on her behalf would be ungrateful at best and shitty parenting at worst.

"It tastes like it too." Tina offered the spoon and Cooper took a slurp.

"Jesus. That's quite possibly the best curry I've ever tasted. You seriously taught yourself to make this?"

Cooper placed the file in her briefcase and lowered her eyebrows. She was certain she'd left the file locked in there. Time for a new access code, she thought, and this time she'd choose something less obvious than Tina's birthday.

Tina shrugged at the compliment as if whipping up a curry from scratch was no big deal. "I had a little help from YouTube."

Cooper's mind drifted back to a few summers ago when she and Tina had visited Cooper's parents in Lanzarote. An eleven-year-old Tina had read that Lanzarote was a Spanish Island and within two weeks had taught herself conversational Spanish. Sadly, she'd been too shy to utter a word of it to anyone outside her immediate family.

Tina nibbled on a cube of beef and tilted her head to the side for a moment as she considered the balance of ingredients. "I read about Mr Parke. The stuff written about him in the toilets; no one really believes it. Hell, Rachel probably wrote it herself."

"So, he's never made you feel uneasy?"

"God no," answered Tina as she double-checked the list of cooking instructions she'd scrawled down on a spiral-bound notepad.

"Because if he has, in any way, you know you can tell me?"

"I know, but he hasn't. Mr Parke's a great coach. Those rumours were made up by bitchy girls with nothing better to spend their time and energy on."

Cooper placed a hand on Tina's back. "As long as you're sure."

"I am. But Mum, it says in the file that you want to examine Linda's car. She's not a suspect as well, is she?"

"Well, we have a number of persons of int—"

persons of interest," she finished on Cooper's behalf while she made air quotes with her fingers. "I'm not a journalist; I'm your daughter. You can't really think Linda had anything to do with this. I mean, I know she's annoying and everything, and God knows what she and Dad see in each other..." Tina paused to look her mother up and down. "Is that what you're wearing?"

Cooper pulled a face and stared down at her jumper dress and leggings. "What's wrong with what I'm wearing?" She was comfortable and - most importantly - warm.

"It's a bit... No offence... Mumsy."

Cooper snorted. "News flash, Tina. I am a mum. Have been for fourteen years."

An eye roll of epic proportions followed as a pinch of salt was thrown into the pan. "You're also a badass detective with a pair of skinny jeans in your wardrobe that haven't seen the light of day for over six months." Tina glanced at her watch then pointed to the living room. "Go. Skinny jeans. Heels. Lose the wig. I'll set the table."

Cooper sighed and once again looked down at her outfit. Perhaps she was playing it a little too conservatively. "Okay," she conceded. "I'll change, but the wig stays."

Tina stuck out her lower lip. "Have it your way, but the buzzcut suits you better. Way more rock and roll. Anyway, go. He'll be here any second."

The scent of lemongrass followed Cooper to her bedroom. The skinny jeans had been relegated to the back of the lowest drawer in her dresser. They were creased and Cooper didn't have time to iron. She pulled off her leggings and tried the jeans. To her amazement, they still fit. She posed in front of the mirror; the creases were hardly noticeable now that the fabric had stretched over her thighs. She slipped her feet into a pair of nude heels and gave herself an approving nod. Not bad. No Kate Moss. But she scrubbed up all right.

Cooper grabbed a Guns and Roses t-shirt and sat down in front of the mirror. She took a long, deep breath and noticed that butterflies had started having a party in her stomach. She sat and stared at her reflection for over a minute. Anxiety built up in her gut until she thought, "Sod it," and pulled the wig from her head. She applied a layer of red lipstick and repeated the words *total badass* three times before heading back downstairs.

She can't have been out of the room for more than five minutes, but Tina had set the table, lit scented candles and dimmed the lights. Jazz played quietly in the background and tall, intelligent Justin Atkinson was staring longingly into the pot of massaman.

"Mum tells me you work in forensics," said Tina. Her voice was soft and quivered slightly.

Atkinson nodded. "That's right."

"That must be really interesting," said Tina. "I want to do something like that when I go to uni. Maybe not forensics but definitely something science-based."

Cooper was impressed. She understood how hard it was for Tina to strike up conversations with strangers; she was clearly pushing herself, and Cooper thoroughly appreciated the effort.

"Well, if you want any advice," started Atkinson before he noticed Cooper in the doorway. His jaw literally dropped. "Erica! You look... Well... Wow."

Cooper looked down self-consciously. "Thanks," she replied, colour flooding her cheeks. "It's all Tina's doing. She wouldn't let me wear what I picked out."

"That's because what you picked out made you look like a Sunday school teacher." Tina opened a bottle of wine and poured three glasses. When Cooper raised an eyebrow, she answered, "What? I was just telling Justin how you've been slaving over this meal for hours." Then she smirked.

There it was: Tina's craftiness. She'd make out Cooper was a domestic goddess in exchange for a glass of Gavi. It was a deal.

"Anyway," continued Tina. She dished out a portion of rice and spooned a large dollop of curry on top. "I'll leave you to it." She grabbed a knife and fork and turned to Atkinson. "It was nice to meet you."

Tina scurried off to her bedroom, and Cooper heard the faintest hint of the theme tune from a Netflix show start to play from upstairs. There was an awkward pause between Cooper and Atkinson. An undercurrent of chemistry kept in check by nerves and trepidation.

"So," began Cooper, shifting her weight and lifting her glass. "Cheers."

Atkinson clinked his glass against hers. "I hope you don't mind, but I have two rules for this evening."

Cooper took a sip and smiled. "Please tell me one of them is absolutely no work talk. The whole debacle with Parke today has me totally riled. "

"Bingo. No work talk."

"Well, I'll drink to that." Cooper took another sip and began to serve up two plates of food. "And the second?"

"No talk of exes." He ran his free hand through his hair and shook his head. "Elspeth's been on the blower today, yapping on about the boys needing to repeat a year at Edinburgh. Honestly, that woman. She wasn't concerned about their grades when she did a runner with that paella-eating toy boy of hers in the middle of their A-levels, and oh, see I've already broken the second rule."

He slapped his palm off his forehead and muttered something under his breath.

Cooper extended an arm and motioned for Atkinson to sit. She'd never met Elspeth Atkinson but she was picturing someone who looked rather like Margot Swanson. "If it helps," she said, "I'd be delighted not to hear the names Kenny, Neil, or Russell, or Aiden, or... Well, the less said about that, the better."

Atkinson sat. He looked rather dashing in the candlelight, and free from his white coveralls, he appeared much leaner.

"You've put my casserole to shame," Atkinson mused as he swallowed a mouthful of beef.

Cooper's mouth twitched with guilt, and she pushed the charade from her mind. She could confess to her culinary ineptitude another day. For now, she could be the chef in high heels.

"I like your t-shirt," he added between mouthfuls. "I remember buying Appetite for Destruction at the old HMV store in town. That must have been, Jeez, eighty-eight?"

"It came out in eighty-seven," said Cooper. "Great album. I've got it on vinyl. Nothing to play it on, of course, but I can't bring myself to chuck it out."

Atkinson was shovelling curry as if his life depended on it. Cooper couldn't blame him; it was beyond scrumptious. "Were you even born in eighty-seven?" he asked.

"Barely."

"How you managed to raise a teenager and rise to DCI by your age, I'll never know."

Cooper put down her fork for a moment. "I didn't have much of a choice. I was seventeen, Megadeath had just reformed, and I had Slipknot's Subliminal Verses playing on loop. One night I was flicking through my study diary to check when my next A-level module was due and I noticed something else was due. I was three weeks late."

Atkinson blew out a long sigh. "I can't imagine how scary that must have been at seventeen."

"I wasn't half as scared as Kenny. He was nineteen and, well I'd be breaking our rules if I talked about him so I'll move on. My parents helped me with Tina until I finished sixth form, but the second I got my results, they left for the Canaries, and I moved in with my gran. It had been their dream for as long as I could remember to open up a bar somewhere in the sunshine. I didn't want to be the one to stop them, so I told them I'd be fine and sent them on their way. I was eighteen, unemployed, living with a sixty-two-year-old and I had an infant to care for."

"Top up?" asked Atkinson, but he poured before Cooper could answer. "I'm beginning to see how you became so resilient."

"Gran was taking care of Tina one evening. I was out clubbing on the Quay Side with my best friend, Cynthia Howes. I used to call her Cindy. Anyway, it was my first night out clubbing since having Tina and we had a great time. It was three in the morning and when we left the club, I stopped by the curb to tie the laces on my boots, and I looked up just as she got into an altercation with a group of bikers over who was next in the taxi queue. One of them shoved her, and she fell off the quay and drowned in the river."

"Oh, Erica." Atkinson looked horrified. "And you were eighteen?"

"Yeah. Just a kid myself really. They never caught him - the man who pushed her. I described the man until I was blue in the face, told them which street he'd run off on and everything. There must have been fifty people in that taxi queue but they never caught him. I spent night after night crying to Gran about how it was criminal that the police hadn't charged anyone. In the end, she got so sick of my moaning, well I was grieving to be fair, but she told me, 'They're doing their best. If you think you can do better, go join the police.' So I did."

———

"Ahem."

The little cough woke Cooper from her dream. She blinked through sleepy eyes and tried to get her bearings. Tina was standing in the middle of the living room staring at her with her arms folded over her chest. She was dressed in her school uniform and had her bag ready to go.

Cooper assessed the situation. She'd fallen asleep on the sofa with her head resting on Atkinson's lap. He was still sound asleep and snoring softly with his head lolled backwards and his lips parted. It wasn't his best look.

"Could be worse," whispered Tina. "At least you're both dressed."

Cooper flashed her a look. "Boundaries," she hissed.

Her head was foggy and a quick glance around the room explained why. There were two empty bottles of wine on the mantlepiece and a couple of tumblers on a side table looked to contain whisky or brandy. After pouring her heart out and telling her life story to Atkinson, he'd reciprocated and they'd turned the sorry event into a drinking game. Sip every time someone mentions a former lover. Sip every time someone mentions work.

She pushed herself to seated and rubbed her hands over her face. She felt grubby and her jeans had dug into her waist, leaving a painful red line. A dawning realisation pulsated behind her eyes; she was about to spend another day hunting a sick psychopath, and the thought of it made her stomach churn. Would all the children of Tynemouth make it safely to their beds this evening?

"Tina, listen. I'm not sure I want you going to school today. How about you come to the station instead? Hang out in the family room?"

"But it's Wednesday."

"And?"

"And Wednesdays are the best. I have maths and double art. And I can't miss chemistry if I'm going to do it at A-level. Mr Price said I need eights and nines if I want to do a science subject at uni."

Cooper could still taste chillies. Bits of rice were caught in her teeth and she had a headache forming behind her eyes. She remembered kissing Atkinson last night. Oh God, they'd kissed - a lot - and all the time she had nuggets of rice in her teeth. Big, sloppy, tongues-down-each-other's-throats, rice-in-their-teeth kisses.

Classy, Erica. Very classy, thought Cooper. She turned her eyes back to Tina, "I'd just prefer it if you had a day off and came to the station."

"Locked in the family room? Sounds more like I'm the one under arrest." Tina's words were still whispered, but her voice was increasing in pitch.

"Is there any chance I can get you to think of it as being under police protection?"

Tina threw herself into an armchair and huffed. "You can't seriously be concerned about Linda? Just tell the guys you have guarding the school not to let her in if she shows up. Besides, I promised Josh I'd help him with his biology—" She paused and mulled something over for a moment. "I'll come to the station if Josh can come too."

Cooper got to her feet. "Nice try. Give me ten minutes and I'll drive you in. I want texts between every class, and I'll have your dad pick you up."

"But—"

"No buts. Now be an angel and make some coffee."

- CHAPTER 29 -

"I AM SPEAKING TO the people of Tynemouth and North Shields. If you know something, say something. If you suspect something, you need to say something."

Cooper lifted her chin and spoke into the television cameras and flashing bulbs of press photographers. It was early afternoon and her stomach was starting to rumble. Hopefully, the microphones wouldn't pick it up. She sat behind a row of tables with the parents of Rachel, Shelly, Jasmine and Reuben, as well as Oliver Martin and a horse-faced member of the press office named Blair Potts. Behind her, a backdrop of royal blue was emblazoned with the badge of Northumbria Police and the slogan 'Proud to protect.'

Lisa Smith and Lou Pearson had delivered tearful statements whilst journalists from the length and breadth of the country took notes or held out microphones. Jasmine and Reuben's parents were too distressed to read their statements so Blair Potts read them on their behalf. For the entire duration Sally Pearson gripped her husband's hand so tightly it caused her arm to shake. She was glassy-eyed and still had the not-quite-present look of someone taking a lot of sedatives.

"We wish to speak to anyone who was near the Spanish Battery at half seven on the evening of Tuesday the thirteenth of November," continued Cooper. "Whittingham Road on the morning of Thursday the fifteenth of November; or on Front Street at five-thirty p.m. on Monday the nineteenth of November."

Cooper lowered her eyes for a moment, then closed her file and tucked it under her arm. "The smallest detail, no matter how insignificant it may seem, could hold the key to solving these murders. Someone is targeting our children. He is someone's son, someone's husband, or someone's father. If you know something, say something. Thank you."

Cooper stood, bowed her head and walked away to a flurry of camera flashes. Blair Potts tapped her microphone, cleared her throat and read out the number for the confidential hotline.

"Sir." Cooper chased Superintendent Nixon along a corridor. He was a lanky man with a paunch that hung over his belt, and his skin had the unhealthy greyish quality of someone who spent little time outdoors. As Cooper caught up with him she saw he was on the phone.

"We're chronically understaffed, dammit," he huffed. "Got at least half a dozen bleeders on maternity."

Cooper's eyes formed into thin slits. Nixon thought calling female officers 'bleeders' was nothing more than harmless banter. He felt the same way when he referred to the newest recruits as fresh meat or his elderly secretary as a coffin dodger. He was of the generation where referring to females on the force as women, ladies - or God forbid - officers, was political correctness gone mad, and no amount of sensitivity training was ever going to change that.

When he hung up, Nixon seemed surprised to see Cooper by his side. "How long have you been there?"

"Long enough," she responded.

"Ah, right." He straightened up and looked down at her; he hadn't trimmed his nose hair in a while. "What can I do for you?"

"You wanted an update, sir. Keaton and Sutherland are staking out Morrison's in Tynemouth. Some pope outfits are due to be delivered to the In-Post lockers between two and half-past."

"Is it our man?" He opened the door to his office but didn't invite Cooper in. Behind him, Cooper spied Commissioner Begum sat in Nixon's leather seat and Chief Constable Davison sat to his right. They were deep in conversation; voices lowered and heads tilted towards each other.

"I'm not sure, sir. I don't know why he would order three of the costumes. Either way, we'll know soon enough."

"Vests?"

"Yes, and a couple of PCs."

Nixon stood aside so Cooper could get a better look at the men in his office. "DCI Erica Cooper, meet PCC Amir Begum and CC Henry Davison."

Cooper stood to attention and Nixon looked like the effort of not looking phased was about to make him burst into flames.

"CC Davison wishes to shadow the investigation today. I think it would be a good idea for him to accompany detectives Keaton and Sutherland to Morrison's. Get to know the team and the lay of the land."

Cooper's jaw clenched. She didn't have a choice here; she could tell by the tone of Nixon's voice that he wasn't to be pressed on the matter. He didn't want CC Davison interfering with the sting, but equally, Nixon didn't want Davison watching over his shoulder every second. Keaton was going to blow her top and Cooper couldn't blame her.

She slid her jaw from side to side to loosen it up. "I'll arrange an extra vest and a car to take him over there," she said reluctantly.

Nixon looked visibly relieved. He shut his door and muttered, "Good, good. Thank you, Cooper."

Cooper stared at the door for a moment before whispering, "My pleasure," and walking off towards CID.

Tennessee looked up from his computer screen. "Christ. You've got bags under your eyes big enough to carry my weekly shop. Been burning the midnight oil?"

"Lovely to see you, too," Cooper replied through pursed lips. "Actually, I had a friend over for dinner. I might have had a touch too much wine."

Tennessee wiggled his eyebrows but stopped short of pushing his luck with any form of innuendo. Instead, he pushed a cup of steaming coffee towards Cooper.

"Cheers. What's new?"

Tennessee sighed. "Not much. Hayley's got it into her head we should raise the baby vegan once he's weaned."

Cooper perched on the edge of the desk and scanned his computer screen. "Christ. Is that healthy for babies?"

"No idea. I'm going to look into it, though. If the doc says it's okay, then I'll not argue. Happy wife, happy life and all that. Can't promise I won't sneak him the odd BigMac now and again."

"I'd be disappointed if you didn't." Cooper tilted the screen so she could get a better look. "Still trawling through social media?"

"Trying to find any other links between the victims. Been at it all morning. I'm going through their recent check-ins."

"Anything promising?"

Tennessee shrugged. "A couple. They've all checked in at Crusoe's recently. You know, the cafe down on Long Sands beach. Jasmine and Shelly both checked-in regularly at the rugby club, they used the gym there, and they were all at the same beach party last month. There're pictures from Jasmine's secret Instagram account showing half the year elevens drinking and smoking down at King Edward's Bay."

"Was anyone in the photos taking drugs? Or did any of them appear high?" Cooper shifted her weight. "I'm wondering if there's a drugs connection; perhaps they owed money to the wrong people."

"Hard to say." Tennessee clicked his mouse a couple of times, brought up the account and zoomed in on a few pictures. "I didn't spot anything other than beer cans and a bottle of Absolut. I'll ask tech to enhance some of the snaps. See if the cigarettes really are cigarettes but to be fair, it's not like Tynemouth kids are short of a bob or two. They'd have to be ordering in some big amounts to be in any serious debt."

"The Pearsons weren't wealthy," answered Cooper, thinking of their dilapidated semi. "And Lisa Smith was raising Shelly on her own. Even with a military pension, that can't be easy."

Tennessee shrugged. "Aye. Maybe you're right."

Maybe she was, but something was niggling at Cooper. There was a doubting feeling at the base of her skull. It might be the hangover but she couldn't help feeling that she should have solved this case by now. Was she rusty from her absence? She must be or she wouldn't have made such a glaring error with Parke. Something was off. She was missing something, or going about the case in the wrong way. Cooper took a gulp of coffee and sneered. The coffee machine in CID was no Starbucks, that was for sure.

Opening the case file, Cooper turned to the notes she'd made about Rachel Pearson. "I knew it," she said. "We took details about Rachel's routine when we interviewed the Pearsons. She had weekly physio sessions for her back. The physio worked out of the rugby club."

Tennessee sucked in a lungful of air.

"Google the gym for me," Cooper asked.

Tennessee clicked and brought up a website. "What we looking for?"

"I'm not sure. Just keep scrolling."

The gym offered studio classes, a boot camp and a spin class. It was fitted with free weights, resistance machines and cardio equipment. Happy, stick-thin women with mega-watt smiles posed with muscle-bound Adonis wannabes. Their website was sleek and encouraged you to sign up at every opportunity.

"Stop," said Cooper. She pointed to the spinning timetable. "There."

"Spin class. Mondays, Wednesdays and Fridays at six-thirty with Duncan Clark." Tennessee's eyes flicked to Cooper's. "Dunk the Hunk?"

"Could well be." Cooper stood up and slopped coffee over herself. "Dammit." She dried her hands on her suit and turned to her DS. "Fancy a work-out?"

-CHAPTER 30-

A HERRING GULL WITH a gammy leg cawed in the face of an Alsatian that dared wander too close to the remains of a Subway sandwich which she was guarding. The sandwich was hers, and she'd defend it to the death.

DS Paula Keaton admired the bird. For some reason, it reminded her of herself in her rugby-playing heyday. She'd never been scared to take on the biggest women on the pitch. Usually, it was the opposite; she'd make a beeline for the burliest member of the opposition and stamp her authority down with a vicious tackle the moment the opportunity arrived. She'd quickly earned herself the nickname Pitbull Paula.

An L-shaped carpark wrapped two sides of Morrison's supermarket. Keaton was stationed at the sliding doors that marked the entrance to the lobby. She leant back against the wall and pretended to play on her phone. Her eyes continuously

flicked between the wall of lockers and the sliding doors where she could still watch the lockers,
only this time, in the reflection of the glass. Sam
Sutherland was resting against the opposite wall.
He was pretending to read the morning paper and
perfectly took to the role of bored husband waiting
for his missus to finish her shopping.

Keaton had the same nervous energy coursing through her veins that she used to feel before an important match. Her legs twitched and
her heart rate skyrocketed. She prayed whoever
opened locker sixteen was their man. Her compet-
itive ego craved victory. She wanted to be the one
to catch him, she wanted the thrill and adoration
of catching the killer, but more than anything, she
just wanted the sick son of a bitch off the streets
and in HMP Frankland. As a killer of children, the
Tarot Card Killer would be dealt with by the justice
system of the other inmates. If he were disembow-
elled with a rusty nail - as horrific a thought that it
was - he wouldn't be the first.

Until the death of Reuben Jones, Keaton had
managed to keep her emotions in check. Well,
mostly she had. The killer appeared to only target
girls until Reuben went missing. Reuben was the
same age as Keaton's youngest brother - Riley - and
he looked a bit like him too. She tightened her fist
at the thought of someone laying a finger on her
sweet, softly-spoken brother and swallowed down
the rage that filled her.

Keaton, Sutherland and two PCs who were waiting in an unmarked car had been at the supermarket since one. The Chief Constable had flounced

in at half past and had tried to take over. Keaton sweet-talked him back to the car and told him that everything was under control. What she'd wanted to say was that until she was instructed otherwise she would only take orders from Cooper, that this was her stakeout, and that she didn't need some geriatric in a fancy suit poking his beak in and ruining the sting.

The Royal Mail had delivered the package at ten past two and they'd been keeping an eye on the locker ever since. Keaton was becoming increasingly antsy and was struggling to stay still. She spent the last couple of hours flittering between anticipation and unbearable boredom. Her adrenaline levels had spiked shortly after three when an elderly lady approached the lockers and used a code to open locker twelve but there'd been no action since.

Sutherland turned a page of his newspaper; it was their code for 'heads up.' Keaton's eyes found a tall male in a black baseball cap, black hoodie and grey jeans. His feet were at least a size ten. He stopped in front of the lockers and took out his mobile. Keaton was between the man and one set of sliding doors. She faked a yawn and stretched her arms above her head, a signal to the officers in the car to stand by. Sutherland dropped his paper into a shopping trolley and moved in from the man's rear.

This is it, thought Keaton. Her chest heaved against the stab vest she wore under her coat, reminding her how dangerous this man could be. She felt like every nerve ending was primed and ready for action. Edging forward, she watched the man type in his access code. The screen changed and writing appeared: *Locker 16 is now open. Have a great day.*

Would he run? Would he fight? Was he carrying a weapon?

The moment the man reached in the locker to retrieve the pope outfits, Keaton clamped a heavy hand on his right shoulder. "Police," her voice boomed. "Don't move."

- CHAPTER 31 -

COOPER'S MAZDA SMELLED OF McNuggets and it didn't take a detective to work out why. Tennessee finished his last chicken nugget in one bite and crumpled the box into an impossibly small ball. Fast food didn't compare to massaman curry but there was nothing quite like Mcdonald's when you needed to soak up last night's wine. They'd visited the drive-thru in the neighbouring retail park and eaten while they drove to LeanLife Gym at the local rugby club.

Cooper finished the box of fries she'd been balancing in her lap whilst watching snowflakes dance in front of the car's windscreen. The temperature had dropped again, and in the time it had taken her to finish her food, the thin dusting of snow that covered the gym's car park had thickened into a blanket. There was something very naughty about eating fast food in a gym car park and she wondered how many of LeanLife's members had done the same. When the last fry disappeared, Cooper checked her phone. She had three increasingly sarcastic texts from Tina as well as a text from Atkinson. He said he'd had a lovely time and hoped to do it again soon. He'd signed off with JA and a heart emoji.

Heat swept up from Cooper's chest to her cheeks. She suppressed a smile and filed the giddy feeling away for now. The sun was starting to set, and as much as she wanted to think about Atkinson, there was tension building in her stomach as the end of the school day approached. How many students would make it back to class tomorrow?

Tennessee walked slightly ahead and held the door for Cooper. A small reception area was staffed by a woman in a cropped top. Her bare belly was taught, tanned and pierced.

Dressing for the weather, thought Cooper.

"Welcome to LeanLife," beamed the receptionist. The woman took in the striking man who stood before her and she battered her - presumably fake - eyelashes at him. "Are you interested in membership?"

Beyond the reception desk, Cooper spotted the triangular frame of Will Harper. He was working out in the free weights area, grunting and gurning his way through a set of bicep curls. He put the weights down and puffed up his chest when he saw the detectives watching him. It was a silverback display by the runt of the litter.

"That damn kid is everywhere we turn with this investigation," said Tennessee. He turned to the receptionist and showed her his ID. "No, thank you.

DS Jack Daniel and DCI Erica Cooper. We need to speak to the manager."

The woman's smile vanished - she wasn't about to sell two annual memberships - but the rest of her face held the paralysed look of someone who had recently used botox.

"I *am* the manager," she said with a hint of insult to her voice. She held out a hand. "Robyn Watson. What's going on?"

Tennessee glanced at Cooper to see if she wanted to take the lead. She gave him a subtle nod, encouraging him to continue.

"We're investigating the murders of some of your members: Rachel Pearson, Michelle Smith, and Jasmine Lee."

Robyn's hand flew to her mouth but her forehead didn't budge. "Oh my goodness. I thought I recognised the blonde girl from somewhere. Did... Did they all go here? You don't think... The killer... He's not?"

"That's what we'd like to find out," said Tennessee, reading what Robyn was trying to say. "Could you check your records? I'd like to know if Reuben Jones had a membership here."

She turned to her computer. Her long nails *tip-tapped* over the keys, then she turned the monitor to face them. "Three members named Jones, but no Reubens."

Will Harper was still peacocking around the gym and constantly turning back to the reception area to see if he was being watched. He was a tempestuous, possessive young man and Cooper didn't trust him as far as she could throw him. Why did all roads lead to Will Harper? He should be in school at this time of the day. Then again, so should over eight hundred other kids.

"Can you find out the last time the girls were in the gym?" asked Tennessee.

Robyn nodded. "The system logs everyone's attendance." She began searching the database and printed off a list of the girls' recent gym sessions.

Cooper scanned the list. "Shelly was here the night before she was killed. So was Jasmine. Do you have cameras here, Robyn?"

Robyn Watson's nostrils flared. Cooper pondered if she was annoyed at the intrusion or if she could smell the junk food on their breath.

"We do. We have two in the gym and one in the studio. We only keep the footage for a month unless there's a problem."

Cooper propped her elbows on the desk. "I'd like to see any footage you have from Wednesday the fourteenth of November." She checked the list that Robyn had given her. "From about four p.m.? That's when Shelly and Jasmine arrived."

LeanLife's manager pulled on a zip-up hoodie and finally covered her midriff. "We'll have to go to the back office. Follow me." She propped a *Back In Ten Minutes* sign on the counter and led Cooper and Tennessee to a dingy box room that smelled of deodorant, Mary Jane, and if Cooper wasn't mistaken, sex.

It didn't take long for Robyn to find the footage Cooper was after. The detectives watched as greyscale images of Jasmine and Shelly moved around the gym. The heads of a number of men swivelled as the girls walked past the weights area and climbed onto neighbouring exercise bikes.

"Do you recognise this man?" asked Tennessee. He pointed at a man who didn't just follow the girls with his eyes. He walked closely behind them and chose the elliptical trainer directly behind their exercise bikes.

"Hmm," said Robyn. "I think so. Can't think of his name off the top of my head, but if I take a look at the attendance log for that time and look at the photos we have on file, I'll be able to get a name for you."

"Thanks," said Tennessee. "If we could do the same for these men as well, that would be great." He pointed at a few others who hadn't been able to keep their eyes in their heads.

Cooper watched the footage as a man in a Lean-Life polo shirt stopped and talked to Jasmine and Shelly for a few moments. When he left, the girls appeared to giggle and whisper something to one another.

"Who's that?"

"That's one of our instructors."

"Duncan Clark?"

"Yes," said Robyn. Her voice was suspicious, and had she been able to lower her brows, she would have. "How did you know that?"

"We need to speak to him. Is he here?" Cooper asked.

Robyn checked the clock on the wall. "He's leading a boxercise class. He'll be finished in five minutes."

It was almost fifteen minutes later when Duncan Clark appeared in the reception area. He wasn't the most attractive man Erica had ever laid eyes on. Still, he had an air of confidence about him, and his toned physique, strong jaw and dark skin tone reminded Cooper of the boxer, Anthony Joshua. She could quite see the attraction.

Duncan wiped his neck with a towel and acknowledged the detectives. "The boss said you needed to see me. Said you're detectives?"

Cooper showed him her ID. "That's right, Mr Clark." Then she showed him a picture of Rachel Pearson. "Do you recognise this girl?"

He took a long, hard look at the photograph. "Aye. She's called Rach. Comes here once, maybe twice a week. Haven't seen her recently, though. She's usually with Benji, our physio."

Cooper took out photographs of Jasmine and Shelly. "What about these two?"

Duncan laughed. "Those two are trouble."

"What do you mean?" asked Cooper, noting his use of the present tense.

"Terrible flirts. The pair of them. I guess it's an occupational hazard, having young women throw themselves at me."

Tennessee lifted his chin. "You sound proud."

"It's not like that," said Duncan. He raised his hands in surrender. "Honestly. If it were the other way round and I was a female instructor and those two were men..." He stopped himself. "Look, they're not my type. What are they? Like seventeen? Eighteen?"

"They're fifteen."

"Oh, shit." Duncan's mouth hung open, and his eyes doubled in size. "Is that what this is about? Have they accused me of something?"

Tennessee looked to be struggling to hide his incredulousness. "No, Mr Clark. They're dead. They were murdered. Rachel too."

He stepped backwards, shaking his head. "No. No, that can't be."

"I'm afraid it's true," said Cooper, "and they'd mentioned you in a number of messages. We're going to need to... Mr Clark? Are you all right? Do you need to sit down?"

Duncan Clark's eyelids fluttered, his irises rolled backwards and he collapsed onto the gym's laminate flooring.

"WHAT DO YOU THINK?" asked Cooper after Robyn Watson had moved Dunk the Hunk to the physio room for a lie-down.

"He's either a good actor or he's been living under a rock for the past week and a half. I can believe not watching the news or never reading a paper, but this story has been everywhere." Tennessee stopped to watch the local first-team run sprints across the rugby pitch. A bit of snow wasn't going to stop these guys from training. Incredibly they were still in shorts and t-shirts. "He voluntarily gave us his phone, and he had an alibi for Monday evening."

Cooper's jacket pocket began to vibrate. She retrieved her phone from her pocket and glanced at the screen. It was Keaton. Hopefully, she had good news.

"Paula?"

"Boss. The In-Post locker was a dud."

Cooper cursed under her breath and looked to the darkening sky. "You sure?"

"Pretty darn sure. The pope outfits were for a bloody tarts and vicars party."

"Tarts and vicars? Are you kidding me?"

Tennessee was pulling faces, so Cooper switched to speakerphone.

"The guy's name is Fin Hamilton. Twenty years old and the captain of Northumbria Uni's ultimate frisbee team."

"Ultimate what?"

"Frisbee. Apparently, it's a thing now. Anyway, Northumbria played Newcastle last week, and Northumbria won the fixture so they get to dress as the clergy at this social thing and Newcastle's team have to go in drag."

Cooper didn't know whether to laugh or cry. What a waste of their time and resources.

"When he realised why we'd cornered him, the kid started freaking out. Wet himself. I'm not joking. Bloody pissed all over Morrison's lobby. They had to get wet floor signs and everything. I'm going to call the universities and Hamilton's teammates as soon as I hang up here and make sure his story checks out, but I think we'll be letting him go within the hour."

"God damn it. I was hoping you had him."

"Me too, boss. Me too. How'd it go at your end?"

"We found Dunk the Hunk," Cooper said.

"And he fainted," added Tennessee. "Managed not to piss himself, though."

Keaton snorted out of the phone. "And he's not our guy?"

"I don't think so. We have a few things to follow up on but it's looking less and less like it. Hold on a sec, Paula, we're going to freeze to death." Cooper opened the car doors and she and Tennessee climbed in. The engine roared to life and Cooper turned the heating up to its highest setting. "You still there?" she asked once her phone had synced to the car's Bluetooth.

"I am."

"So what the bloody hell are we missing?" asked Cooper. Kenny's name flashed on her phone's screen and she tapped a button to send him to voicemail. She couldn't stand the thought of going to bed that night not knowing if she might wake up to the news that some poor kid had been strangled to death and dressed up as a hierophant.

"Let's start at the beginning," said Tennessee. "Rachel Pearson, killed after her yoga class, dressed as a magician and left in a boat at Prior's Haven. A former gymnast who broke her cervical spine, had physio here at the rugby club and dated Will Harper."

Cooper drummed her fingers on the steering wheel. "Michelle Smith, known as Shelly, suffocated in her own home after her mother left for work that morning. Dressed as a priestess. Worked out at the same gym, captain of the netball team and was also involved with Will Harper."

"Then there was Jasmine and Reuben," said Keaton. "Taken after attending an after-school arts club and going for fish and chips with a friend. Killed in the early evening, Reuben was stabbed and Jasmine was strangled. They were kept somewhere until around four forty in the morning and moved to the track behind the park. A witness saw a dark-coloured estate car pick up Jasmine and Reuben and we have door-cam footage of what is presumably the same car."

"What other evidence do we have?" asked Tennessee. He clenched his fists and flexed his fingers in front of the heater vents a couple of times. "We have a print from Reuben but the killer isn't in the system. There was charcoal residue on Rachel and a hair that could belong to Jasmine in Pete Parke's car."

"But Parke had an alibi for the times of each of the murders," said Cooper. Frustration was taking hold, and she could feel the beginnings of a tension headache. "You know. When I visited Linda Webb on Tuesday she was making a smoothy. One of the things she put in it was activated charcoal."

"You're shitting me?" asked Tennessee. "And she's still giving us the run around?"

"But," said Keaton before Cooper could confirm. "We're almost certain that the killer's male. Based on the fact he crushed Rachel's windpipe and overpowered Reuben. He was also able to not only move the bodies but to dress and style them, and in Rachel's case, lift her into a sailing boat."

Cooper closed her eyes and sighed. "You're right. I'm not sure Linda Webb's strong enough to move those bodies, but she isn't the smallest of women either, and let's not forget she had no alibi for the time of Jasmine and Reuben's death, or the times their bodies were moved. What else do we have on the killer?"

"The tarot card obsession," said Tennessee, who was still warming his hands. "He, *or she*, is on some sort of a journey. Isn't that what the old woman told you, Coop? That he's killing young people to absorb their youthful energy in some bid for immortality."

"Or as I like to put it," said Keaton, "he's a few pasties short of a Greggs."

Tennessee took his warmed hands and cupped them over his cheeks. "Nutter or not, he has a flair for the dramatic. He's leaving bodies all over Tynemouth like it's some sort of grotesque sculpture garden."

Sculpture, thought Cooper before repeating it aloud. "Sculpture, sculpture, sculpture. You know, when Rachel's body was discovered, I described it as having been dumped in the boat but Atkinson corrected me, saying the body had been displayed."

"He wants the world to see his work," said Tennessee with a nod.

"Because this is, what, his art?" asked Keaton.

"Fuck," said Cooper. The inside of her chest began to thunder with heart palpitations. "Are you thinking what I'm thinking?"

Tennessee nodded. "And the charcoal residue on Rachel's skin. Keaton, are you by a computer?"

"Looking at one right now."

"Look up that PVP chemical. See if it's found in glue?"

"I can tell you now, it is. glue-sticks and spray adhesives, fixatives, hairspray."

"Fucking hell!" Cooper shifted into first gear and wrestled the old Mazda across the Rugby club's icy car park. "He's treating the bodies as art projects, and the victims had trace amounts of art materials on them. Brian Fucking Hutchins."

Kenny's name flashed on the mobile's screen again. Cooper placed Keaton on hold for a second. "Not now, Kenny. I'm following a lead," she snapped.

Kenny's voice was breathy and low, and his tone chilled Cooper to the bone. "Erica. I can't find Tina."

- CHAPTER 32 -

NOW IT WAS COOPER who felt like fainting. Not Tina. Not her baby girl.

"Kenny? What are you saying?"

"She's missing, Erica. I went to pick her up from netball club but it was cancelled. I must have called her fifty times. She's not picking up."

Cooper gasped for breath but none came. Had Tina been missing since half three? That was over an hour ago. She stammered but the words got caught in her breath. Tennessee's hand fell on her shoulder and he took over the conversation.

"This is DS Jack Daniel. Have you checked Cooper's home?"

"Yes. Yes. I've just come from there."

"I'll call it in. We're heading straight to the school. Kenny, are you okay to drive?"

There was a moment of hesitation. "Yes."

"Check everywhere you can think of. I've heard Cooper mention Tina going to Woods cafe and the library on Front Street. Check the boyfriend's house and call all of her friends. Then you need to go to Cooper's and wait there in case Tina shows up."

"Like hell am I waiting around."

Cooper manhandled the car onto Queen Alexandra Road. The parent part of her personality was battling with the detective part. The parent wanted to cry. She wanted her bright little girl back in her arms, but if that was to happen, she had to be the detective.

"Do as you're told, Kenny. Go to Front Street, call Josh and get back to mine."

She hung up and jumped into the driver's seat while Tennessee made some calls. She drove as fast as she could on the snowy roads and heard her DS request backup.

"Oliver, it's Jack. What car does Hutchins drive? A Mini? Right, check if any other cars are registered to his address or if he access to any other cars. Now, dammit."

The car skidded as it turned into Tynemouth Academy and bumped a Mini Countryman that was still in the otherwise deserted carpark.

"That's his car. He's still here," whispered Cooper.

"Thanks, Oliver," said Tennessee as he ended the call and turned to Cooper. "Hutchins lives with his mother. She drives a dark blue Volvo V60."

PCs Andrew Underwood and Nate Lewis met them at the car but Cooper barely noticed them. Her breath billowed around her face as she stepped out of the car and began running across the forecourt towards the sports fields and the gymnasium that the students liked to call the shed.

The men followed closely behind. Cooper could hear their boots crunching through the snow. She grabbed a lamp post and slid around it, bringing herself to a standstill.

"Wait," she said, extending an arm to her side and almost clotheslining Tennessee. She pointed to footprints in the snow. They were small and shaped like women's shoes. Some heeled, some flat, some with pointed toes.

"There. You see?"

Tennessee and the other officers turned their heads downwards and studied the snow-covered tarmac.

"The footprints, there're at least eight sets." Cooper pointed a finger and traced the route. "They get to the door, then they change their minds and turn towards the school gate."

"Not all of them, Coop." Tennessee pointed at a lone set of footprints that belonged to a pair of flats. The prints turned in the opposite direction.

PC Underwood approached the door to the shed and read a paper note that was pinned to the door. "Says here, *Netball cancelled this week. No* coach."

"I'm guessing Parke wanted a day off after we marched him out of here and accused him of being a paedophilic serial killer," said Tennessee. Snowflakes danced around his head and caught in his hair.

"*We* didn't do that. *I* did. It was my mistake." Cooper followed the lone set of prints around a corner and stopped when she saw them meet a larger set of prints. There were signs of a scuffle and handprints in the snow. Taking a torch from her keyring, Cooper illuminated the snowy ground and yelped at the sight of snow that had been tinged pink from blood.

"Here," grunted Underwood. He pointed to a rock that was about the size of his fist. It was covered in viscous red liquid.

"The prints lead back inside," Tennessee remarked. "It looks like she was dragged in."

Cooper made to run towards the school but Tennessee held her back. "Coop. We're dealing with a dangerous killer. We're not wearing vests. We can't just go—"

Cooper pulled away from him. There was no way she was waiting for backup. Not when it was her own daughter's life at stake. She slipped into the lobby, wincing as the soles of her wet shoes squeaked on the tiled floor of the lobby. She stopped to remove her shoes, wanting to stay silent for now. Tennessee followed suit and spoke calmly into his handheld radio. Cooper could hear Sutherland's voice crackle in response.

"I've just arrived at the school. The other units aren't far behind."

Cooper mouthed her instructions to Tennessee. "Tell him to surround the school and seal the exits."

She turned her gaze to a photo of Brian Hutchins, smiling down at her from a display of all the school staff. She wanted to punch a hole in it. Her endocrine system released a torrent of hormones and she felt like a lioness protecting her cub. Cooper would fight tooth and nail if that's what it took. Did Hutchins know Webb would jump ship when the bodies started to mount up? Surely his motivation for murder went beyond simply wanting her job? Cooper and Tennessee turned on the spot, four corridors branched off from the main lobby, and two sets of staircases led the way to the upper floors.

Tynemouth Academy was not a small school by any stretch of the imagination. The cuboid building had three floors of classrooms, offices, studios and laboratories. At full capacity, the school held over two-thousand pupils and over 150 members of staff. It served not only the village of Tynemouth but the neighbouring towns of North Shields and Whitley Bay. With a building of this scale, it was hard to know where to start.

Outside, Sam Sutherland hugged the external wall of the school building as he approached and he stuck to the shadows until he reached the lobby.

"Christ. Cooper, are you okay?"

It was a ridiculous question. She was far from okay. Her girl had been taken by a madman. A man she was supposed to trust and who had killed four of her classmates. How would Sutherland feel if it had been Caroline? No, was the answer. She was not okay.

Cooper pushed her negativity to the back of her mind. She had to stay in police mode. "What areas of the building have lights on?" she asked.

"We did a lap as we approached. Keaton's watching the doors on the western side of the building and Martin's not too far away. He's in a squad car with Nixon." He was out of breath and needed to take a second before he could continue. "The eastern side on the ground floor. There're a few lights still on there, the first floor too, almost directly above. There's a cleaner making her way along the top floor. She's turning off lights as she goes, and we think we saw someone still working in the labs."

Cooper looked down the corridor that led to the art department. The hallway headed east, towards the North Sea, and towards the illuminated windows. "Do we have numbers?" she asked.

"More arriving every second," said Sutherland.

"Have a team come in and clear any remaining staff. Keep everyone without a badge away from the art department."

"Roger." Sutherland spoke into his radio for a moment then followed Cooper.

She led Sutherland and Tennessee along the darkened corridor. They moved quietly, checking each abandoned classroom as they went.

Cooper's mouth was dry; her heartbeat pulsated in her ears. She was acutely aware that she was unarmed. They'd come straight from questioning a gym instructor, and there'd been no time to organise guns or even tasers. The three detectives got into formation when they reached the door they were looking for, the two larger men flanking their underweight chief. They listened for a moment but no sound came from the other side of the door. Cooper gave the nod and Tennessee charged in, followed by Cooper and Sutherland. It didn't take long to establish that the room was empty. No one was here. Instead, they were surrounded by freshly painted clay pots and some sculptures made of soda cans and tin foil.

"Fuck." Cooper was beyond terrified. "Where is she?"

"Let's head upstairs," suggested Sutherland. He pointed at the ceiling and then frowned, his eyes flicking back down to the floor. "I thought that was paint, but it's not. It's blood."

A breadcrumb trail of red droplets snaked across the tiled floor, and Cooper struggled to keep the panic at bay. For years it had only been her and Tina. No parents around, no Kenny, no siblings to act as aunts and uncles. If she lost Tina, she lost everything. Something primal surged through her and she let out an almighty roar. "TINA!"

They stood in silence, listening for any signs of life. Cooper could hear footsteps on the gravel outside, she could hear a faint droning noise of an industrial vacuum cleaner somewhere in the building, and there, a thumping noise. Rubber on metal. Thump, thump, swish. Thump, thump, swish.

"There," said Tennessee. He pointed to a store cupboard. The noise was definitely coming from inside.

"Police!" boomed Cooper. She tried the handle but it was locked. She slammed her weight against the door, once, twice... Tennessee shoved past her. There was no time for "Allow me, ma'am." He shoulder charged the door, knocking it off its hinges.

Tina Cooper was curled on the floor in the fetal position. Her mouth gagged, her arms and legs bound, masking tape covering her eyes. She thrashed violently; the thump, thump, swish coming from her shoes banging and sliding against the tiles. Cooper dived at her, relief flooding her body. Tina was alive.

Cooper scooped Tina's head in her hands and soothed her. "It's me, Tina. It's Mum."

She gently removed the gag and peeled the tape from her daughter's eyes as her own eyes filled with tears. Tina flinched and turned her gaze away from the fluorescent lighting in the art studio. "It's Hutchins, Mum. It's Hutchins!"

Sutherland had found a pair of scissors and was working around Cooper to sever the cable ties on Tina's arms and legs. The plastic had cut into her flesh, leaving it raw and painful. Once freed, Tina flung her arms around Cooper and repeated herself. "Hutchins."

"We know." Cooper delicately pushed Tina's hair from her face. "Where did he go?"

Tina's jaw moved up and down, but words didn't come out at first. "Drama," she eventually managed. "Drama department. He... he said he needed a costume."

Cooper had to prise herself from Tina's grip. "Get her out of here, Sam."

"Mum! No!"

"Tina, sweetheart, go with Sam. He'll keep you safe. I'll be back soon, I promise."

Sutherland pulled Tina to her feet. She was sobbing uncontrollably. Tears stained her cheeks, and she struggled to catch her breath. Cooper recognised the beginnings of a panic attack, and it broke her heart to move away from Tina when she just wanted her mother to hold her.

"Which way?" she asked her daughter. "Come on, Tina. Focus, sweetheart. Which way?"

Tina pointed to the ceiling.

"EYES ON." Tennessee's radio crackled. "We have a runner."

Tina broke free from Sutherland's protective arm and pressed her face up against the window. Brian Hutchins's bleached hair was visible in the moonlight. He sprinted across the carpark and fumbled with his keys. The squad cars illuminated as half a dozen men ran towards him.

"That way," said Tina, her arm extending to point at an emergency exit.

Cooper and Tennessee barged through the emergency exit and gave chase. Hutchins had made it to his car. The engine was starting as Cooper reached the edge of the carpark. In her socks, she slid on the ice and fell head-first onto the curb. Tennessee faltered but chose to pursue Hutchins. It was the right choice. Cooper pushed herself back to her feet and wiped blood from her forehead.

The Mini Countryman surged forward and knocked a PC off his feet. Thankfully, he rolled out of the way before the car's tyres could roll over him. Sirens blared. The Mini collided with the first squad car, spinning in circles on the slick ground, almost taking out another officer.

Another squad car moved into position at the end of the road, cordoning off the street. Young Oliver Martin jumped from the vehicle as Hutchins fell out of his driver's side door, making a run for it. Keaton sprinted across the school field, the grass gripping her boots better than the road ever would. She was gaining on them. Cooper's heart was in her mouth as she watched Keaton overtake Martin and tackle Hutchins to the ground. She let the full force of her fullback's frame slam into him; the sound of the man's ribs cracking could be heard from twenty metres away.

Cooper sank to her knees and burst into tears. She didn't give a damn if anyone thought it was unprofessional. They had him. It was over.

Keaton held Hutchins in place by digging her knee into the small of his back and pinning his shoulders with her hands. Tennessee, Martin and at least ten PCs caught up and surrounded him.

Tennessee looked over to Cooper. "Want the honours?"

Cooper shook her head. Sutherland was carrying Tina into the back of an ambulance and wrapping a blanket around her shoulders. Keaton could have the pleasure of cuffing Hutchins and reading the bastard his rights. Cooper had a daughter to comfort.

- CHAPTER 33 -

THE NORTHUMBRIA EMERGENCY CARE Hospital was a short ambulance ride north on the A19. Due to the winter vomiting bug, visiting hours had been reduced to just one hour per day and limited to immediate family only. Poor Josh had turned up with flowers and a box of Tina's favourite chocolates, only to be sent away by a stern-looking nurse with crow's feet deep enough to swipe a credit card through. Cooper took the gifts from Josh and gave his hand a squeeze.

"Tina will love them, Josh. I'll have her call you."

The young lad's cheeks flushed and his eyes dampened. "I was so scared," he said.

"She's going to be all right. You don't need to worry anymore."

He nodded and shuffled his feet, toeing the shoelaces of one trainer with the other. "It was definitely Mr Hutchins?"

"Definitely. But it's over now. He's going to jail for a very long time, probably the rest of his life," she assured him.

Cooper bid Josh farewell and followed the same nurse to ward four. Tina sat up in bed when she saw her. She smiled but there wasn't much emotion behind it. Cooper kissed her forehead and handed her the gifts.

"From Josh. He's a sweet one, that lad."

"Can you tell Dad that?" she sniggered and it was nice to see a hint of Tina's usual sass.

Cooper pulled a curtain around the bed to give the pair of them some privacy. She wished who-ever was in the neighbouring bed would turn their television down or have the decency to use head-phones. She didn't think her daughter should need to listen to the swear-laden Sopranos or whatever mob drama he was watching after her ordeal.

"The nurse said your wrists and ankles will heal before long."

Tina examined the bandages on her wrists. "They itch like crazy." She opened the box of chocolates and stuffed three into her mouth before offering one to Cooper. "Don't shake your head. You need the calories too."

Cooper chuckled and did as she was told. "These are great," she said with her mouth full. She swal-lowed and continued. "I've arranged for a trauma counsellor—"

"Ah, Mum, no. I can't."

"I know you hate talking to strangers, sweet-heart." Cooper rested her hands over her heart in a pleading fashion, "but she's an expert in this sort of thing. She'll be able to help you in ways I won't."

Tina drew her hands up as if she was going to slam them on the bed in protest. She paused and folded her arms over her chest instead. "I'd rather not." She turned her head back and forth several times, then added, "but I will if it makes you happy."

Cooper sighed. What a relief. "It will. Thank you, Tina."

Tina took another chocolate and unscrewed the lid off a bottle of water from the side of her bed. "You know what was weird? He kept apologising."

"Hutchins?"

"Yeah. We had art in the afternoon. He'd barely done any teaching since taking over from Linda, but the substitute was sick, so I guess he didn't have a choice. We were finishing up our sculptures and Hutchins wasn't paying any attention to the class. He was properly distracted with his own project. The class was basically running riot. Anyway, his fingers were all blackened because he was sketching a charcoal drawing and I remembered reading something about charcoal residue in the file you had on Rachel. So, I turned to Josh and whispered a joke about Hutchins being the Tarot Card Killer. I didn't mean it. I didn't really think he was and I didn't think I'd said it loud enough for him to hear me but when I looked back at him he was staring at me. And you know how I misread facial expressions all the time? I couldn't tell if he was angry with me for making the joke or if he was panicked because I was right. Either way, he gave me the creeps."

"Oh, Tina."

"The bell rang, and I got out of there as fast as I could. I was going to call you from the toilets in the shed when I got to netball."

"Only netball was cancelled, and the shed was locked."

"Yeah. The other girls decided to go get hot chocolate at Woods and I... I didn't. I thought it was best to call Dad and have him pick me up early. So, I walked back towards the school and that's when he grabbed me and hit me over the head with something." Her hand instinctively went to the back of her head to feel the scab that had formed in her hair.

Hearing the story sent chills down Cooper's spine. All the fear and pain she'd felt not knowing if Tina was alive or not came back to her. If she'd just kept her off school, none of this would have happened.

"He wasn't making any sense." Tina lowered her voice and her mother had to lean in to hear what she was saying. "He apologised over and over. Kept saying sorry and jabbering on about how I wasn't part of the plan. That I was a good student."

Tina shrugged and took another swig of water.

"Then he started saying that I wouldn't look right. That he didn't have the right clothes with him and how he'd have to make do with whatever he could find in the drama department."

Cooper swallowed. Her imagination was forcing images of a dead-eyed Tina dressed as a hierophant to the forefront of her mind. White robes and a pointed hat, blood oozing from a deep cut in her chest and coating the robes in scarlet. Cooper swallowed again but her mouth had dried up. She pictured a laminated card reading *The Lovers.* She wouldn't have been able to handle losing Tina. She'd been through a lot in her life but there was no way she'd be able to come back from that.

Cooper scooted Tina to one side of the bed so she could lie down next to her. "I think he was telling the truth, Tina. I don't think you were part of the plan. But if he suspected that you knew..." She paused for a moment and rolled onto her side to look at Tina. "If only you'd gone with the other girls. Safety in numbers and all that?"

Tina shrugged and began to play with the edge of her bedsheet. "I wasn't invited. I never am. I'm weird little Tina Cooper."

Cooper wiped a tear from her eye. "To hell with those girls," she said. "As far as I'm concerned, you're perfect little Tina Cooper.

The answer comforted Tina like a bowl of hot noodles on a cold day but it did nothing to ease Cooper's guilt. She'd been one of the popular girls during her own time at high school. She was the first to be invited to parties, she had the most fashionable friends, and boys paid her a lot of attention. Looking back, it was no surprise she'd been knocked up before she could finish sixth form. The ugly truth was that the Erica of old would not have been friends with someone like Tina; the Erica of old wouldn't have known she existed.

BRIAN HUTCHINS LICKED HIS lips and blew bubbles through the film of saliva. He did it over and over, creating a rhythm of pop, pop, pop noises. His glasses were askew and the brown stubble that covered his jaw didn't match his bleached head. He'd removed his shirt and was sat tethered to his seat in just a vest. Hutchins's entire upper body was covered in a spiderweb of tattoos. Cooper counted at least twenty pentacles from where she stood behind a sheet of one-way glass. As well as the pentacles, he was decorated with a handful of seeing eyes and the number 666. Down his arm, in cursive script, read, *He who drains the power of the youth will dine with Satan and know his truth.*

"So, the old woman was right," mumbled Cooper to herself as she read his tattoo. "Is he talking?" she asked Tennessee.

"Not since we last spoke." Tennessee twirled his mobile between his fingers. "They have a doctor coming to assess if he can be held in general population or if he needs a bed in the loony bin."

Cooper shot him a sideways glance. "Been taking vocabulary lessons from Nixon?"

He smirked. "I say we dump him in gen. pop. I won't shed a tear if he doesn't make it to trial."

"Agreed," said Cooper, "but the families might. They deserve to see him sentenced. Did we hear back from Martin?"

"We did. The mother's car's with forensics. I'd bet my house it's what he used when he picked up Jasmine and Reuben."

Cooper turned her back on Hutchins and rested against the window. "Even if forensics can't find anything, we have all the evidence we need. I just spoke to Keaton. Hutchins's house was crammed to the rafters with fortune-telling hooey, voodoo dolls, books on witchcraft, devil worship stuff. You name it, they found it. His diary's going to make interesting reading; he'd convinced himself that each time he took a life, it brought him closer to the devil."

Tennessee shook his head as if he could wake himself from this bizarre dream. "I heard they found a bunch of fancy dress costumes too."

"Yeah, they did. And drawings. The bastard had a list of who he wanted to kill and sketches of how he wanted to display the bodies. He was saving the fool until last. That card was marked out for none other than Linda Webb."

Tennessee blinked in disbelief. "Dare I ask?"

"She was destined for the ninth hole at Tynemouth golf club."

"And Tina?"

"She wasn't on the list. Neither was Reuben."

"So we were right about him only taking Reuben as a means to get Jasmine. How is Tina? She doing all right?"

Cooper dipped her head. "I can bring her home tonight. She's milking it. Demanding we get a Chinese takeaway."

"Good shout. Might have to head home via the Silver Moon myself." He switched his phone to his other hand and resumed his twirling.

Cooper tilted her head back, indicating Hutchins. "He and Linda Webb both went for the head teacher position when it became available last year. Linda got the job and twisted the knife by diverting funding from his department. He knew she'd flake the second the shit hit the fan. I checked her employment record and she looks to have a history of it. If all went according to plan, he'd get to kill her off and play the hero who saved the school. But, if it all went wrong and he got caught, well, he'd still be closer to his beloved Satan and his murderous art exhibition would make sure he went down in the history books as the most notorious killer of the century."

"The Tarot Card Killer," mused Tennessee to himself. "He's going to be infamous."

The pair stood in silence as they contemplated the loss of life over the previous few weeks. The sad truth of the matter was that the press office was already inundated with writers wanting to pen Hutchins's biography. His name would be forever etched into the British psyche, but by the time the case came to trial, no one would remember the names of the victims. Say the names: Mary Ann Nichols, Annie Chapman, Elizabeth Stride, Catherine Eddowes, or Mary Jane Kelly and faces turn blank. Say the name Jack the Ripper and everyone nods in recognition.

Cooper's mind was still in nineteenth-century London when Tennessee's phone rang loudly. She jumped and clasped her hands to her chest. Tennessee was equally shocked as he dropped the phone and cursed as it bounced off cheap, wiry carpeting.

"DS Daniel," he said, retrieving the phone and pressing it to his ear. "Really?" he asked, taking in a sharp inhalation. "Jesus. Okay. I'll be right there."

Tennessee fumbled with the phone again and slid it into his pocket.

"Jack?" asked Cooper, concern forcing her to use his real name for a change. "What's wrong?"

Tennessee was halfway out the door when he turned back. "Nothing's wrong." A look of merry wonder passed over him. "That was the mother-in-law. Hayley's gone into labour." He grabbed Cooper and kissed her on both cheeks before she could protest. "Baby Alfie's on his way. I'm going to be a Dad!"

-CHAPTER 34-

KENNY ORDERED ENOUGH CHINESE food to feed an army. Plastic cartons formed a jigsaw pattern over the dining table and bowls of spring rolls, spare ribs and fortune cookies spilt over onto the kitchen worktops. A *welcome home* banner stretched from one corner of the ceiling to the other and the living room appeared to have been turned into a botanical garden, such was the number of flowers that had been delivered.

"Dad," laughed Tina when she walked through the door and took in the scene. "I've only been gone two nights."

Kenny wrapped his arms around Tina and shrugged. "Did I go overboard?"

"You went overboard, swam up the Tyne and started racing the salmon."

Cooper gave Kenny a friendly punch on the arm. His over-the-top gesture stank of overcompensation, but if Tina liked it then that was all that mat-

293

tered to her. "You should have brought Linda," she said, thinking the former headteacher would want to celebrate that Hutchins was off the streets and that she was no longer a suspect. "Justin'll be here in five. Josh too."

Kenny checked his watch and his head lolled from one side to the other. "We kind of broke up?"

"Kind of?" Cooper gave him a sceptical look.

"When I told her Hutchins was the killer, that he'd been caught but that..." he lowered his voice to a whisper and looked back at his daughter, "that another five minutes and Tina might have been killed. Well, the first thing she said was how the governors would be begging her to come back to work. It made my blood boil. I couldn't believe it."

Cooper shook her head. "I can believe it. I know you liked her Kenny, and I'm sorry, but she was the most self-involved person I've ever met."

Before Kenny could agree or disagree, the doorbell chimed and announced the arrival of Josh. Tina opened the door and planted a sloppy kiss on her boyfriend's cheek. Josh chewed his own lip and tried to avoid Kenny's eye.

"Come on in, lad." Kenny's friendly tone caught the youngster off guard and the can of cool lager he was handed almost finished him off.

"Erm, thanks, Mr Roberts." He opened the can as if it was a test; he probably thought Kenny was about to rip it from his hands and announce that no daughter of his would date an underage drinker.

Tina was about to close the door when Justin Atkinson trotted up the front path waving a bottle of Champagne.

"Justin, Kenny. Kenny, Justin," introduced Cooper.

There was a brief awkward moment where the two men sized each other up. One, obviously the brains; the other, the brawn. One, the past; the other, the present. Atkinson would never be able to haul breeze blocks like Kenny could, and Kenny couldn't use a dictionary if it came with instructions and a helpline.

Atkinson broke the silence first. "Good to meet you," he said, his voice a few bars lower than normal.

Kenny responded with a grunted "Aye, same to you," and a handshake that probably crushed Atkinson's fingers, not that the forensics expert showed it.

Cooper ignored them and grabbed Champagne flutes for those not drinking lager. She took the bottle from Atkinson, popped the cork and poured three glasses. "We have a lot to celebrate," she said with a genuine smile. "My brilliant daughter is back from the hospital."

Everyone clinked their glasses and toasted, "To Tina."

"My brilliant mother caught the demon headmaster," said Tina.

Clink. "To Erica."

"And our colleague welcomes new life to the world," said Atkinson.

"To baby Alfie," Cooper toasted and they all clicked their glasses once more before taking a drink.

After an hour of overindulgence where Tina experimented with just how much crispy duck she could fit into a pancake and Josh opened fortune cookie after fortune cookie until one vaguely predicted Newcastle United would win their next match, Cooper began to clear the plates. She changed into skinny jeans, boots and a slinky top, and applied bright red lipstick.

"Are you sure you don't mind us going out?" she asked Tina who was trying to stop her father from showing Josh her baby photos.

"Of course. Go celebrate solving the case. You've earned it... Dad! Stop it. No, I don't look cute. I look like a Cabbage Patch Doll."

"Kenny?"

"We'll be fine." He pulled another album from a shelf. "Oh, look at Tina's little dimples."

"DAD!"

Atkinson put his arm around Cooper's shoulders. "Where are you taking me, anyway? You've been very mysterious."

"We're going to a gig. There's a band I've wanted to see for ages but they've only just started touring again. They're called The Screaming Dolls."

Justin's lips pinched in confusion. "Right. That sounds rather shouty."

"Oh, I hope so," said Cooper, taking her wig off and tossing it into the kitchen bin. She didn't want to hide behind it a second longer. "I haven't moshed in forever."

Atkinson pulled her in close and kissed the top of her head. "Part of me hopes you're joking."

"Just part?"

"Yeah," he shifted his weight and tucked his free hand into his pocket. "The other part is telling me to shut up right now and not jinx this."

Cold air flooded the house as they walked arm-in-arm into the chilly Tynemouth night. Kenny took a long swig of his sixth beer and marvelled at how stunning his ex had looked as she left. It had been a lifetime since they were together but she hadn't aged a bit, not in his eyes. She'd been his first real love and no one since had come close to comparing, especially not Linda, that self-obsessed snob. He'd been a fool in letting Erica go. He'd been a bigger fool in not coming back until now. He took another drink and savoured the numbing effect of the alcohol. He let his head fall back and rest on the back of the sofa while Tina selected a film on Netflix for them all to watch. He'd win her back, he thought. One way or another, Erica Cooper would be his.

DCI Erica Cooper will return.

Keep reading for the first chapter of Rock, Paper, Scissors. The second book in the DCI Erica Cooper series.

- ROCK PAPER SCISSORS -

THE CITY DIDN'T LOOK right to Macey Gallagher as she stumbled out of the club. The lights of the traffic left red and white snakes across her vision as if her brain was set on long exposure. Her eyes couldn't keep up with the world and her body couldn't keep up with her brain. Every movement required meticulous concentration. Right foot. Left foot. Right foot.

A neon pink sign blinked at Macey but she couldn't read it; the letters looked jumbled and they didn't make sense. All around her, Newcastle's party people were enjoying their Saturday night. They hugged, kissed and danced, oblivious to the nineteen-year-old's worsening state. Pearl would be around here somewhere. She must be. Macey just had to find her.

"Watch it." A woman with an angry face and impossibly black eyebrows shoved Macey out of the way and into a brick wall. "Look where you're going."

The bricks grazed Macey's arm and tiny globules of blood popped to the surface turning her skin into a Lichtenstein artwork.

Where was Pearl? She didn't like feeling like this. She'd only had a couple of drinks. Hadn't she? Two glasses of wine with dinner before switching to Diet Coke in the club. It wasn't that much but her head pounded and she desperately needed to pee.

It was April in Newcastle upon Tyne and bright, clear days gave way to chilling, teeth-chattering nights. In these parts, the locals declined to wear coats despite the night-time temperature barely reaching five degrees.

"Coats are for southerners," Alison told her on her first day at Newcastle University. "If you want to fit in, leave your coat at home. Besides, who wants to cover up an outfit as cute as yours?"

An ambulance raced past with its lights flashing and siren blaring. Macey covered her ears and closed her eyes. Everything was louder and brighter than it should be. She could hear people laughing and paranoia told her they were laughing at her. Across the road, two squat men got into a fight. Their heavy fists flew at each other's heads in great arcs until a ginormous man in black with an earring in one ear separated them. One stormed towards the taxi rank, the other marched towards Macey.

Macey backed herself as far into the wall as she could, hoping to make herself invisible.

"Alreet, pretty lass?" His scowl turned to a smile and he edged closer. Macey tried to focus. He was old, not granddad-old but probably mid-forties at least, maybe fifty. Lines carved across his forehead and whilst his head was bald, his beard was mid-brown with patches of white. "Now, where've you been all my life?"

Macey clutched her bag to her chest. Her mouth was drier than the Sahara but she managed, "For most of it I wasn't born."

It was a mistake. The man's scowl returned. "Bitch," he spat, edging closer still.

It wasn't the first time Macey's mouth had got her into trouble. She was quick-witted, like many of her Dubliner compatriots, and while some thought of her craic as endearing, the insecure could react badly.

A slender woman with brown spiral curls walked by.

"Pearl?" Macey called. *Thank God*. She ducked under the man's arm and made a run for it, though it could hardly be called a run, a stagger would be more accurate. "Pearl?"

The woman turned and looked Macey up and down. She wasn't Pearl. "You all right, love?"

Macey rested her back against the wall and nodded. The gesture satisfied the woman but Macey was far from all right. She wasn't well, the bald man was still staring at her and her flatmate was nowhere to be seen. They'd promised to travel back home together, to share a taxi and order a dirty great pizza to finish off the evening. Pearl would be mad that Macey had gone home without her but the doorman wasn't going to let her back into the club and she couldn't stay out in the cold all night. She took two steps towards the taxi rank and teetered over in her heels. What a total waste of money. The shoes looked amazing but they were nearly impossible to walk in and God knows why anyone would design something so uncomfortable to wear. She tried again. Right foot. Left foot. Her ankle buckled once more and Macey was falling; falling straight into the arms of the woman who wasn't Pearl.

"Oops. I've got you." She had a kind face and wore a fluorescent vest, the sort a workman would wear. "You don't look like you're doing so good. Do you need help?" The good Samaritan propped Macey back upright and supported her around her tiny waist. "What's your name, love?"

"Macey." The word didn't come easy to her. Her brain was becoming foggier by the minute and her jaw wasn't responding how she'd expected.

"Great accent. Where in Ireland are you from?"

"Dublin."

"Oh, fantastic." The stranger helped push Macey's blonde, wavy hair behind her ear. "I've been there for the odd boozy weekend. Great place. You here for uni?"

Macey nodded. She felt nauseous and bewildered and she didn't want to be sick, not on the street.

"I'm with the Tyne Pastors," the woman said, pointing to a logo on her yellow vest. Did you have too much to drink, Macey?"

She shook her head. "No," she managed. "No, I— I don't think so."

"We work with the police. We help people who could do with a sit down and a glass of water, or people who are lost, that sort of thing. We have a van across the road." She pointed to a dark van with sliding doors. "If you want to shelter from the cold, we have blankets and can make you a nice cup of tea while we try and get a hold of your friends. Sound good?"

The thought of a warm drink drew Macey over the street as if she were being pulled by a magnet. She was steered away from a kebab that had been dropped in the road and supported as she stepped up the kerb.

"Careful of your footing here." The stranger waved to an amicable-looking man who was holding a pile of fleece blankets. "This is Macey. I think she'd like some tea and to rest her feet."

"Hi, Macey," he said as he handed her a blanket.

Macey wrapped it over her shoulders and pulled the ends tight to her chest. Instantly, she felt comforted.

"Take a seat." The woman smiled and indicated a bench that ran the length of the van. A slim woman with mascara running down her face was sitting on the bench and sobbing into her mobile. She hiccoughed and continued crying. Between her feet, some strong-smelling coffee steamed into the cold air.

"Thank you." Macey smiled at her curly-haired new friend. She looked blurry, but she was gentle and she had a familiarity about her. It was like talking to an aunt or a cousin.

"Where do you live? We usually stay out until four. If we can't reunite you with your friends by then we can give you a lift."

"H-Heaton," she stammered. Heaton was a popular suburb that sat to the east of the city centre and was only a short drive away. "Rothbury Terrace. Near... Near the mosque." Macey sat on the bench and tried to make herself comfortable. The bench was hard but the fleece cushioned her bottom and she was already feeling warmer. She slumped back and closed her eyes for a moment, then looked at the screen on her phone and tried to make out the logos that no longer made sense to her. Pearl and Alison were probably dancing. Had they even noticed she'd gone?

"Here you go." She was handed a mug of tea by the man. He screwed the lid back on the flask and returned to the driver's seat. This would all be over soon, she told herself. Either Pearl would come and find her, or she could wait an hour and the pastors would drive her back home. She craved to be back in her bed. A trip to the medicine cabinet and a pint of water and she'd be right as rain.

Curls returned to the van. "Any luck with your boyfriend?" she asked the crying girl. The girl shook her head and tucked her phone into a pocket. "How about we stop this awful draught?" She reached behind her and slid the van door until it clicked closed.

The driver looked over his shoulder, Curls nodded at him. The engine started, and the van pulled away.

"Are you taking me home?" Macey asked.

The driver didn't answer. Nothing sobered a person up quite like the sickening knowledge that something awful was about to happen. For as Macey Gallagher's hands were bound with a cable tie, she realised all too late that these were not the Tyne Pastors and the good Samaritan was not so good.

- MESSAGE FROM THE AUTHOR -

IF YOU ENJOYED CUT The Deck, I would sincerely appreciate it if you could take the time to leave a review.

Following the release of The Only Weapon In The Room, I was keen to write another book set in my local area. Many of the places described in this book are real. Priors Haven, the Spanish Battery, Longsands, King Edward's Bay, Northumberland Park and North Pier are some of my favourite places in Tynemouth to take my naughty terrier for a stroll. Tynemouth Academy, on the other hand, is a figment of my imagination. I didn't feel comfortable tarnishing a real school with a serial killer, a self-obsessed headmistress and a bunch of disruptive kids.

B BASKERVILLE

Connect with me online:

Mailing list: betsybaskerville.com

Twitter: @B__Baskerville

Facebook: B Baskerville - Author

Instagram: b_baskerville_author

- ACKNOWLEDGEMENTS -

I MUST GIVE SPECIAL thanks to everyone who has read and provided feedback for Cut The Deck.

Dibz, Christine, Emilia, Anne, Ian and Jennifer, thank you for reading through the earliest of drafts and for being so warm and positive in your feedback.

Thanks to my fellow martial arts addict, Amanda. Sorry there's not as much 'ninja stuff' in this one.

Shaun, thank you for the encouragement and support and for calling me a rising star. Now to live up to it!

Mum, (who took months to work out why DS Jack Daniel is nicknamed Tennessee) thank you for reading and rereading everything I've thrown at you.

Rob, I love you and I'm so pleased the first novel you read in ten years was mine.

- ABOUT THE AUTHOR -

BETSY WAS BORN AND raised in Newcastle upon Tyne. She describes herself as a crime fiction addict and UFC geek of epic proportions.

When not writing, Betsy loves hiking with her boyfriend and their very naughty Welsh terrier.

- Also By B Baskerville -

The DCI Cooper Series:
Cut The Deck
Rock, Paper, Scissors
Roll The Dice
Northern Roulette
Hide & Seek

Stand Alones:
The Only Weapon In The Room
Dead In The Water

Printed in Great Britain
by Amazon

19474824R00181